The Dick and Jane

The Dick and Jane

Abby Robinson

Delacorte Press / New York

Published by
Delacorte Press
1 Dag Hammarskjold Plaza
New York, N.Y. 10017
Library of Congress Cataloging in Publication Data
Robinson, Abby.
The Dick and Jane.
I. Title.
PS3568.02775D5   1984   813'.54   84-14203
ISBN 0-385-29361-5

Manufactured in the United States of America

First printing

To another Jane and Barry

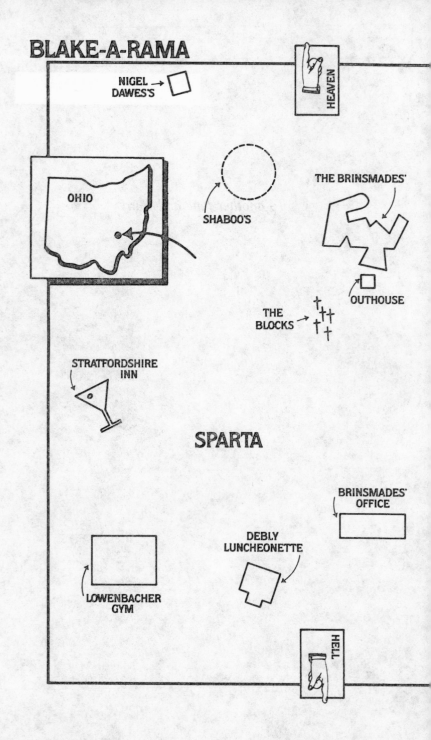

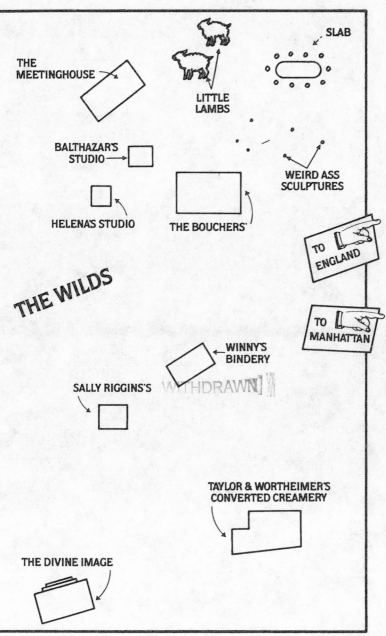

THE MEETINGHOUSE

LITTLE LAMBS

SLAB

BALTHAZAR'S STUDIO

HELENA'S STUDIO

THE BOUCHERS'

WEIRD ASS SCULPTURES

TO ENGLAND

TO MANHATTAN

THE WILDS

WINNY'S BINDERY

SALLY RIGGINS'S

WITHDRAWN

TAYLOR & WORTHEIMER'S CONVERTED CREAMERY

THE DIVINE IMAGE

SCALE: 1" = 1 BIG SHLEPP

Love interest nearly always weakens a mystery because it introduces a type of suspense that is antagonistic to the detective's struggle to solve the problem. It stacks the cards, and, in nine cases out of ten, it eliminates at least two useful suspects. The only effective kind of love interest is that which creates a personal hazard for the detective—but which, at the same time, you instinctively feel to be a mere episode. A really good detective never gets married.

Raymond Chandler
Raymond Chandler Speaking

The Eye sees more than the Heart knows.

William Blake
"Visions of the Daughters
of Albion"

The Dick and Jane

Trouble

Summertime and the livin' is easy, huh? Bullshit. It was hot as Hades and I'd just been canned. Not that my job as in-house photog for a big corporation was any great shakes. I sure as hell wasn't going to miss taking pics of employees like Clara Clammer holding the humongo zucchini she'd grown in her postage stamp backyard or Dan Owens all kissyface with his prize-winning dachshund Baxter. I have to admit though, I did develop a soft spot for Estelle Murphy with her skyscraper dye job that defied gravity; she'd been a hatcheck goil at the old Stork Club. Her gossip about Tallulah Bankhead was as passé as her coif.

But then there were those depresso award luncheons where the food was lousy and the likes of Amelia Johnson and Philip Thurston, Jr., would receive gold-plated pins with microdot rubies for fifty years of devoted mailroom slavery or twenty-five of editorial perseverance. It was the two-bit corporate buyoff and the suckers were always grateful. The only thing that got me through that crap was the bartender. He stirred up a martini that knocked my cynicism on its ass.

The Phone Call

It was a steamy Monday night in mid-July. I was sitting on the couch, scantily clad, figuring angles to hustle dough. Poverty made me jumpy. I had some 16 × 20 prints sticking to my lap that were supposed to go into a show in October. For the past few years I'd been making photos of body parts—hands, legs, feet—and getting a rep in art circles as the Frank Perdue of photography.

I was praying there were still some Medicis left when the telephone jingled. I transferred the prints from my lap to the floor and headed for the extension by the bed. I try to take as many things as possible lying down, but some sixth sense told me this call might mean business. I did some fast footwork, aboutfaced and picked up at my desk. Hoisting the receiver to my ear, I noticed my nails needed a high gloss of Jungle Red. Photo chemicals are hard on a girl's hands. The mystery caller, speaking with a nasal twang, plunged into conversation the way a hungry man dives into meat and potatoes.

"You Jane?"

"Yeah. You Tarzan?"

"Sorry, kid, I ain't. Domenic Palladino's tha name. Private investigator." I heard that and wondered which buddy was in a jam this time. "Call me Nick."

"Okay, Nick, what can I do for you?"

"I'm workin' a case with yer friend Rosenblatt."

Marvin Rosenblatt wasn't a friend exactly. He was a slightly overweight, balding lawyer who'd taken a shine to me. He promised to throw legal work my way. All he'd thrown so far was legal typing. Big deal.

"I'm callin', see, 'cuz I need photos and Rosenblatt sez yer good. Whatchya doin' in a coupla weeks?" The shamus was a graduate of the snappy dialogue school.

14

"Well, to tell you the truth, I'm kind of busy right now." That was a crock, but if you don't bluff, you don't play poker. "But maybe I can squeeze your job in, seeing as it's for Marv. What exactly did you have in mind?"

"A sheet smeller."

"A laundry job?"

"Uh uh, sweetheart, a sheet smeller means matrimonial. Like in divorce. Like adultery."

"I get the drift."

"I gotta do some legwork first, ya know, get tha laya tha land." He snorted at his own crummy joke.

"What are we talking, Nick? Working a day? A night? A week? What?"

"If everything goes down like I plan, we're talkin' a night. Worst comes ta worst, maybe two. How much?"

"My rate's $150 a day plus expenses." How the hell did I know what to charge? All I knew were the going rates for weddings and bar mitzvahs.

"No dice, babe. Too steep. How 'bout comin' down ta $50."

"Too cheap. Remember I'm good. $100."

"$75 and no more hassle."

"$100's my final offer." I worked hard on sounding ballsy.

"Ya drive a hard bargain there, sweetheart, but okay, yer on. I'll let it go at a C 'cuz there ain't travel expenses. I provide tha wheels. I'll give ya a buzz next Sunday with some definite info." He hung up abruptly. The dialtone said goodbye.

Deadly Fantasy

I was fatootsed. The chance to meet a real-life private eye made my pulse race the Indy 500. I'd been into detective novels for years, so I knew a thing or two about dicks. Hopefully Palladino'd be the direct descendant of Sam Spade or Philip Marlowe. He'd be strong and lean, tough but tender. Rather than talk he'd smolder. He'd have cold, penetrating eyes that would see right through me, and he'd move like a cat. A man "neither tarnished nor afraid." A man of honor and a man of danger. My hero.

I was so caught up in my fantasies that I didn't hear my main squeeze come in. He bent down and planted a smooch on my boob. I torpedoed out of my seat.

"Jesus Christ, you scared me half to death, sneaking up on me that way."

"And here I thought my kiss stirred the Inner Fires of Lust."

"Well, it did some of that, too," I admitted sheepishly, and more than a little surprised. Lately, Hank had been acting remote and strange. "So now that you've stirred them, what do you intend to do about it?"

He double O'd the loft bed.

"Nah," I said. I was pleased when he looked disappointed. "Too far. What would you say to the rug here?"

He didn't say anything, he acted. It was too humid for fancy moves so we minimized the buildup and missionaried to the max. It was hot, the way it'd been when we became an item a year and a half ago.

I met Hank Gallagher, a.k.a. Golden Boy, during my corporate stretch. He was the gee at the custom lab crosstown who handled my account. For the first six months all I knew about him was he had a sexy d.j. voice, a beano sense of humor, and an efficient M.O. When a coworker reported that she'd met him and he was to-die gorgeous, I decided to check him out myself. It took a week to screw up the courage to invite him to lunch.

The guy turned out to be a dish all right—golden hair that perfectly matched his luxurious golden soupstrainer and bright, honey-colored blinkers, broad shoulders, slim hips, long legs, and a great ass. He sent my erotometer into the ozone. And after shmoozing over burgers about life, art, and photography, I was convinced he was Mr. Right. Except he had two strikes against him: (1) he lived in Hoboken and (2) he lived there with a woman. Geography I could deal with, the girlfriend I couldn't. The only thing I poach is eggs.

I cooled my jets and we went back to being phone mates. A letdown but I'd live. Bored out of my gourd one day at HQ, I put a funny note and a dime store squirt camera in with my order. Gallagher started sending notes and presents back. That gave the 9–5 routine a boost and made us pen pals.

We slid to chumdom. I don't remember whose idea it was, but we started spending a lunch hour a week going to galleries and taking pictures. We always had loads to talk about and those lunch hours usually went into overtime. Meetings of the mind were better than no meetings at all.

Around Christmas time I ran into him at a cocktail party. He looked particularly hunky and he was alone. I was all dolled up. We had a few drinks and lots of holiday cheer. The cheer was high voltage when the bar closed. I knew he was broke but he was into the big gesture. He sprang for chow in a tiny French joint he knew in the Village. After that we went to a movie, then to a bar, and then to another. It got to be late and the next move was obviously to bed.

"But I won't," I said with difficulty. "You're living with someone."

"Not for much longer," he said.

A week later the girlfriend and all the furniture were gone.

That resolution made for a helluva happy new year. Though I felt a twinge about Hank's breakup with his ex. Sure, it wasn't my fault. His relationship with Cary'd hit the skids before I ever entered the pic. All I did was meet the lug and have everything in common with him. Still, the frail deserved sympathy; nobody digs her man hanging out with another dame.

In the whambang beginning I felt like I'd turned up thirty-six aces on a contact sheet. Gallagher was romantic, funny, smart, sensitive, attentive, talented, and a dynamite lay. We were as compatible as Dektol and Selectol. We worked together, hung out together, and made art together. We didn't quite live together. Gallagher kept his digs in Hoboken so we could each have privacy when we wanted. We almost never did; who'd be jerk enough to spend nights alone when there was nuclear fission to harness in bed.

The fishy stuff started when Gallagher got laid off in June. He went on unemployment and had time on his hands. That's when he took up with Blake. William Blake, English writer and artist, born November 28, 1757, and croaked August 12, 1827. In certain circles the late lamented was hyped as a genius and a visionary. In others, Mr. B. was billed a kook. Hank thought he was the berries. He started talking Art—big A—instead of making it. He spouted off a lot about Truth, with a capital T, and Beauty, cap B. He became Serious. Worse yet, he started critting my photos with highfalutin' lingo. He said they lacked "Fearful Symmetry" and "Radiance." Who needed to hear that kind of crapola? Who even knew what it meant?

Way back when, I'd read some of this limey's scribblings and said "cornball." More vividly than the poems I remember a Doctor Kildare episode that copped one of Willy's catchy titles: "Tyger, Tyger." Richard Chamberlain fell in love with Yvette Mimieux, an epileptic surfer. The story was hokey but I was sad when Yvette found the perfect wave, had a fit, and washed up dead on the shore. It wasn't Blake's fault she kicked. It was the doc's. He was some kind of killer. No woman he ever got involved with survived the show start to finish.

The long and short of it was that Willy Wonder hadn't made it to the top of my charts. I was putting up with Gallagher's jag because I loved the guy and the good stuff still outweighed the bad. I hoped it was like what moms say about "the terrible twos"—just a phase the boy was going through. Only it was going on awfully long and I was beginning to worry. I thought I could wait it out; I thought so right up to the P.I.'s phone call. Suddenly I was thinking matchruptcy and itching for adventure.

Later that night I curled up in the sack next to my spoonie and had dick fantasies that wouldn't quit. The moxie of a Philip Marlowe all my own had me in a spin. Could it be that a sexy Italian private eye would make a better *numero uno* than the one currently lying next to me, rereading *The Marriage of Heaven and Hell?*

"Let me read you some of this," Hank said, nudging me out of my illicit evedreams. "It's got such Purity and Proportion."

"Okay, shoot," I said, feeling collared and confused.

" 'Drive your cart and your plow over the bones of the dead.' "

Oh, brother. All I could think of was driving off into the sunset in Palladino's two-toned Impala, his dirty socks, underwear, and soiled shirts balled up on the backseat, his guns, my photo equipment and makeup case crammed into the trunk.

" 'The road of excess leads to the palace of wisdom.' "

All systems "go." I was en route and forget the seat belts.

" 'Prudence is a rich, ugly old maid courted by Incapacity.' "

Ugh. None of that, thank you.

" 'He who desires but acts not, breeds pestilence.' "

I had my hands full already without adding plague to the hopper.

" 'Dip him in the river who loves water.' "

Well, he wasn't *all* wet.

If my life was about to change, let it. If Super Sleuth wanted to take me away from all this, let him. If Hank insisted on droning on like this, screw him. I was going to sleep.

The Offer

The next a.m., I pumped up on java and hit the bookstores. I arrived home several hours later slaphappy with reference material and ready to bone up on my new line of work. I didn't need a thermometer to tell me it was another scorcher. All I had to do was sit quietly and watch the paint blister. I went to the fridge and brought myself a sugarfree. I took it and my haul to the couch and smoothed down for a good read.

Golden Boy'd been in Hoboken signing for his unemployment check and moseyed in around 3:30. Unemployment wasn't a half-bad scam for artists. It was the next best thing to a National Endowment for the Arts grant. It gave you enough mazuma to scrape by, stay home, and make work.

Hank planted a soggy one on my sweaty neck and said "Hi." No fires of lust today unfortunately. As soon as he got a bead on the stack of new detective novels at my feet his eyebrows went into conference. "How can you read that trash?"

The heat made me prickly so I traded him a scowl.

"You know what Blake would say about you?"

"You know what Raymond Chandler'd say about you?" I rummaged around for my notebook where I kept literary ammo. "He says, 'Show me a man or woman who cannot stand mysteries and I will show you a fool, a clever fool—perhaps—but a fool just the same.'"

We were playing with dynamite when the phone let loose. Nick to the rescue? Instead it was my kid sis, Sara, calling from the City of Brotherly Love.

"Hi there." She sounded cheerful, which bugged me.

"Hi," I groused.

Sara said: "You sound lousy. What's up?"

I said: "Nothing much. Hank and I were just sitting around having a fight."

"Serious?"

"I'm not sure yet."

"Over what?"

"The new love in his life."

"He's seeing another woman?"

"That I could probably deal with. This is worse. He has this thing for William Blake." There was a sharp intake of breath on the other end of the line. "No, no, he's not gay. William Blake, the poet. The mystic. The dead one. He's all Hank talks about. Blake this, Blake that." I ended with a yell.

"You know what you need?" Sara was always fast on the draw when it came to advice.

"What?" I was usually not fast to take it.

"A vacation."

"The only trip I can afford is a quickie around the block and that's only if I bring my lunch."

"I have an offer you can't refuse."

"Oh, yeah?"

"Remember I said I was going to take a vacation before I started medical school?"

"Sure. You made it sound like the last vacation of your life."

It was sis' turn to get scrappy. "You only hang out with artists. If you knew any doctors, you'd know I wasn't exaggerating. You don't have a life once you're in med school."

"Aw, c'mon, Sara, give me a break. You make med school sound worse than the slammer. Even prisoners get time off for good behavior. Besides, you *want* to go to med school. You *like* suffering."

"Don't give me a hard time, all right? I'm trying to be nice. Anyway, I wanted to spend a week somewhere warm where I'd be pampered."

"So you're checking into the folks' condo."

"No, smartass, I'm not." The kid had the resilience of a Spauldeen. "I'm going to Club Med in Guadeloupe."

I once eyed a Club brochure photo. Bronzed young professional gods and goddesses lolled around a flossy pool, sipping booze in every pastel shade. Finding Mr. and Ms. Average Tourist was like finding the hidden bunny in a puzzle. Everybody modeled a lot of skin and what looked at first glance to be native jewelry. Jewelry, nothing, the caption explained; plastic poppit beads, Club Med's answer to wampum. The pitch was for the hotblooded to poppit the days away, bake in the sun, and shake in the sack.

"Great," I said, holding up my end of the conversation like Atlas.

"The hitch is Mom and Dad don't want me going alone. That's where you come in."

"Me?"

"Yup. They said I could go if you went with me."

"Sorry, cutie pie, but like I said, I don't have the scratch."

"I know that and they know that. That's why they said they'd pay for your trip. So I tentatively booked us for the week of August the thirteenth through twentieth. The flight leaves Kennedy, Thursday at 11:45 A.M. How's that sound?"

She had me by the short hairs. I could make my bimonthly appointment at unemployment, sign for my measly $115 a week check, have my friend Viv drive me to Kennedy, and be out at the airport with time to burn. "Okay," I conceded. "How can I stand in the way of your happiness?" Besides, a Blake break wasn't a half-bad idea. Possibly it was exactly what Hank and I needed. So what if I could think of a thousand places I'd rather visit faster than you could say "photojournalism"?

"You won't regret it. We'll have a great time, you'll see," Sara chirped.

I hung up feeling like I'd been hit by a Mack truck.

Opportunity and Inclination

I spent a lazy Sunday in bed with Hank, doing a bit of the old in and out, skimming the *Times*, and wondering when the hell the shamus would call. He didn't. Ditto for Monday, Ditto^2 Tuesday. Club Med D-day crept closer. If Nick didn't make his fingers do the walking soon, he'd be out a photographer. And I'd be out a joy ride into the sunset in a beatup Chevy. Not to mention a paycheck.

I let the earth rotate one more time before I took matters into my own hands. I dialed the gumshoe's number. When his answering machine snarled "Leave a message," I snarled one. I was no ordinary shutterbug, I was a tigress.

The ding-a-ling came Thursday while I was peeling off Gallagher's jockeys. "Don't answer it," I hissed. Too late. Hank had already launched himself Minuteman style at the receiver.

"Hello . . . Yes . . . Who? . . . Oh . . . She's right here." His beautiful face went ugly. He pointed the phone at me like a pistol. "It's that detective."

I looked down at the dropped trou, sighed, and put the horn to my ear. "Ya called." Not a question, not an apology for the late hour. Your basic no-frills treatment. Just the facts, ma'am, just the facts.

"You were supposed to call me days ago." I sounded like a jealous girlfriend and I hated myself.

Palladino spit out his end of the conversation like so many watermelon pits. "Sweetheart, I hadda lotta work ta do. There were some, uh, complications. See, tha husband . . ."

"Husband?" My skin goosebumped. "I thought we were working for the wife." You hang out with feminists and artists long enough, you assume you're siding with the skirt or the underdog. Usually they're one and the same. Now it was sisterhood versus a bank book so light it floated like a helium balloon. The money took the round on velvet. I made shredded wheat out of my lower lip.

"Yeah, guy named Dewinter, Troy Dewinter. Businessman. Big bucks. He offered his old lady a coupla thou a month alimony but she nixed it. Said it stank. Smelled okay ta me; I could retire smellin' bad like that, fa Chrissake.

"In any case, Rosenblatt makes a suggestion. He sez ta Troy, 'Troy, baby, we could save a lotta bread and hassle if she's gettin' a little side action.' Dewinter sez nah, his wife ain't tha type ta fool around. Marv's heard that one before."

"And then?" I watched Gallagher odalisque on the bed, fingering the *Songs of Innocence* by the usual.

"Then Big Marv convinces him and hires me ta sniff round and dig up tha dirt. Only problem's I followed tha wrong dame for a week."

"You what?" That knocked me for a loop; mistakes like that never went down in movies or books.

"Ya don't hear so good, I gotta broadcast it? I tailed tha next-door neighbor. Look, Dewinter's description was flimsy. Ya'd think after livin' with tha broad five years tha guy'd know what tha hell his wife looks like.

"It was a bad break, I admit it. Specially 'cuz tha other broad was better-lookin'. But there's a happy ending, dollface. Turns out our princess is hanky-pankyin' with a good-lookin' model type— younger guy—name a Jack Price."

"So now what? We go to the apartment and jump out of the closet and photograph mid-fuck?" Golden Boy shot me a beam of pure disgust and shoved his nozzle deeper into his Blake.

I featured the scenario: a naked couple balling on designer sheets. A closeup shot of their faces freezing in horror. Long shot: frail weeps, clutches sheet to bony, shaking bod. Dude leaps out of bed, whips on pants, fumbles with fly. Pan to closet. See flash from camera take one last damaging evidence shot. Tight shot on photog. Ta-da, my big moment. But wait! Oh, no! Instead of cute little me, I see a chunky male. Five o'clock shadow, bags under the eyes, fat cigar dangling from slack mouth, scuffed shoes, soiled tie, rumpled trenchcoat. Camera is an old Speed Graphic. The face and rig are absolutely Weegee, the famous press photographer of the '30s, the guy who gave us *Naked City*.

"Are y'kiddin'? Nobody jumps outta closets no more. Only on TV; audiences eat that shit up. Nah, tha law's been changed, babe." I was relieved. "All ya gotta do nowadays's show Opportunity and Inclination." He creamed over the legalese, it sounded so legit.

"Which means?" I ran my index finger up and down Hank's spine, a reminder we had unfinished business.

"They don't gotta be doin' it; ya just gotta show they coulda. Ferinstance: ya see 'em in tha buff. Or ya show 'em spendin' two, three hours tagether in a motel room that ain't got but one waya enterin'.

"We got nuthin' ta sweat with this Dewinter job if tha hot stuff I saw in tha bedroom last night's tha usual. It'll be like takin' candy from a baby."

"What do I need to bring?"

"Our stakeout's a block from tha chick's penthouse, so bring tha longest lens ya got. I'll be by your place tamarra night, say round tenna clock. Oh, yeah, don't wear nuthin' flashy." Click.

Triangles are trouble and this one had turned nasty. The vengeance and greed angles were film noir material. By comparison, Hank's and my triangular past had a plot line that was straight Disney.

I braced the gig to loverboy. He got churlish.

"I don't like your working for that guy. I'm afraid for your 'Divine Likeness.' Exposure to all this Wrath and Fury could do real damage to it. It could change you."

"You're making a mountain out of a molehill," I said, eager to chuck the discussion of my Being and De-Being. Spiritualism wasn't my strong suit although I was experiencing powerful vibrations. Not from the Beyond. From the Nether Regions. Like below the belt. It took some effort to get the boy off the high-toned intercourse and down to the physical kind. That communicated better.

The Loan

Rise and shine early the next morning and POW. Disaster. I'd told Palladino I was good and I was. What I didn't tell him was I didn't have the wherewithal. What I needed was a bazooka-size lens. Quick. I wasn't flush enough to rent one and I didn't have a friend with one to lend. In the art circles I traveled, there wasn't much call for Big Bertha telephotos. We all wideangled from the hip and from the heart.

There was nothing to do but whine. Maybe he wanted me to shut up or maybe he'd eased up on the "Divine" razzmatazz. Whatever, Hank responded like a prince. He gave me a hug and said he'd square things. His solution was simple: hit up his old prep school pal Parker.

Parker was a tall, skinny, horsefaced trust fund kid. He had so much dough, he was a retiree from birth. He busied himself cashing dividend checks and telephoning his accountant, broker, lawyer, travel agent, and drug dealer. Every now and again he played footsie with the notion of becoming a professional f-stopper. He was into photography the way stereo junkies were into music. Parker bought technical gear; they bought the latest components. Parker didn't just have a shitload of equipment, he had a goddamn arsenal.

Around lunchtime, Hank took a breather from *A Vision from the Book of Job* and stretched his underpinnings over to Parker's Sutton Place triplex. He waltzed back a few hours later, high as a kite, his pupils dilated at f1.4. Under one arm was a 400mm lalapalooza. Under the other, some flashy tulips.

First he handed me the necessary. My tiny biceps could barely pump the iron. Then he pushed the posies under my schnoz. He looked the way he often did when he's apologetic—soft and loyal like a golden retriever. My heart melted.

"I'm sorry if I gave you a hard time last night. It's just that, I get nervous we're drifting apart, you know?"

"Yeah, I know. I worry too." I cuddled up next to him. Even in a heat wave, body warmth is comfy.

"Maybe it's like Blake says: 'Without contraries there is no progression.'"

That sounded jake enough. "I'm all for progress. But maybe we could try to minimize the contraries a little, huh?"

"Okay," Hank said and gave me a squeeze. He moved over to the couch and sat down. I lay with my head in his lap. He stroked my mop. "The most incredible thing happened." He sounded animated. I lifted an eyebrow.

"Parker had this really terrific woman over who's part of a Blake community called Golgonooza out in Ohio. Isn't that amazing?"

My eyebrows did a duet. Not exactly in amazement.

"The place sounded fan-tastic. Everybody there lives and breathes Blake. She invited me to come out and visit."

This was the first I'd heard of Parker being mixed up with Blake. Or Blakettes. I wasn't totally surprised though—he went for spacey chicks. Spacey and pretty. I knew zip about his literary tastes. "So you think you'll go to this Gorgonzola?"

"Golgonooza, Jane, not Gorgonzola. Golgonooza is the City of Art. Of course, I'm going. It's an offer I couldn't refuse. I thought I'd go there while you were off in Guadeloupe."

"Oh." Not only was it an offer he couldn't refuse, he couldn't accept it fast enough. I was frightened plenty going to Club Med, a multimillion-dollar operation that billed itself "an antidote to civilization." Religious communities, communes, and cult retreats scared the bejesus out of me. Golgonooza, the City of Art? My ass. It sounded like Guyana and I didn't want to lose Golden Boy to mystical mumbo jumbo or Kool-Aid.

"You sure you want to go? It might be real weirdo."

"You should have heard her. The place sounded great."

27

There was no squibbing Gallagher's enthusiasm. "Well, then, I guess that's the best time for you to go." "Tit for tat" is what I thought. "Fearful Symmetry and all that" is what I said. Hank's gash split open in a smile. Bingo.

Sniper

The air was stale as a bad joke. It made you long to spend the day in an airconditioned movie, fuck the feature, and all night in an airconditioned bedroom, fuck whose.

Around 9 P.M. I stopped picking at the rabbit food, got up from the table, and began assembling the doodads of my trade. I screwed the killer lens on the Nikon, then secured the whole shebang on the Gitzo. My instructions were to look unobtrusive, but this baby was showy. High-class camouflage pros could disguise the sucker; all I could come up with in a hurry was covering it with a lawn-and-leaf-size garbage bag. Carrying the dingus, I looked less photographer than sniper.

Gallagher's fork escorted a piece of iceberg around his plate. He was nudgy again about my "Divine Likeness" but laboring to keep his Organs of Perception open.

When the clock's little hand nuzzled X and the sweep slipped past III, I heard honking. I couldn't wait to catch my first look-see at the dick of my dreams. I was as excited as a girl on prom night but squelched it. Gallagher was potentially explosive and I didn't want him to detonate. I ambled over to the window on locomotors of rubber. Parked in the street below was a four-door Monte Carlo with Jersey plates. The blinking red, yellow, and green disco lights of the Pussy Cat Lounge, the topless go-go bar I lived above, danced on the shmutzy blue hood.

My pump segued close to my ribcage when a man wearing a cruddy-looking raincoat poured himself out of the passenger side and beelined to my doorbell. From my second-story perch he seemed on the short side, somewhere in the five-foot-six to five-eight range, with hair patent-leathered with Wildroot. I didn't get a good shag of the face. Suspense mounted along with my pulse rate.

My buzzer squawked. I slalomed past the oak table where Hank and the dinner dishes looked like they had the mopes. I hoisted my camera bag; the strap adhered like a label to my moist collarbone. The camera rested on my opposite shoulder for balance. The metal of the tripod felt cool against my skin. Hank parked his eyeballs on the rigging, walked me to the top of the stairwell, and told me to be careful. He put me in a liplock. He was always a right guy in the kissing department but tonight I had bigger things in mind. I had to meet the Man.

Insta-Death

I'm no gazelle—and even without photo regalia, getting past the bicycles in the hallway is a job for a professional contortionist. By the time I reached the street door, I was in a lather. Perfume is always handy to have when you're out to charm the pants off someone special. I'd forgotten to douse and I wasn't packing a purse. I couldn't go back upstairs for a splash; it might make Gallagher suspish. Kismet au naturel; it was a risk I had to take.

Dizzy with anticipation, I planked my most dazzling smile across my thin mug and danced my 5'4", 110-pound bod out the door. The person in the mac lounged against the car's fender, pulling on a Lucky. One gander and I turned a color that matched my hennaed hair.

What you see is what you get and I wasn't lamping any Philip Marlowe or Sam Spade. Nor for that matter Nick Charles, Lew Archer, Travis McGee, Mike Hammer, the Continental Op, Philo Vance, Ellery Queen, Hercule Poirot, Lord Peter Wimsey, Sherlock Holmes, Nero Wolfe, or even Charlie Chan.

Nope. Domenic Palladino was a dead ringer for Ratso Rizzo, the sleazo character in *Midnight Cowboy*. Ratso in real life had the decency to turn into Dustin Hoffman. Nick had no out. We were both stuck.

The corner of a powder blue, polyester leisure suit snuck out from under his raincoat and light glinted from the gold chain around his neck. The slight bulge at his waist didn't come from any secreted Smith & Wesson. It came from Milwaukee. Dash Hammett, Ray Chandler, and the pulpsters had set me up for a fall.

Okay, so I'd been sucker bait. But I looked at it this way—Nick had done me a favor. By queering my romantic notions, he'd slapped the Golden Boy weld back into true. The caper was now strictly on the up and up, a matter of purse strings and not heartstrings. It wasn't the first time jack in the pocket beat peter in the pants.

Palladino dumped my gear in the trunk and climbed back into the car. P.I.'s were supposed to be loners but Nick wasn't alone. Not by a long shot.

Once I adjusted to the short's arctic air, I checked out the wheelman. There was a large globe that was his head, rolls of fat that were his neck, and a limo-length expanse that was his back. On his blubbery right arm, peeking out from his short-sleeve drip-dry, was a faded tattoo that looked like an anchor. This leviathan made Sidney Greenstreet look skinny.

The gumshoe twisted around to introduce me to Frank "Flash" Ferrara. Flash's moniker suited him the way "Tiny" fits a sumo wrestler. El Rotundo was Palladino's operative and a per-pound bargain at any price. Ferrara's specialty was close-range tailing. No one suspected that she or he was being followed by a blimp. Flash had been working the Dewinter case with the peeper from the beginning. Tonight he came along for the kill.

The glow from the Pussy Cat shed dim light on the wavy-haired blade sharing the backseat vinyl. He was in the twenty-five to thirty zone, had a pencil moustache, and was decorated in a tight tank top and a pair of calf-clingers that'd done time at the drycleaners. Sal Martino was the name, disinterested witness was his game.

So much for intros, on to the tough stuff. Ferrara pointed the Buick up Sixth. Driving required his total concentration. The sleuth, no Mr. Talkative, went on beaver patrol. I sized up Sal.

Disinterest

"So, Sal," I started, my voice sounding louder than normal against the quiet hum of the A.C., "you freelance this kind of gig a lot?"

The clotheshorse spoke softly. "Nah, I'm a hairstylist. I'm kinda doing this as a favor. Uncle Frank came by the shop this afternoon and sez, 'Wanna make some easy money tanight?' I wasn't doing anything so I sez 'Sure.' "

"But if Flash's your uncle, how can you go into court and testify as a disinterested party? You're not supposed to have any connection with the case or any stake in the outcome, right? I mean, if you go into court, won't the judge toss your testimony?"

Fleshpot flapped his chins in my direction. "Ain't no big deal; Sallie here's my nephew. Tha kid'll do tha job good as anybody. Besides, his last name ain't tha same so who's gonna know, huh?"

Palladino cast his heavy-lidded eyes backseatward. "And ain't nobody gonna know if nobody opens her big, fat mouth. Kapish, sweetheart?"

"10-4."

Gaining Entry

Ferrara squeezed his gas guzzler snug between a Caprice and an Accord on West 84th. That put us smack in front of the Seymour Arms Hotel, a certified New York City landmark. That meant the place had history going for it. It went as far as the building's exterior and not a centimeter further. Erected in the early 1900s by a rich industrialist, it was a mishmash of architectural styles garnished by French froufrou. The guidebooks pushed its "fanciful silhouette against the night sky." And no wonder. Street level was an eyesore, polka-dotted with winos, weirdos, and hookers.

Inside was an even harder-luck story. The lobby smelled of slow but certain death. Once upon a time, entertainment muckity-mucks lived in palatial suites. Now it was riffraff in cubbyholes. Of course, architectural history marches on—hand in glove with real estate values. In a few more years the hoi polloi'd reclaim, renovate, and recycle the Seymour into a chichi coop.

We weren't sent here by the Landmarks Commission to study gentrification feasibility. We were interested in the stairway to the right of the main entrance, the one covered with an awning whose white script read "The Cosmopolitan Baths." The Cosmo was another kind of Gotham landmark. Its historical antecedents were Greek. The strictly male clientele, however, wasn't into historic preservation so much as penetration. There were other tubs in town but the Cosmo was one of the classiest.

Nick came across with the scam. "Lefty—thatsa guy workin' tha gate—he lets us in, we go through tha baths fast, headin' for tha door in tha back. Keep your eyes right and traps shut. And you"—he faced me now—"do whatchya can ta keep you and that thing" —he pointed to the photo gizmos—"outta sight. Under no conditions do we get anybody in there agitated. We take tha elevator upta tha roof and set up for action. Any questions?"

A sawbuck changed hands at the door and Lefty, a bulletheaded ex-marine, waved his hand permissively in the direction of a blue-lit stairway. I teamed up with Flash, using his flab to hide my weapon and my unappreciated feminine merchandise. I kept my optics glued to the hankshaw's Florsheims. The floor had a nice geometric pattern. I couldn't help noticing the pool; it was a biggie that had less to do with swimming than with olympian pretensions. Three beautiful young men floated languidly. Even over Ferrara's labored breathing, I heard Sal sigh.

We breezed toward the door at the end of the bar. Flash was no jigtimer. His phiz was a Niagara of *shvitz*. Melon-size stains grew under his Carlsbad Cavern armpits. He sucked in air like an Electrolux. It was just his way of demonstrating the second law of thermodynamics: Everything wears down. Fat things faster than others.

We scrunched up in the cramped corridor by the freight elevator, waiting for Lefty. He treated us to a view of his pan ten minutes later. He spoke a wicked Brooklynese and looked cheesier under the fluorescents than he had outside. The motherfucker liked his line; it showed in the way he muscled open the freight car and shoved us inside. He punched the controls for "blast-off," Mach 1'd us to the Seymour's top floor, pushed us out, slammed the door, and rocketed back to AquaWorld. A sawbuck doesn't buy service with a smile anymore. Detecto novels lied about that too; they said it bought the red carpet.

Up on the Roof

The merc in the thermometer sizzled. The moonlight was molten. Tar oozed under our feet as we headed for the roof's west end. There were three folding chairs already set up behind a chubby stone railing. Ferrara's caboose camped in the middle one. Nick's keister claimed the chair on the right. I spread the tripod's legs in front of the remaining and eased off the wraps.

Sal brushed a square of roof off with his hand, then daintily wiped his palm with the red nose-wipe he'd pried from his pocket. "I'm gonna catch up on my beauty sleep," he announced. "Don't wake me unless there's something worth looking at."

Talk about disinterest. Sal couldn't have looked more disinterested if he practiced in front of a mirror.

The gumshoe pulled a trio of binocs out from his leatherette attaché and he and Fatso put their thick fingers right to work fiddling the focus. The boss signaled me to do likewise. Using the hand with the diamond pinky ring that televised his initials, the P.I. pointed to the corner apartment building on the Drive. "See tha penthouse up there?" I swung the glasses hard right. "Tha one with all them flowers on tha terrace? Okay, ya see tha window ta tha left?" The air was so thick it puckered when he jabbed at it with his index. "That there's tha bood-whar. Now, ya see tha flowers? Paula, that's tha chicklet's name, Paula, she comes out every fuckin' night 'bout eleven thirty ta water 'em. Y'ask me, tha dame's daffy when it comes ta leafy stuff. Wonder what she'll do with 'em when Troy stops sendin' her tha lettuce? After Rosenblatt gets through with her, ain't no way she's gonna afford ta stay up there."

I made a noise like a death rattle.

"Now whatsa matter with ya?" Nick asked.

"Oh, nothing," I said, feeling a traitor to my sex. Benedicta Arnold.

"Anyways, every night she comes out and like it's weird. She's always wearin' somethin' lavender color. It ain't that she looks bad in it, but Jesus, enough's enough. So then maybe five minutes go by and it's loverboy's turn. He comes out . . ."

"To shpritz the plants?"

"Hell, no, angel. He comes out with, get this, a paira binoculars. The sonofabitch's a Peeping Tom. He peeps fifteen, twenty minutes a night. Whaddya bet he tells tha broad he's stargazin'?"

Ferrara made ha-ha sounds. "Bet 70–30 for."

"Make it 90–10 and ya'd be in tha ballpark. After tha stargazin' routine, they go in. When they're futzin' around in tha fronta tha apartment, we can't see squat. They futz a hour, hour 'n' a half, get nackered, and head for tha bed. Lucky for us tha perverts like fuckin' with tha lights on."

"That's the whole setup?"

"That's it, sweetheart; that's what they do every night we been watchin'. So what you gotta do is be all set and ready ta go when they are."

"Opportunity and Inclination in action."

"You got it, sister."

Now that I had the skinny, I trained the F1 on the high window. My hand St. Vitus danced and my head throbbed like a discothèque. What was a nice girl like me doing on a roof like this? I was an Ivy Leaguer with a B.A., for Chrissake. A fancy shmantsy M.F.A. to boot. I could teach college. I had talent. Imagination. Occasionally I thought I even had good looks. What I definitely didn't have was money. The root of all evil.

That explained why a nice girl like me was in a mess like this. Being paid to do something I shouldn't be doing and being professional enough to want to do well what I didn't want to be doing at all. What did I care if Paula was getting it on with Price? Touchy-feelies were okay with me. I'd been known to go in for the same myself. Besides, who knew? Hubbikins probably was getting some tail on the side himself. Alimony made the situation hyper dicey.

Why couldn't the Dewinters kiss and make up? Or let the alimony baloney slide and ease on the sleaze? Send me home to Hank and Willy Boy. That triangle was pain city, too, but at least it was *my* pain city.

Or maybe Romeo and Juliet wouldn't Adam and Eve it. I was being paid for time, not results, right? No action between the sheets, so what? It wouldn't be the first Friday night I'd spent in Dullsville.

Adultery, Garden Variety

"See, whad I tell ya," the detective boasted when sure enough, 11:30 P.M. on the dot, the woman in question drifted onto the terrace. I checked the slat out through the magnifiers. The lanky brunette was nice-looking though nothing to make you spin a cart around in the supermarket. Thirty-fourish. Delicate facial features. Mouth, pouty. Graceful; the product of years of ballet lessons. The backstraps of her sundress made a big lavender X against her white skin. She ranged among her plants, plucking a leaf here and there the way she'd straighten a guy's tie. She was the sappy kind who treated new blossoms like little kids.

"Get down," the P.I. hissed when Jack Price made his debut. "He sees us, we're dead." Price looked to be in his early twenties, clean-cut, dark hair, aquiline nose, square jaw. All-American.

He stood at the corner of the terrace, dressed in a pair of skimpy cut-offs in a pose that'd look a million bucks in a boating ad. Planted, the only part of his he-manly body he moved was his noodle, and that he swiveled on one very supple neck. He did fifteen minutes' worth of social studies and then, as if choreographed, put down his spyglasses just as Paula lowered her watering can. Terrific timing. They seemed to glide toward the sliding door. I waited for a pas de deux, but they were no Rudy N. and Dame Margot. Instead they linked arms and strolled indoors, airheads to the peril that surrounded them.

Killing Time

Stakes take up a page max in books, five minutes maybe in flicks, and in TV shows, blink and it's goodbye. Media hype. Real-life surveillance is a drag. Big chunks of zero happen. Something breaks this side of tomorrow if you're lucky. Usually you're not. You snap gum, smoke too many cigs, give the thumbs plenty of twiddle. You want a drink so bad you can taste it. But nature's against you; what goes in must come out. Peeing is a no-no. You might miss what you've been waiting for while you're on the can. In the sleuth biz killing time is no joke. Dicks kill more time than people.

The crew wasn't talking much. Where was my Dick Tracy two-way wristwatch so I could check in—and up—on Golden Boy? Dangerous leaving him alone with Blake so much. Although even Mr. B. seemed exciting from the aerial.

"Hey, Nick," I said, antsy to pass time. "How'd you team up with your sidekick?" Where had Holmes met Watson?

"Fat Boy and me, we go way back, don't we, Flash?" Tub o' Lard jiggled his jowls affirmatively. "We grew up tagether in Little Italy, over on Mulberry. I was a real sweet kid till Flash baby corrupted me in grade school. I was gonna be a priest, make my mother proud."

"*You* were going to be a priest?" My think machine went "tilt." Palladino, a dick like G. K. Chesterton's famous shamus, Father Brown? That was a hoot. "Seriously?"

"Cross my heart, sweetheart. But Ferrara, he taught me how ta lie ta tha nuns, cheat on tests, play hookie, and smoke cigarettes." Nick dragged hard on the weed he was working on for emphasis. "Not much help with tha girls though, were ya, Fat Boy?" The big fella's solitary incisor sparkled in a homecoming queen smile. "I always say Flash here broke my mother's heart."

"So how'd you wind up a private eye?"

"It was either be a punk or take tha job cousin Mario got me as a insurance investigator. Nine ta five was safer. I knew if I got in serious trouble, my mother, may she rest in peace, woulda killed me."

"Who knows what evil lurks in the hearts of men?" The Shadow knew. And Mom.

I Spy

Time moved slo-mo. Without a tube, talk, sex, drugs, and rock 'n' roll, a little voyeurism goes a long way. Tonight it was the only game in town.

I binocu-cruised around the concrete fjords. With no fixed itinerary, I put in at some nifty ports of call. Sightseeing included:

Stop #1 (balcony): See paunchy middle-aged native jerk off among begonias.

Stop #2 (kitchen): Watch Samurai warrior demonstrate swordsmanship on rare roast-beef sandwich.

Stop #3 (bedroom): Observe bizarre mating dance. Sultry tigress decked out with a great pair of gams and little else wiggles seductively on unmade bed. Nordic tiger knocks himself out doing situps. Bodybuilding TKO's body chemistry. Babe on bed has a long night ahead of her.

Stop #4 (dining room): Visit with elderly chief as he instructs pimply teenage brave. Rite of passage refreshments: Coke and Twinkie.

Stop #5 (hallway): Participate in celebration of household gods. Young virgin boogie-woogies with vacuum god, purifying sanctuary.

Stop #6 (study): Watch craftsperson at work. Forty-five-year-old writer pounds at typewriter, molding the Great American novel.

Stop #7 (living room): Catch a view of typical domestic life. Father plays horsie with chunky toddler. Mother puts bawling brat to beddie-bye.

Return to point of departure. Pronto.

Stymied

Suddenly light blazed in the Dewinter bedroom. Palladino kicked Sal back into consciousness. My blood pressure did the shimmy. Our Lady of the Flowers sailed into the pale-lilac-colored room—the gal was no piker when it came to color coordination—and plunked two fat plum-toned pillows from the king-size. She doused the glim and floated out. A whopping three-and-a-half-minute event. We waited around for an encore.

It was 3:45 A.M. when the P.I. pushed the field glasses into his attaché and slammed it shut. Moonbeams punched up Palladino's puss frozen in fury and Ferrara's doughy features sagging with exhaustion. Sal appeared world-weary, but then again, Sal cultivated that look. I relawned and leafed the Nikon.

Eros only knows why the couple's night moves changed venue. We left the chairs behind to find out. Meanwhile, we hopped the Seymour's passenger elevator to the ground floor.

We hurried past the desk clerk. He was as old as the building itself and his actuarials read "high risk." Gramps gave us the once-over; disgust showed through his cataracts.

Flash's Buick, as silent as a hearse, barreled downtown. The streets were empty so we clocked it to my place in record time, the night's only run of luck. As I jumped out of the car, Nick put it to me: "Tanight, same time, same station." It wasn't just the postman, who only rings twice.

Fear

As soon as I got upstairs, I stashed my munitions and stripped down. Honeybunch was a soggy mound on the bed, snoozing soundly, the sheet twisted around his feet like rope. *The Portable Blake* was open to *For the Sexes: The Gates of Paradise*. Nice to know he was thinking of me before he conked out. I cuddled up close and ran my hand over Hank's stack-up. Then I stared at the contours of the city out my curtainless windows. Fear stalked my Walker Street loft through the naked panes. Four happy years I'd lived without blinds or shades and never thought twice about it.

Now all I could think about was a stranger sitting up on a nearby roof spying on my baby and me. A peek freak like Jack Price. Or a blackmailer. Or a psychopath. Or a photographer. Or some hired snoop putting together a dossier for some unknown reason for some unknown client. Or worse yet, for my parents.

"Hank," I whispered, then supplemented with an elbow jab. "Help!"

Golden Boy rolled over. "What's the matter, Sherlock?"

"I'm scared."

He pulled me to him. His sweat made him slippery. "Don't worry, I'll protect you." He was barely awake but halfway to a hard-on. His mouth and hands sleepwalked breastward.

I groaned softly. "Hank, stop. Not tonight."

"Huh?" he murmured, then "mmmm" in my ear.

"I'm afraid there's somebody out there watching."

"Fear and Hope are Vision." He wasn't as asleep as I thought.

Now I was really frightened. Not only of voyeurs but that *For the Sexes* was a kinky Blakean sex manual. "It's too dangerous."

Gallagher's hand parted my thighs and began undercover work.

"Danger," I mumbled. I'd learn to live with it.

Thwarted

Saturday, July 25th, the lady vanishes. No flower and peep show; no twinkle of light in the bedroom. At 1:15 A.M. Nick split for the lobby. He would ring the penthouse and hang up if one or the other answered. Neither did. Paula's Mercedes wasn't in the garage. The kids had skipped out and stayed out past curfew. 4:30 A.M. we called it quits.

July 26th, Sunday. The usual routine, then both in the bedroom. It looked like a good time for buzzing in the Brillo. Paula wore a knockaround lavender jumpsuit and Jack kept his privates tucked up in cut-offs. Price lunged. Not for his lady love but for the windowshade. Down it came. Curtains for us.

Another washout on Monday. A screwup with the central A.C. and there was a pissant window fan blocking our view.

Lady Luck was on Lady Lavender's side. The lovers were rating high on the P.I.'s S.H.P.O.S.—subhuman piece of shit—list.

It was only 11:30 P.M. when Flash plugged his wheels into a slot in front of the Pussy Cat. Palladino'd been swearing a blue streak for blocks and his voice was hoarse. He rattled gravel around in his throat. "Tanight's tha last goddamn night we spend on tha goddamn roof. It ain't worth it ta Dewinter ta shell out more dough."

"Terrif," I said, still rooting for the home team. Nick glowered.

"We got enough dirt on tha dame for Rosenblatt ta mincemeat her in court no matter what."

"Nuts," I whispered. You can run but you can't hide.

"Hey, yeah," Roly Poly concurred. Sal sided with unc.

"Shaddup, fathead." The shamus said it with starch. "Drive."

Parting Shots

Night patrol number five, morale at the Seymour fell to subbasement level. What a chump, I'd been falling for those lurid cover drawings of handsome hankshaws, tawdry women, smoking pistols, and exotic poisons that hinted at fastpaced action.

Around 1:00 A.M. we got a break. Lothario entered the bedroom in his birthday suit. Nick and Flash slapped their mitts together and yelled "way ta go." Sal and I went gaga. We knew the guy was well built but well hung was something else again. Of course, size per se means zilch. We'd see—it was our last chance—how well the same threw his weight around.

Our prey went over to the mirror. He swiped at his hair and smoothed the sides with his palms. He flexed his pecs; they were in good working order. He turned sideways to tradelist his profile. The guy had a big crush on himself.

The gidget appeared in the doorway panoplied in a filmy lavender—natch—negligee, the kind that looks throwaway but was Hollywood big budget. She turned on a dime and headed off toward the Drive side of the apartment. Nick growled, "Fuckin' piss shit, not again." She was gone what seemed a week. Fat Stuff was so tense his blubber looked taut. I was breathing hard, my trigger finger stroking the Nikon's shutter button as tenderly as a baby's bottom. Sal was in heaven but heading toward heartache. There's no future in unrequited love.

Paula hit the boudoir carrying a bottle of bubbly and two glasses. When the tide turns in a case, it turns with a vengeance. The celebration of today becomes the kick in the teeth of tomorrow. I wished I could have warned them they were wasting the French fizz.

I didn't like doing it but I squeezed the shutter. Adonis in the raw toasting sylph in skimps. Classical painting always shows dress situation reversed. Manet for one would turn over in his grave. This was a sicko time to think art history.

"Okay," I said after a fast five frames. A small number would only do small damage; that was as convincing as only being a little pregnant. "I got what you needed, so let's go."

"They just got warmed up," Flash slavered. "I waited days ta see this show. What's tha rush?"

"I've got a weak heart. It can't take the excitement." Ferrara thought I was kibitzing. Sal wasn't gung ho to watch either. He was jealous. Even his pencil moustache drooped.

"Dollface," Palladino said, "a picture's worth a thousand words. You should know that. Why settle? We can give Marv a whole fuckin' *Encyclopaedia Britannica*. We're gonna stick around and make Rosenblatt one happy guy. Hangin' in for tha hot stuff's tha least we can do." A grin spread ear to ear.

I was having an A-1 approach-avoidance conflict. "So what else is new?" my old shrink would've asked. "Huh?" my present company would wonder. The only psychology they understood was "shut up and deal."

Paula and Jack sat on glitzy patterned sheets getting looped. Price polished off his hooch, set the glass down on the night table, and made the big move toward his broiler. Click, click went my camera. There was a mini-tussle—click—and Jack pinned his victim to the bed—click. The broad liked that and laughed—click. Jack bussed her hard and rubbed his leg between hers—click. He disengaged a hand and hiked up her nightie—click. I half expected to see lavender pubes but the dame had limits.

Price's labials pony-expressed across his lover's bodyscape. They cut a trail between her hilly breasts—click. Then they cantered over ridges of ribs—click—and passed along a mesa of stomach and headed into the sagebrush—click and double click. Meanwhile, his meat hooks ran maneuvers in the southern territories. I had to hand it to Mrs. D., she'd picked herself a live one. She was pretty sexpert herself, hand jiving on Jack's back and ass—click—and then putting lipstick on his dipstick—click thrice. "Get a good shotta that, honey," Palladino directed. Our disinterested witness groaned. He thought Romeo had put himself in the wrong hands entirely.

The duo didn't miss a trick. I wondered if they banged their brains out all the other nights we'd missed or whether they were making up for lost time. "I wouldn't mind a night of him myself," I mumbled loud enough for Sal to hear. "Me, too," he seconded.

The sex machines ran out of juice; I ran out of film. I'd shot them in enough different positions to illustrate the Kama Sutra. Palladino yelled "More." Ferrara gave a football cheer. Sal sulked.

"C'mon, let's blow," Top Banana commanded when the bedroom blacked out at 3:22 A.M. "Time tha resta us got some shuteye." He and Ferrara were still chuckling as they packed away their binocs.

Streetlevel, Sal announced he wasn't going home. He was off to the Cosmo to drown his sorrows in the pool. If he couldn't have Jack, at least he'd be in the vicinity.

My colleagues were cheerful as we zipped down Broadway. Why shouldn't they be? Their job was over and they could collar a nod. Lucky me—the one leaving town in a day and half for a week of sun and fun, ha ha—I had work up the wazoo. My motto was the same as Pinkerton's: "We never sleep."

Figure me for exhausted. Then chalk me up as a nervous wreck. What if I made some dumb-ass techno goof and none of the conjugals came out on the film. I wasn't exactly a neophyte when it came to photo disaster. There were those wedding shots I developed in the wrong chemicals. Or that time I forgot to reset the lightmeter's ASA. And what about that press party when my strobe went on the fritz and only half of each frame got exposed? How I talked my way out of that one was a long story. I knew if I screwed up tonight's shoot, Palladino'd have me fitted for a cement overcoat and shoe ensemble. And I'd be splashing around in the Hudson, not the Caribbean.

The Pussy Cat was still pumping the promise of sex a-go-go and flat beer into the street when Flash dropped me at my door. The shamus helped carry my gear to the curb. "Guess this is goodbye, kiddo. Hava good trip. Ya getta chance, drop me a line. Nice workin' with ya. I'll be in touch." He slapped me on the back, backed into the Monte Carlo, and was gone.

Skulduggery

I felt like a pack mule lumbering up the stairs. The loft was candlelit. Romantic. Gallagher stood, staring out the window.

"Aw, hey, you didn't have to wait up for me. But I'm glad you did."

Golden Boy seemed to be doing a rigor mortis imitation.

"Hank?" No reply. I shed my equip and rushed toward him. "Hello?" Nobody home. Cuddles' eyes were glassy as aggies. "Earth to Gallagher, earth to Gallagher, do you read me? Come in Gallagher. Over."

No go.

"Hank-o, what happened?" I tried not to shriek.

"Hap-pen-ed?" His voice sounded as far away as a satellite.

"Babycakes, you're a zombie."

"Zom-bie," he telecommunicated. "Oh." Long pause. "No. My Or-gans of, uh, Per-cep-tion are," pause, "wide . . . o-pen."

"Open, huh?"

"Wa-nna . . . know . . . what I . . . saw?" He modeled his dominoes in a goofy grin.

I didn't see as I had the option.

"I . . . saw . . . ," fade out, "the Tor-ments of . . . Love . . . and, uh, Jeal-ou-sy." He sounded like a 33⅓ platter played at 16.

I thought I'd seen exactly that, and more of it, at the Seymour but this wasn't the time for one-upmanship.

"I . . . saw . . . Ob-scure . . . Se-pa-ra-tion." His vocals demonstrated the Doppler effect.

Separation from reality.

"I . . . saw . . . Et-er-nal . . . My-ri-ads."

I saw red.

"Okay, okay. But how did you get to see all this stuff? Where were you tonight?" While I was out busting my superego earning a living.

"With Par-ker." He stopped, opened his mouth, tried to speak, clammed, and wet his lips. "And . . . his . . . girl-friend . . . Win-ny." Another station break. "She . . . brought these . . . ," brief spell of amnesia, "these . . . uh . . . ma-gic," very long pause, "mush-rooms . . . from . . . Gol-gon-ooooo-za. . . . They were . . . ," aphasia time again, "fa-aaar . . . out."

"Very."

"Yeah. . . . Fa-aaar . . . out." The guy was a primo jargonaut tonight.

"Look, sugar plum," I interrupted, "I think you're wanted in the sleep department."

"Sslee-eep?" The concept took a while to penetrate. "O-kay."

I undressed him and put him to bed. This was *not* better living through chemistry.

Speaking of chemistry, there was an A.P.B. out for me in the darkroom. First I rolled the film on a steel reel and dropped it into the tank. Poured in the D76, let it do its thing for aeons, then poured it out. Did I get the whole enchilada or *nada?* Cartier-Bresson, the honcho frog photojournalist, didn't have exclusive franchise on decisive moments.

The film sat in the fixer the longest four minutes in Guinness record. My hands shook holding the souped celluloid up to the light. There they were, tiny negative images of the penthousers committing their tiny crime of passion. I was glad-sad, up-down, pleased-pissed, calm-crazed as I hung the strip up to dry.

I checked on Golden Boy; he was dead to the world. I was still worrying about him when I went back into the darkroom an hour later to mix chemicals and begin printing. The work was sandpaper on the morals and a bitch on the hormones.

The snaps made me horny. Too bad I didn't get a chance to try out all the new moves I'd learned while they were still fresh. I thought about do-it-yourselfing but my hands were covered with chemistry. It might cause warts.

Legal Tender

Hank was still comatose when I shoe leather expressed the three blocks to Rosenblatt's office at 353 Broadway. The decor was wall to wall legal paper. The mouthpiece was reading a brief and had his feet up on the desk when I came in. I tossed the envelope onto his meatbag. "I couldn't send these through the mail; they're porn."

Marv's chair creaked as he arranged his anatomy. He flipped through the prints and whistled through his nicotine-stained chompers. "Nice," he cooed. "Very, very nice."

"Let's face it, I'm gifted." I got serious. "Listen, Marv, I know Paula's not the client, but how bad are these going to make things for her? In court, I mean."

"Tell you the truth, Janie, I don't really know. Most people, when they marry money and divorce it, they gotta wind up ahead of where they started, if that's what you're worried about. Look, she won't get as much as Dewinter offered in the beginning but she'll probably make out all right. She's got a decent lawyer. Not as good as me, of course, but decent. And who knows? Maybe it won't go to trial. My guess is Troy's still soft on her, the jerk.

"If it's any consolation for you, I don't plan to use the photos unless I have to." He picked the evidence up again. "They're good, though, really good." I was convinced when I handed Esquire the bill. He didn't even bellyache.

The rest of the day was strictly low profile. All I had to do was pack. It was no lather throwing two bricks of film, string bikinis, mysteries, and Kodak's *Photographic Surveillance Techniques* into a suitcase. Hank was the hard part. He'd returned to the planet—minus most memory of last night's magic—but was still distant. I didn't have to go all the way to Club Med; I already missed him.

We had a quiet dinner at a local chophouse, where high tech complemented high prices. The feed went down fine; it was the conversation that left a bad taste. I tried putting Gallagher off Golgonooza; his trip upset me more than my gastric juices.

The Rolling Stones tried to warn me: You can't always get what you want. I got a sermon; the man was determined. Readjusting to nightlife on terra firma—rather than observing it through a lens and up in the air—was no snap.

We were back at Walker Street about the same time Paula and Jack would be doing their terrace thing. And we were between the lily-whites and balling the same time as the Upper Westsiders, assuming they were on the same performance schedule as yesterday. How did we compare bedwise? Only photos would tell. Only they never would. I'm camera shy.

The Getaway

8:45 A.M., Thursday, July 30th. The getaway car screeched to a halt in front of the homestead. Viv Steiner, my old college roommate and best buddy, was behind the wheel. She tooted.

"Guess it's time to breeze."

Gallagher was leisurely tossing Blake masterpieces into his grip. Winny wasn't picking him up until noon.

"I wish you were coming with me," I said and meant it. Better there than There.

"C'mon, Jane, we went through all that last night."

He was right. Why stage a rematch. Losing once was bad enough and I'm a poor sport to begin with.

"Besides, it'll be nice for you to spend time with Sara."

"Stop with the altruism. I'm allergic."

Viv honked again. "I really ought to go." I stayed to smooch instead. There was another blast on the horn.

"You'll be careful?" He nodded.

"And take good care of yourself, right?" Another shake.

"Promise?"

"What do you want, blood?"

That was exactly what I was afraid the Blakeans might be after. "Well, then, have a Radiant time." I did my best to sound jaunty.

"It's my Firm Persuasion." I was afraid of that, too.

"I'll miss you."

"I'll miss you too." More slobberation. Exit.

I cakewalked through the unemployment line and Viv was a crackerjack driver. She'd been a cabbie awhile after graduating *summa* from *Alma M.* Now she was a Legal Aid lawyer, but she still drove like a maniac.

We made the airport in nothing flat. It was swell seeing Sara, although my new surveillance skills didn't help my conversationals any. Like I said, I'd gotten used to watching, not gabbing. Mid-flight Captain Skip got on the squawk box and announced we were cruising at an altitude of 35,000 feet. I was way beyond sheet smelling.

Grounded

A micro bus shuttled us from dinky Raizet airport in Pointe-à-Pitre to Le Club. We were met at the gate by wackos dressed in loud floral items, chanting a strange atonal ditty and dancing a spazzy hokey pokey. Only hours ago I'd been scared shitless about a Blake cult? I must've been crazy. That raised another hideous possibility. "Is this a loony bin?" I interrogated Sara. "I thought there was something bizarro about Mom and Dad sending me on this trip." Sis denied everything. My terror increased. That meant these were no ordinary berserkos, just relaxed vacationers doing the official Club welcome bop in official Club drag. Worse yet, lessons in this song and dance routine were given daily during happy hour. Thank God I had two left feet, sang off key, and planned to nap religiously between five and seven every day, including Sunday.

The staff was a hands-across-the-waters conglom that gave the U.N. a run for its money. The poppit bead moolah system was as primitive as petrodollars. The thatched huts I'd imagined were up-scaled into squat yellowish buildings with casement windows. The vegetation had leaves like shiv blades, especially the draecenas. If it was heavy going with the flora, the fauna was worse.

Surf 'n' Turf

The smear of white sand was ringed with picture postcard palms. Sit under one and get beaned by a coconut. The water looked calm as a bathtub's and blue as Sani-Flush. I unpacked, bikinied up, and shot into the surf. I didn't know about sea urchins. Imagine being attacked by a swarm of killer bees and you'll have a clue what happened to my feet.

More disaster followed when I limped to the dining room. Club Med was big on Mingling. The place was always lousy with it but dinner was when it went on full blast. Eyes swiveled like klieg lights. Tabletops groaned under Himalayas of food. The Americans oohed and aahed. The French ooh lala'd.

I was feeling ho-hum when I was seated at one of the large round tables next to a liquor salesman from Hawthorne, New Jersey. He fronted as Vince and he'd had a crummy day too.

"You go to the nude beach?" was the way he led into it.

"Nope," I replied. "Not yet."

"You have to be real careful, you know what I mean?" I didn't and said so. "That sun'll fry you. Take it from me." He pronged a fried shrimp. "I know from experience, believe me."

I did. His face was lobster-colored. "Caught a few too many rays, huh?"

"It's not my face that's the problem." He leaned toward me conspiratorially. "I sunburned my pecker. You know what that feels like?"

I told him about the sea urchins but empathy wasn't what he had in mind. He wanted handholding and then some. All I wanted to do was crawl into bed with Raymond Chandler's *The Simple Art of Murder*. Sometimes the dead in bed are more exciting than the living. Or in Vince's case, the living dead.

The Fixup

Sports and meals put the only dents into the day. You could knock yourself out playing volleyball and tennis, scuba diving, snorkeling, sailing, swimming, and/or doing yoga or calisthenics. Sara was ready; she took off right after breakfast to surround herself with brawn.

Me, I hoisted a couple of Bloody Marys. Promo material claimed "Our cuisine helps you rediscover your appetite for life." I'd wait for lunch to find out.

That, as it turned out, was no meal. It was a three-ring circus with food acts. I was gimping past the crepes when I bumped into the frog. We got into a rap. Jean-Pierre was a Parisian-based TV producer, had salt-and-pepper hair, eyes that Ansel Adams would call Zone V, and a last name—LeCoq—that made you wonder. His tight, just-under-six-foot body organized itself around a bathing suit that made a fig leaf look rococo. I had to remind myself that it was Sara who was shopping in the men's department; I was only browsing.

I made it a point to introduce him to sis. She'd been a French major in college and here was the perfect way to bone up on the parlez-vous. Though I suspected body language would interest her more than Berlitzing.

"Yummy," Sara assessed when the swoony'd gone off to wind surf. "Nice going."

"Wrong number, toots. He's a nice guy but I'm into bedlock with the boy back home. Even if he is weird-ass lately."

"I'll bet J.P.'s great in bed."

"On what do you base your diagnosis, doc?"

"French tradition. And the vibes are right."

"Why don't you give him a test drive and let me know." Medical curiosity on my part.

"Are you sure you're not interested?"

"I'd feel like a heel two-timing."

"You're on vacation. Hank'd never have to know."

"Nah, I couldn't, Sara." Paula, Jack, and Troy suddenly flashed on the mental monitor. "With my luck, there'd be complications."

"I'm not going to argue. Mind if I make a play for him myself?"

I felt a teeny twinge of regret. Ignorable. "Go for it, honey. He's all yours."

She did but he wasn't. He hung around, seemed to like her but the bozo didn't make his move. Holidays don't last forever. By Monday night it was time to fish or cut bait.

In the Heat of the Night

The palms wigwagged in the starlight and the tropicals pumped heavy perfume into the air. There's a Blakism that goes: "The weak in courage is strong in cunning." Cunning was what the J.P. caper called for and I was the right wimp for the job.

What I wanted to do was mosey over to the bunkhouse and read Patricia Highsmith's *Little Tales of Misogyny*. Instead I was at the disco with Sara.

The overhead fan did a half-assed job. The crepe paper hung like *al dente* lasagna noodles. I was standing on the sidelines when a hairy hand grabbed me and pulled. An invite to cement-mix from a graduate of the Fred Flintstone Academy of Dance. I liked primitive art but that was as far as my taste for the primitive went.

Frenchie came to my rescue and told the caveman to crawl under the nearest rock. That's what I assume the blah blah meant translated.

"You have not luck with men here." J.P. waved his flipper in Fred's direction.

Why should here be any different? I commented, but only to myself.

"My English, it is not so good. I do not always say properly. Men, *les hommes*, they do not understand you. You are *peut-être un peu difficile.*"

According to my script, we were supposed to discuss Sara, not me. "Sara's much less difficult and a helluva lot nicer." It wasn't the smoothest transition but there wasn't time to get fancy.

"Ah, *oui*, your *soeur*. A very nice girl."

"She thinks you're very nice too." Not subtle but hopefully effective.

"*Merci*. But you are more, how shall I say, *intéressante.*" His Zone V's flashed.

"Oh" was my first response. "Uh oh" my second. "Excuse me a minute, okay? I'll be right back."

I zigzagged across the dance floor. J.P. had gotten under my skin like a tropical disease. I had a bad case of Opportunity and Inclination.

Sara didn't need a CAT scan to diagnose the ailment. "I prescribe action," she said in an I-told-you-this-would-happen tone. Smug.

Now I had palpitations. "I was afraid you'd say that."

"Didn't you ever have the urge before?"

"Sure. There was that hot flash over the dick. But that didn't count. That came out of love of literature. One look at him cured me double quick."

"Any ideas about Hank?"

"High fidelity as far as I know."

"Look, Jane, Hank's a million miles away in some crazy cult commune."

I wondered what my squeeze was doing with the Blakeans. Or what was being done to him. "Don't remind me."

Junior sawbones continued. "He never has to know. And it's not like J.P. lives in SoHo and you're going to bump into him every week at the Laundry Loft. So you can fuck him and have a lot of fun. Or you can suffer."

"I'm already suffering. I feel nauseous and dizzy. This goddamn conversation is taking years off my life."

"It's your vacation and your choice, sweetie."

"What would you do?"

"You have to ask?" She shot me a glance reserved for mental defectives.

The result: LeCoq and I waltzed to the beach. We horizontalized and did more than swap spit. Preplug, I called "Halt!"

"*Quoi?*"

"I have a problem." I had to spill.

Panic registered on Frenchie's index. He fished a deck of smokes from his shirt and fired up a butt. "First the good news," I said. "No, it's not herpes." He looked relieved. "Now for the bad news." Bad? It was the bad acme. "I, uh, don't have my, uh, diaphragm."

"*Pas de problème.*"

"Sure," I thought. No *problème* for you, fella; ten-carat *problème* for me.

"We put back on the clothes and get it in your room. *C'est facile, n'est-ce pas?*"

"Yeah, it should be, but it isn't. Because I didn't bring one. At all. See, I'm into this guy back in the Apple, and . . ."

Frogman looked famisht. "And this man, he keeps for you this *truc?*"

"Of course not," I snapped feministically. "How about I'm just the true-blue, old-fashioned-girl type?"

"*Pardon, mademoiselle,* but I think this is shit." He pronounced "shit" "sheet." Cute but it didn't help.

Too bad the magic of moonlight goes only so far and no further. "Okay, you win. I'm not old-fashioned. I'm an asshole. I didn't figure on blanket drill with somebody else."

Parley-voo ran his lunch hooks over my sandy breadbasket.

"There are *les capots anglais. Les préservatifs.* How do you say in English?"

It took a bit to crack the language barrier. He meant rubbers. Only he didn't have any.

"The souvenir shop, *peut-être?*" Everything here came printed with the official trident insignia. Trojans probably did also. Maybe embossed; Le Club's very own French tickler.

Jean-Pierre checked the luminescent dial on his Rolex. "*Merde,* too late. *Fermé.*"

I ruled out rough riding as too risky. I wasn't cut out to be the mother of tadpoles.

To make a sad story short, we put the big love scene on the back burner. I went back to my room feeling guilty *and* frustrated. It was a combo that cried blood.

"What are you doing here?" I asked when I found little sister in bed with face cream. "I thought for sure you'd be off with one of your hot boys."

"More to the point, what are *you* doing here?"

I gave her a blow by blow.

"No problem," she assured me. "I'll fix you right up." She hopped up, yanked her wallet out of her bag, and threw me a package of 4X.

Sara was as prepped for disaster as the Red Cross. "You always carry rubbers?"

"A girl can't be too careful."

I'd learned my lesson.

"And sometimes I get sick of taking all the responsibility. There are times the guy should deal with it."

"Roger."

"Besides, who likes shlepping all that paraphernalia around. It takes up all the room in your purse."

"How do men respond when you whip one of these thingies out?"

"I was afraid you'd ask that. I'm strong in theory, poor in actual practice. Can I ask you a question now?"

"Anything. Shoot."

"What the hell are you standing here asking me stupid questions for? If I were you—and I wish I were—I'd be in J.P.'s room doing it."

My knees turned to Jell-O. "You think I should? It's so late."

This time it was a look that would've thawed the polar ice cap. "You have a pressing business appointment first thing in the morning?"

It was a Section 8 and I dusted.

You could've knocked the dude over with a feather when I arrived in his room, flagging my trophies. On went #1. We were off and phallicizing.

The French have a rep as great lovers. Not just for their high C *hautes*—couture, cuisine, and culture—but of *l'amour* itself. LeCoq did me and his country proud. Savvy Sara apparently hadn't been a French major for nothing. I woke up late the next bright and *voilà* I was a Francophile *aussi*.

Aftermath

Did I get off scot-free on the guilt end? Does shit cling to a shovel? I'd be having a ball—sunning, shooting, snorkeling, sailing, shtupping—and suddenly guilt would gum the game. Guilt laced with fear.

I'd feel a stab in the labonza and bang, I'd be thinking "Hank." Here I was living it up and for all I knew Golden Boy's life was in grave danger. I was cheating on him while Blake-crazed maniacs might be doing a number on him. And even if they weren't, I hoped he was having a rotten time. I didn't like his going off without me.

Sara, meantime, was canoodling with a shrink from D.C. That

justified my sending a postcard to the folks saying we were having a wonderful time. I didn't tell them exactly why it was wonderful. They liked to think Sara and me pure as the driven snow. America is a free country and they were free to believe whatever hooey they wanted.

Since he'd asked, I popped a quickie off to the bloodhound. The front featured sand, surf, and skin. The back read: "Nick, This sure beats the Seymour tar beach. Wish you were here?" Damn straight, he did.

No sooner had I mailed the notes and turned around than playtime was played out. Jean-Pierre and I said *adieu* Thursday by a clump of dracaenas by the tennis court. The vegetation had softened during the week; I no longer worried about puncture wounds. Monsieur rolled his tongue out of my smush and ripped his lips from mine like Velcro. "You know, Jeanne"—he'd taken to frenchfrying my moniker—"I come to New York soon to make business. You give me your address and *téléphone* and we see each other, *oui?*"

Sara'd said that once we left Guadeloupe the LeCoq episode would be *fini.* The escape clause had been one of her strong selling points. Arranging a rendezvous on home turf, under Golden Boy's aquiline, would be playing with fire. I gave him my number. "Burn" was my middle name.

This time it was Captain Biff on the Eastern Airlines squawker and Sally Reardon demoing lifesavers. Neither pitched the kind of support I needed as we approached Fun City. Fun City? The hell it was. Not after where I'd been.

Don't get me wrong. Doing time in the Big Apple wasn't a total bringdown. I had rolls of film to develop and a buzz that I'd shot some beauts. And of course, there was my One and Only. Whom I was creaming to see. No matter how Blaked up or out.

Before I cracked open *Photographic Surveillance Techniques* for a skim, I had my angle. I'd say Club Med'd been quiet and restful.

Not quite a lie, more like fluff. After all, I *had* spent a healthy slice of time in bed and the activity *was* relaxing. I just didn't snooze much. As for the bags under the blinkers, the deep tan gave them the downplay. Sara examined me and found no telltale post-nookie marks. I rechecked in the lav. Nope, no hickies anywhere. I'd land with a clean bill of health.

"Jean-Pierre threatened to come to New York for a visit," I told Sara before we landed.

"They all say that," the heart specialist claimed. "Talk's cheap."

D.O.A.

After Sara caught her shuttle to Philly, I boarded a Carey bus to Manhattan. I was met at my front door by Razor, the Pussy Cat's scummy owner/manager. Razor's pan advertised his handle. A close shave with something bigger than a Gillette Techmatic had left a line like a weathercaster's cold front along his right cheek. He once offered to show me his other uglifiers in the bar's back room. Seems he collected them the way blue serge collects lint.

"Hey, doll," he drawled, undressing me with his lizard eyes. "Looks like ya been somewheres with that color. C'mon in and hava drink on the house. An' while you're at it, you can show me your tan lines." He waved his gums.

Summertime, he always makes gab like that and I have to resist the urge to do a tap dance on his dome. His attention span is seasonal; no skimpy sundress, no lip. In winter he's mute. Razor's no good when it comes to remembering faces.

I charged upstairs and found hot air. No honey. No note. No flowers, champagne, no bonbons.

Where the hell was my B.F.? He was supposed to be back the day before. I cursed and stamped my 6½'s. The setup was suspicious. I doodled on a pad as I rang Golden Boy's Hoboken pad—

curlicues between rings one and four, jagged shapes between five and nine, and stabs with the Bic from ten through fifteen. N.G.

I paced, picked off my nail polish, and began to unpack. I'd reached the lingerie when Ma Bell squealed for attention. I did a Haley's comet, lifted the receiver, and cooed: "Hi, baby. Did you miss me?" I felt like a solid becoming a liquid.

"No." The monosyllable was lethal. "Hullo? Ya there?"

"Barely."

"I called ta welcome ya home, sweetheart, not ta hurt your feelings."

By this time the damage was done. "Oh, no, you didn't."

"Good. I didn't think ya was tha fragile flower kind. Didya hava good time?"

"Yeah, great." My delivery was as flat as a poorly exposed negative.

"Ready ta do a little work?"

Checkmate

My shrug wasn't audible. Palladino figured the silence for the green light. "Good. 'Cuz I got another case."

"Yeah, what?" My mind was on Golden Boy. Or lack thereof.

"Drugs."

"We get to take any?"

"It ain't right, sweetheart, ya just gettin' back and soundin' crappy. What's eatin' ya?"

"Nothing my boyfriend couldn't fix. But that's not your look-out." There was no percentage in kvetching. "Go ahead, tell me about the case."

"It's like this. Rosenblatt's got this client, see, and this flatfoot sez he sees our guy givin' some other guy some junk on Fifty-first between Tenth and Eleventh. Our guy sez he wasn't passin'. Besides, tha street's so dark, nobody can tell shit from shinola even close up. Let alone from tha corner tha blue stood on."

"Which means we do what?"

"Ya go up there at midnight, stand where tha copper stood, right, and fire off some shotsa tha doorway where tha supposed deal went down. Ya make tha place look dark—real dark—and that's all there is to it. Couldn't be simpler."

"Back up a minute, buddy. What's this 'you' business?"

"Whaddya mean 'you business'? I just told ya, didn't I? I want ya ta go up ta Fifty-first and take some photos. I'm talkin' English, ain't I? Or didya forget tha mother tongue while ya was away?"

"You want me to go up to that raunchy neighb *alone?* At midnight? With my photo gear? Are you shitting me? My camera'd be ripped off in three seconds and we're not even discussing what might happen to the rest of me. No way, José. You couldn't buy me enough life insurance to get me up there solo. Uh uh. Come with me or I don't go."

"Ya know, yer a real pain in tha ass."

"Gee, thanks. The soft soap will get you everywhere."

"But I admit ya gotta point. Sometimes I forget yer a girl."

"Watch it, peeper. All these compliments will go to my head."

"Okay, okay. My apologies, kid. Look, I'll level with ya. Tha problem's I'm tied up with tha wife and kid and I can't go. Tell ya what, though. I'll send Flash."

"That's perfect. I can just see it. I'm setting up the shot, right? Somebody comes up from behind and grabs the Nikon. Flash takes off after him. The thief could run from Fifty-first to Florida and back before Flash's blubber waddled a block. C'mon, Nick. That sucks. You go or it's no deal."

"Jesus Christ, I need this shit like a hole in tha head," the sleuth muttered.

"I'm cute when I'm angry." Twice as cute since I was pissed at Nick *and* Hank.

"You win, sweetheart. For tha record, tha only reason I'm gonna do this is 'cuz the job's rush. Ya got that? I'll pick ya up, say round eleven thirty."

"Hey, wait, don't hang up! Eleven thirty when?"

"Tanight."

"Tonight? I can't do it tonight," I yelped.

"Come again? I just switched round my whole goddamn schedule and probably pissed off tha wife and kid and *now* ya tell me it's no go. What kinda crap ya pullin', huh? Tha case goes ta trial Tuesday and Rosenblatt's gotta have tha shots this weekend. Lady, we don't got time ta fart around."

I was triple ticked now. "Look, I just got home. I haven't even unpacked." I looked over at my suitcase for confirmation. "And I want to see Hank, goddammit!"

"That tha boyfriend? See him tamarra. Here I thought ya could use tha dough. But hey? If yer gonna go all prima donna, I'll find myself another photographer. It's sixa one and a half dozen of tha other ta me. There'ra lotta hungry guys out there dyin' ta make a buck."

It was eat or be eaten. "Go ahead, you bastard, kick me when I'm down." I knew I was licked. "See you at eleven thirty." I slammed down the phone. Not with a bang but a whimper.

In town three crummy hours and where was I? Back in my loft and right back behind the eight ball. There was nothing to do but unpack. I tried Gallagher's number again. And again. And again. Bad. Worse. The pits. From the pits it was a turkey shoot to shallow graves, macabre cult rites, brainwashings.

Then I had a brainstorm: Call Parker. Could be he'd have a bead on the boy's whereabouts.

I skipped the social prelims. "Do you know where Hank is?" I steamrolled when the trust funder answered.

"Nope."

"Do you know if he's back?"

"Nope."

"Did you hear anything from him during the week?"

"Nope."

This was no conversation; it was dental extraction. "Nothing at all?"

"Nope. Not from him or Winny. Strange. She usually calls once, twice a week."

"Maybe they tried while you were out. You sure your answering machine's working?"

"Yup." Parker threw money around, but that was it.

"Can you give me Winny's phone number?"

"She doesn't have a phone."

Of course not, why should she? Blake never had one. "Anybody else you know out there have one?"

"I dunno. I've never been out there."

He took drugs. I would have thought him a natural for the place. "How come?"

"Winny said I wasn't ready. I still lived too much in my 'Mundane Shell.' "

So Hank aced the entrance exam and Parker was stuck doing remedial reading. I had to tread lightly now. It's cheeky calling somebody's squeeze—especially one you fear and have never met—a Mansonite.

"Parker, do you think this Golgonooza's on the up and up? I mean, don't you worry that maybe something kind of sicko's going on out there?"

"Nope. Not on your life."

But it wasn't my life I was worried about.

Shooting Up

I wasn't sure how to proceed. I could call the cops and report a missing person. No, premature. I could call Golden Boy's parents in

Providence and put them on the case. No, potentially messy. I could eat dinner. Nope, the cupboards were bare. I could drink dinner. Sold.

The booze was beginning to smooth down the nerves when Nick pulled up in a mud-puddle-colored VW. I scribbled a note to snookums on the off chance he'd show while I was working the night shift.

Compared to the roof job, I was traveling light this time. All I packed was a tripod, the trusty F1, a normal, and a meter. As soon as the stuff and my butt were stowed, Nick started in. "I just want ya ta know, honey, it's 'cuz a you I got domestic problems. I got one helluva rib roast 'bout this here change a schedule."

I apologized. "No homewrecking intended."

"Tha boyfriend turn up?"

"Nah" and I sketched the situation.

"I wouldn't worry too much if I was you. I been ta places like this whatchamacallit when I was trackin' runaways. Sounds like tha run-a-tha-mill commune bit ta me, sweetheart. Hippy dippy. Folks in that kinda arrangement, they ain't too swift keepin' tracka time. Tha boyfriend, he probably got, whadda them flakes say? Oh, yeah, 'like mellow.'"

"Like hell."

Conversation bottomed out when we reached our destination. Hot polluted air hung like a grimy curtain across Fifty-first. The tableau was Lowlives on Parade and it gave me the jumps. The doorway we wanted was seventy-five feet-ish from the corner. The streetlights didn't spread many footcandles of glim on the subject. Layman talk, that meant the doorway was dark. Getting technical, it meant pushing the film and making long exposures. Logistically speaking, it meant setting up on the southwest corner of Eleventh and praying a creep wouldn't elope with my equipment. Translated back into layman lingo, the job was a total drag.

Nick grumbled when I stationed him nearby for protection. The hankshaw was no brute but his dukes were the only weaponry. A couple of sleazoids got a little too close for comfort but he fought them off with his yap. Twenty-five minutes, start to finish, the job was over. I dialed Hank from a phone booth on the corner. No reply and I was close to the weeps. We got back in Nick's heap and lurched downtown.

"Nick," I said. "I have a question about these pics. I don't know how to print them."

"That's great, kid. Now ya tell me. What tha hell ya do up there tha whole time? Take in tha scenic view?" The shamus's hands strangled the steeringwheel.

"Hang on, snoopie. It's not that I *can't* print them. I'm not sure *how*. What I'm driving at is this: How dark should I make them? I can print them forty ways to Sunday, depending on how I futz in the lab."

"Lookit, Jane, all's ya gotta do, make 'em look dark. Like tha place." He sneered. "How come ya gotta make everything so damn complicated? It a disease with ya or somethin'?"

"Yeah, it's been diagnosed as intelligence. Malignant. Probably fatal. Listen, Nick, this is serious. See, what I don't get is how I reproduce 'darkness' in a print. If I'm called in to testify, what do I say? 'May it please the court, shlepp my print to Fifty-first at midnight and hold the sucker up. The print will seem to disappear; it's such a perfect tonal match.' Think the judge and jury'd believe that? For all they know I could've taken the shot any time of day and just made a dark print. I'm not making it complicated. If you think about it at all, it *is* complicated. Actually," I mused, "it sounds a lot like a conceptual art piece."

Nick looked like he'd taken a bellyful of lead. "Conceptual art, Je-sus, gimme a break, will ya? Just make tha fuckin' thing dark. Dark so's ya can't see down the block. Not black black 'cuz that'd look phony. Go for inky. Kapish?"

Enough to keep my brainwork to myself. The best I could figure, evidence photog and art both diddled around with slippery characters: Reality and Illusion. Any shutterbug could tell you that fooling around with lenses, angles, and viewpoints can make the same object look tall or short, fat or thin, near or far, pretty or ugly. But that's just the tip of the iceberg. The same photog can go into the darkroom and monkey around even more.

There was plenty to philosophize about but I'd save that rap for more responsive ears. Still, the shamus had it right, gut level. Art and evidence depended on context. And in the context of Nick's short, evidence = sense, art = baloney.

"Asshole," Nick signified, cutting his crate's motor adjacent to my building. I took it personally until I spotted the boozician fandangoing his way into the middle of Sixth to hail a cab with his life. I'd seen it happen before; some gees, they go into the Pussy Cat for topless and come out mindless.

"How's about a nightcap at Dave's?" Nick made friendly. Dave's was the twenty-four-hour quick-and-dirty on Broadway and Canal. The specialty was egg cream. "When your (sic) are drinking a Dave's Egg Cream," the promo read, "you are drinking a legend."

"Thanks, but I'll pass," I said. Hank was the only sugar I craved.

"Okay, dollface. Guess ya had a hard day, huh? Another time."

"You're on."

"Drop that conceptual art stuff off at Rosenblatt's by Saturday, all right?" He flashed his snappers.

"Sure."

"And don't worry too much 'bout tha boyfriend. He'll turn up."

Blissed out or in a box?

Close But No Cigar

Finding Dreamboat in the bed was another conceptual piece that had to be dropped. All there was between the percales was lonely atmosphere. All the dust was in place; the note on the table sat unmanhandled.

"Aw, hell, give it another whirl," I coached myself and buzzed New Jersey for the skaty-eighth time. The phone rang a few shy of a zillion. Then it stopped.

I said hello to some heavy breathing. "Hank, you there?" Rustling noises, then the 201 area code receiver crashed to the floor. "Hank? Are you okay? Speak to me!!" The scary part was it was all too possible he *was* speaking to me; this might be the way magic mushrooms sounded long distance.

"Hank, baby?"

Fumblings, rumblings, panting, and finally, "Jane?" The voice sounded more low-down than I remembered.

"Thank God." I stopped white knuckling Ma Bell. "You're there." Whether he was all there was the question. "I had the wimwahs worrying. How come you didn't come back yesterday the way you planned?"

"The Energies out there were too intense to abandon. And . . . Winny decided to drive in."

"Is she training for the Trans-Am or is she here to square things with Parker? When I talked with him he was pretty miffed she hadn't called all week."

"You talked to Parker?" He didn't sound pleased. Then the vocals fizzled. I knew the phone was in the bedroom but I thought I heard a toilet flush.

"Hank, you still there?" The sigh meant yes. "How come you didn't have her drop you here?"

"I, um, needed some Space."

"But you just had a humongo dose of it, for Chrissake. And I'm dying to see you. And do some other things to you as well." Can I help it if I had a dirty mind?

Very faint music started playing in the background. The neighbors having a late-night party? Funny, I didn't remember the walls in Hank's apartment being so thin.

"C'mon, Jane. Don't be upset. Please. It's just that, well, Golgonooza had more Labyrinthine Intricacy than I expected, and I needed time to"—I had a lousy feeling about what was coming—"make Peace with this Barren Clime."

"Gee, thanks a bunch."

"I need a little time to pass through this Silent Melancholy. I thought you'd understand."

It'd sure look bad if I said I didn't so I said I did. Except now the melancholy was making a hullabaloo that sounded like pots and pans.

"Hank, what's all that racket at your place?"

"Racket? Oh, nothing."

"Are you alone out there?" Was it possible the Blakeans sent a secret agent to keep their newest convert in line? I couldn't quite shake the feeling.

"Somebody here?" He sounded alarmed. "Why, no. You think . . ."

"Forget it." I hated sounding the suspicious bitch. "Here's what I think. You should get your ass over here as soon as possible to restore Love and Harmony, fill the Abyss of the Five Senses, and experience Eternal Delight. And what was it that you talked about before you left? Oh, yeah, Gratified Desire. That sounds jake too."

"I'll be there in the morning."

"First thing, promise?" Did something land on the waterbed? Was I so bushed that I was imagining things?

One more funny noise tickled the tympanum. It sounded like a plunger on a clogged drain. A goodnight smooch via wire from the wilds of Jersey.

I gave "Space" an exclusive as I rattled around the queen-size. How much did Gallagher need? There was space in spades in the kip and two thousand square feet of it in the loft. Ample for two, I calculated, but I'm a literal thinker. That's no great asset where your lovelife's concerned. Especially when the competition's talking "Immensity," "Eternity," and "Infinity." The debate didn't get much airplay before I knocked off for the night.

Reunion

As a wakeup, the wiggling in the sack sure beat the alarm clock. Warm, familiar jibs nibbled my ear. I'm a pushover for a kisser with the knack, and Gallagher was a solid sender. He wasn't a puckerer, slobberer, or noisemaker. He had an extensive repertoire for his tongue and a few quality routines for his teeth. Once his mouth was in gear, activated mitts welcomed other parts of me home.

I'd woken up enough to spark back. I did a little oral work around the head and neck and then began digital investigative reporting in the erogenous zone. I felt there was a problem. The hardware had gone soft. I double-checked with a knob-job but it was no go. Golgonooza may have done more damage than I suspected.

Golden Boy looked green around the gills and stared at the roof beams. "I hoped that wouldn't happen."

"Well, it's not exactly the express route to Gratified Desire but it's no big deal, Hank-o. Honest." Best to take it slow and low. No need adding insult to injury. Besides, after LeCoq I wasn't horny and I could afford to be generous.

Deflated One blew up a Marlboro. His inhaling and exhaling were the loudest sounds in the room, aside from the jackhammer din the Con Ed men made directly below my window.

The ceiling panorama didn't hold much interest. Gallagher rallied and propped himself up on an elbow. From behind his smokescreen he gave me a squint. "No tan lines, I see."

"The joys of nude sunbathing."

"Guess you did a lot of it, judging from the color."

"I went for Sara. She wouldn't go by herself." Keep up this line of questioning and I'd soon be the one with a problem.

"You two must've had a good time."

"Sara had a ball."

"And you?"

"Better than expected," I flimflammed. Then proceeded with jabber about Vince, the surf, the sports, and the eats. I left out the fling. The come-out: a travelogue as innocent as a nun's. Amend my résumé to read visual artist *and* con artist.

"So what's going on with you and Golgonooza?" In a religious war, know thine enemy. "Start at the beginning and tell me everything."

Squeeze Plays

Presto chango. One minute I was in bed with loverboy, the next, a Holy Roller. Gallagher went off on a blab bender that lasted an hour. Stripped down it doped out like this:

Blake's Take	*Hank's Take*	*My Take*
"I must create a system or be enslaved by another man's."	Golgonooza was held together by a Fearsome and Powerful Vision.	So was the Manson crowd.
"Imagination is My World; this world of Dross is beneath my Notice & beneath the Notice of the Public. I demand therefore of the Amateurs of art the Encouragement which is my due; if they continue to refuse, theirs is the loss,	The only Great Art was Blake's Art; Golgonooza was the only real Art Capital where the Great Tradition continued.	Burn the art history books. Fuck Modernism. Death to the Impressionists, Cubists, Dadaists, Surrealists, Abstract Expressionists, Color Fieldists, Minimalists, Pattern and Decorationists, Conceptualists, and Photo Realists.

Blake's Take	*Hank's Take*	*My Take*
not mine, & theirs is the Contempt of Posterity."		
"Nature & Art in this together Suit: What is Most Grand is always most Minute."	The life-style was Integrated and Organic. Everybody lived in log cabins or handbuilt houses.	Back to the land; only softies had indoor plumbing.
"The Goddess Fortune is the devil's servant, ready to Kiss anyone's Arse."	Here was a haven uncontaminated by Crass Commercial Concerns. People raised sheep, grew and sold dope, did odd jobs, waited tables, or taught at nearby Gatewood U.	The old mystical bromide: Be Poor. Be Pure. And vice versa.
"What is it men in women do require? The lineaments of Gratified Desire. What is it women in men require? The lineaments of Gratified Desire."	Golgonoozers took Immense Delight in each other's Eternal Individuality.	Strange sex rites. Group gropes. Orgies.

"The Imaginative and Creative Affinities were extraordinary."

"I can hear."

"I can't wait to get back." Gallagher's irises glinted.

He had the Spirit. I had the spooks. "Back?" I quasi-croaked. "You're going back?" This was not what I cleaned wax out of my ears to hear.

"I have to."

"What do you mean, 'have to'?" The situation grew more dire by the split second.

"They want me to come out and work."

"What kind of work do they have in mind?" This was turning into a nightmare.

"They, we, want to do a Book. A quality art book. Fine design, fine text, fine reproduction. On Blake and Golgonooza."

"A coffee table book?" Blake might have been poor but there was no reason his disciples shouldn't make a buck off his wealthy fans.

"If you want to cheapen the Concept, you'd call it that."

"Are they paying you?" Maybe green persuaders were the reason for his enthusiasm. Golden Boy was as broke as I was.

"Money's not the point. It's important to Inform and Educate people about Spiritual Beauty and Personal Truth."

The Gospel according to St. Willy. It didn't look good for us nonbelievers. Religious cults wage crusades. "When are you planning to go?"

"I thought I'd stay and help you get ready for your show and leave about a week after the opening."

When the going gets tough, the tough get going. "I'm going with you," I stonewalled. He was going alone over my dead body. Although I certainly hoped it wouldn't come to that. I had a low death threshold.

Hank's daylights tore out of his head like they'd been hot-wired. "You want to come? Really?"

"I'm dead serious." I shuddered at the pun.

"But you can't." He sounded agitated. "You're not ready."

I was prepared; Winny'd laid that line on Parker. "But I will be. I'll read, I promise. I'll go cold turkey on the detective novels. You'll see." My grandstand play.

"Jane, you don't understand . . . the Situation . . . I don't think . . ."

"That's right. Don't think. It's settled."

"Jane, really . . . the Situation . . ."

"I want to go." Hell, I had to go. Somebody had to protect him from the cult's clutches.

Now that I was in bodyguard biz, I might as well have the body I was guarding closer. Blake wrote, "The nakedness of woman is the work of God." So I worked with that. A little well-placed godliness did the trick. Gallagher and I picked up the he and she-ing where we'd left off. There was a lot of skin sliding on skin until there was no way to separate whose flesh from whose. Mine was tanner but when the earth moves, who pays attention to small things like color?

We lay around after the flesh session. At some point I caught sight of the clock. "Jeez, it's late. I have to get up."

"What for?" Hank snuggled up.

"I've got to print."

"Your Guadeloupe film can wait," Hank kvetched.

"It's not my stuff. It's a job."

"Job, sure. You just got home." My patootie started canoodling.

"I did some work for the dick," I confessed.

The fondling stopped. "That scumbag didn't waste any time."

"Aw, look, don't go all sourpuss and spoil the morning. If you'd been here"—I bit my tongue before adding "when you were supposed to instead of being off with those crazies"—"I'd've turned the job down. When I couldn't find you, I went for the shinplasters." We misguided materialists couldn't afford to work for love alone.

Hank was grumpy when I hauled my nakedness out of bed. Dressed and in the darkroom, it took me a while to figure out how dark to print the street scenes. Palladino was right, inky did it. The photos may have been out to lunch on the art end, but as far as I could tell, they made honest evidence.

On Trial

Exactly how honest was the reason I got called in to court Tuesday to testify in *The United States of America* v. *Andrew Scudd*. I'd been raised on Erle Stanley Gardner but what I got instead was the Case of the Cockeyed Casting Couch. Rosenblatt was no stand-in for Perry Mason, physically or oratorically. His devoted assistant, Manny Shapiro, might've passed for Della Street if he'd done himself up in drag and Della'd taken massive doses of testosterone. Nick made investigator Paul Drake look like a smooth operator. The only piss whiz in the pack was District Attorney Bruce Drummond and that was bad for our side. He was probably the original model for Gardner's snarly DA, Hamilton Burger.

Erle was a talented writer but he never would've put Justice Mahoney in the high seat. Women in his books sat in the dock, not on the bench. It was a damn good thing she sat where she did; she was a lot easier on the retinas than the defendant. Marv's client had as much oomph as a dirty sweat sock. He was a scrawny punk in a baggy suit with a face that begged for Clearasil. He looked the type to torture furry housepets. Still, being ugly as sin didn't prove he was guilty as same. Scudd claimed he was innocent.

Normally I get myself up on the arty side, but today I was in witness wear. I'd put on my only straight-arrow dress and pair of pumps—the rig-out that certifies me for official family hooplas—and manacled my frizz with a tortoiseshell barrette. It was trust I was trying to inspire, not lust.

Marv's prep was minimal: "Answer all questions yes or no. Don't volunteer any info and keep your mouth shut." Sometimes the simplest things are the hardest.

"Are these the photographs you took between midnight and approximately twelve thirty A.M., the night of August sixth?" Marv asked, holding up the artwork I'd delivered Saturday.

"That's correct." Dammit, wordy.

"And you took these in the company of private investigator Domenic Palladino?"

"I did." Better, but not good enough.

"That's all, Your Honor."

Marv sat down, Drummond popped up. The DA wore a tight-ass three-piecer that flattered his burly build. I was willing to bet an ulcer lurked behind the gray flannel.

Drummond took his time approaching the witness stand. He stood in front of me and pulled down his vest. "Miss Meyers, while I'm not disputing your credentials, it does seem that your photographs exaggerate the sinister atmosphere of the crime site." He shot a "we-know-her-kind" look at the jury's eight men and four women. "Could this possibly be the case, Miss Meyers?"

"No." Emphatic. I was getting the hang of it.

"We're not quibbling that the street was dark, Miss Meyers. Just that you've made it excessively so."

I didn't like Drummond, his tone, or the way he punctuated sentences with my handle. I got hotheaded and Marv's advice went out the window. "Cut the insinuendos, *Mr.* Drummond. I didn't fake evidence." As backup I launched into a techno spiel about film speed, light readings, exposure time, all the how-tos on the snoreboard.

"Miss Meyers," he persisted, his voice icewater, "I have here some prints of the very same site taken by our photographer." He shoved them under my nozzle as if I had to smell them as well as scan them. "Surely you can't help but notice that these pictures look considerably lighter than yours. And that the doorway in question is far more visible. Just how do you account for that discrepancy, Miss Meyers?"

My sweaty mitts had trouble grasping the glossies. The other f-stopper had to be an old vet and I was only a rookie. Maybe I *had* screwed up. The sinking feeling in the gut didn't signal confidence.

I stared at the prints; I quick-overed at Rosenblatt. He looked the way I felt. The prints were different all right. As different as night and day.

Suddenly there was a way out of the tangle. "Easy," I bragged. "The streetlights are on in my photos, right?" I held one up in my right hand and pointed to the lights with my left index. "Now in your set"—I wanted to add "you motherfucking pig" but Marv said keep it simple—"they aren't." I held up one of the DA's exhibits. It was like "show and tell" in grade school. "That means yours were taken before the lights were turned on. Before, say, what? Eight o'clock? And the only reason these shots look nightlike at all is because they were printed down in the darkroom by your 'expert.' I think mine are more accurate, wouldn't you say, *Mr. Drummond?*"

That put the pin to Bruce baby. The judge, a sour expression on her squash—from disgust, indigestion, or both—told me to step down. Court was adjourned for an hour.

Nick strolled over for congrats. "Hey, sweetheart, now I dig what ya was drivin' at tha other day with that conceptual shit."

"Stick around, big boy, and I'll teach you everything you ever wanted to know about art."

"I'll take a raincheck, doll. Right now alls I wanna know about is lunch."

By the time we got back to court, Marv was slicing up the prosecution's case, starting with the rival photog's testimony. Sonofabitch, it had turned into a Perry Mason episode after all. The next day the jury delivered a verdict of "not guilty." Scudd was so happy his pimples gleamed. Marv put me in a bear hug and told me we were celebrating over dinner.

Poison

Outside, the Hai Ho on West Thirty-eighth was no great shakes. Inside, some slick decorator had done it up like a walk-in Hershey bar, the whole shmeer in cocoa brown. The legal eagle was sitting near the bamboo in the main dining room. The light level was so low—it rivaled Fifty-first Street—that the maître d' had trouble locating him and Marv was no drink of water.

The Esq. was perusing the oversize menu when I dropped into the seat opposite. We gassed about the Scudd win and then got down to basics.

I cracked the *carte*. "Jesus Christ," I yelled. Three quarters of the patrons looked up from their chow in horror.

"Is this a joke?"

"Is what a joke?"

"You call this a Chinese restaurant? It's fucking kosher!"

"What, you got something against kosher cuisine? You haven't tried it yet."

"Why here of all places?"

"Why not?" he rebutted talmudically.

"Why don't you just go ahead and do the ordering." I was defeated by three thousand years of dietary tradition.

"Then I think we'll have the number four, Dawn Chicken." I read the description on the menu—fried chicken breasts stuffed with pastrami, bamboo shoots, snow peas, and Chinese mushrooms. "The Moo Shu Veal." It was a good thing the soup jockeys were all illegal aliens from the Borscht Belt; better they shouldn't know from the real McCoy made with pork. "And how about an order of Pho-Nee Shrimp in Mock Lobster Sauce?"

I agreed to that without a read—it was less painful. "You sure you don't want one of the American Favorites? Meatballs and kasha?"

"My dear, this is a feast. Order anything you want."

What I wanted most was to get my tush out of there, but what I said was, eating red meat was against my religion. To keep the faith I ordered a stiff martini.

Later, when the lawyer was rolling some ersatz Moo Shu into a latke, he said: "By the way, Janie, you interested in another job? I got a quickie."

"Legal typing or photo?"

"Photo."

"With Palladino?"

"No, with me this time."

Playback

"After the Rodriguez caca? Have you gone completely mental?"

Once upon a crime, Rosenblatt had a client tagged Santiago Maria Ignatio Rodriguez. A regular Joe who allegedly pulled a B-job. I'm not sure why I bother with the "allegedly" except it gets to be a habit when you hang around the defense men.

The four bankrobbers were either dumb, vain, or both. Each pulled off a cameo in front of Chase's security cameras. The dude in the army jacket and hard hat looked a helluva lot like Marv's boy.

Rosenblatt's defense had Shakespeare rubbing elbows with James Cain. There was a mistaken identity bit right up the Bard's alley. Seems Santiago had a twin, Ernesto, a creep with a police record as long as his arm. The bro'd been picked up on the same charge, been tried, and got off on a technicality. From there it was a hop, skip, and a jump to Cain double indemnity territory. Convince the jury Ernesto was the villain—it was no skin off his sniffer since he couldn't be tried for the same crime twice—and Santiago'd be free.

The crux was the bank pictures. They were surprisingly good. Which was bad. Which was where I came in.

My shtick was to shoot a second set of prints. I stood on a chair on top of a desk in the middle of Marv's office and made like a bank camera. The shark had Ernesto suit up like the stickman in the evidence pic. Duping the duds was a piece of cake. We hit grief with the heavy metal. The holdup man held a gat. The lawyer

77

didn't own a rod and Ernesto wasn't carrying. We fudged with an office Swingline. Believe it or not, the final product foxed some witnesses. Not the jury, however. Esquire's argument went down the tubes; Santiago went up the river. Three to ten, Ossining.

Counsel's headaches had just begun. Not only did he lose the case, he almost lost his shirt and shingle. Rumor had it that outside the courtroom Marv used less than one hundred percent kosher procedures showing witnesses my handiwork. The state disbarment panel got on his ass and for a while it was touch and go. Some days it looked like Marv would be Santiago's cellmate in the big house; others, that he'd be out on his duff on the street. It took months for the scales of J to tip Rosenblatt's way and a few more for his legal life to swing back to normal.

Massacre

"It's a lead pipe cinch."

"Sure, and Colonel Mustard did it in the billiard room. Marv, old buddy, what're we playing, Clue?"

"No, really, Janie, this one's a snap. All we have to do is take pictures in a Food Fair where there was a murder."

"During a price war?"

"I'm being serious. Five guys came in and held up the cashiers. The manager hit the alarm button and one of them—not my client, knock on wood—panicked. He'd been in 'Nam and came back with a plate in his head and a screw loose. The vet flips, thinks he's back in the jungle, strafes the meat department, and kills a lady shopper."

"They say vegetarians live longer."

"Jane, please. Some respect."

"Sorry. The MSG must've gone to my head. Go on."

"They all run out the back and get caught in the parking lot. The other guys want to stand trial. What I want to do is split my case off. When my guy sees his buddies getting sentenced to ten to fifteen, he'll wise up and cop. That way he'll wind up doing two, maybe three." Rosenblatt scarfed some of number four's deli trimmings. "So what do you think?"

"Miss Scarlet did it in the conservatory with the rope."

"Saturday morning early all right with you?"

I mulled it while Marv grubbed the last Pho-Nee. "Sure," I said reluctantly. We inter-mitted to clinch the deal. "We get fortune cookies in this joint?"

"I don't see why not. They should be *pareve*," the advocate speculated.

The Judeo-Sino variety came with the check and looked more like a macaroon. I crumbled one open and read: "The only thing you can count on nowadays is your fingers."

Tour de Force

9:30 A.M. Saturday: I went downstairs expecting to find Rosenblatt's green Honda Civic. Instead, I traced out a familiar Beetle. "What happened to Big Marv?" I asked the gumshoe as I jumped in shotgun.

"He finked out on ya, kid. Last minute his mother told him he hadda cousin's bar mitzvah out on tha Island." That made our Hai Ho date a limbering up exercise for the nice-Jewish-boy marathon.

The change was jake. Palladino had the personality of an emery board but better that than the beak's kvetchiness. I told the dick I was glad to see him. If he took it as a compliment, he didn't let on. He just bent the throttle north, then east, then north some more. In my geography book anything north of the International Center of Photography on East Ninety-fourth was Alaska. "Are we headed for Nome?"

The sleuth answered matter-of-factly: "Harlem."

Harlem had snow too but not the Nome brand.

"Here's what we do," the P.I. went on. "A shotta tha front where tha door's at, one a tha checkout, a coupla tha meat—specially where tha deceased got plugged, and tha aisle from tha meat ta tha exit door inna back. Nuthin' fancy, 'cept maybe a little fancy footwork."

"Fancy footwork? What for? Marv got permission for this shoot, didn't he?"

Nick shook his head in a disturbing way.

"He didn't call?"

"He called. But he didn't exactly get permission."

"So we go in cold. Aren't we going to look, how shall we say, conspicuous up there?" I cocked my noggin Harlem way.

"Sister, even if we walked in two weeks apart, they'd know we came in tagether. Do what ya gotta do in there quick and there'll be no problem. Y'ain't gonna go Nervous Nelly on me, are ya?"

"Damn straight, I am." The clammy feeling at the base of the neck could only mean one thing: hysteria. You don't wear good intentions like clothes: food shoppers, not knowing what I shot or why, might get the wrong impression. Might get superpissed and swing. Nuts, all somebody'd have to do was yell at me and I'd cower.

"Do just like I tell ya and it'll be fine. I wait in tha car. First ya do tha outside, then go inside and look—"

"Like I just dropped in for collards?" I gave my hazels a tour of their sockets. "Where's your ass during all this?"

"Around, don't worry."

"Don't tell me 'don't worry.' I was weaned on Maalox."

"Look, sweetheart, if somethin' goes wrong, I'll handle it."

When I looked skeptical, the gumshoe laid the blast on. "Ya think yer friend Rosenblatt hires me 'cuz I don't know my business? Ya think he gives money away for kicks? If yer plannin' a future in this lina work, sugar pie, yer gonna havta calm down and trust me."

I stared out the VW's window. The numbers on Park Ave. ran up; the buildings ran down. I gave "trust" a play and decided to buy it. Point to Palladino.

"Something else bitin' ya today or what? Tha boyfriend givin' ya flak 'bout this kinda job?"

The guy was hitting all the sore spots. "He isn't the most supportive." I didn't bother explaining that Gallagher's "anti's" tumbled from high-hat aesthetics, not from petty concerns like mere mortal safety.

"Ya can't pay it much mind, honey," the dick advised. Warmly, for him. "I've been doin' this kinda work for a lotta years now and tha little woman, she still don't like it. Ya gotta teach 'em ta shaddup."

"No soap. Hank's got a learning disability."

Flapping plastic pennants were strung up used-car-lot style around the Food Fair's facade. The flags jazzed up the place the way new cellophane spiffed up old Wonder bread. "Okay, honky," I said to myself. *Cotton Comes to Harlem.* Now it's your turn." I slid out, jockeyed around, crammed the whole exterior into my viewfinder, and punched the shutter. One shot down, I was loaded for bear. Eyes in the nearby hit on me half 'n' half—half curious, half hostile. Nothing personal—any fay north of One Hundred Twenty-fifth Street would get the treatment.

Shoving the Leica under my jacket, I pussyfooted into the market. I was never so happy to see chitlins, ham hocks, and pigs' knuckles. Twenty-seven years old and it was the first time I'd ever seen any of the above. The shag alone was an adventure.

I tried to pass as a serious shopper by poking assorted cuts, chops, slices, and slabs. I snuck out my light meter. The overheads didn't impress the needle.

Nick peeked out from behind the cereal display at the top of aisle six, wagged a stumpy finger in the direction of the exit door, and skiddooed. Most of the cart pushers wheeled around me like I was diseased. Ground chuck was on special so I had a long wait for the aisle to clear. Finally I whipped out the M2, plugged it to my eye, and popped off a quick one of the poultry case. That was where Mrs. Elvira Jackson was thinking "Fried chicken for dinner again this week?" when she took the slug.

I backed up for a long shot, twirled, and fired at the exit door. I was just starting to feel at home when I heard a growl behind me. "Hey, you, whatchya think you're doin', huh? You ain't got no bizness sneakin' 'round ma store."

I aboutfaced. A six-foot-two bruiser was beelining two hundred twenty-five pounds of unadulterated fury my way. He was built like a balanced equation: what he lacked in neck he made up in huge, hamlike hands. They weren't the kind of squeezers you wanted anywhere in a twenty-block radius of your chokable. Or the rest of you for that matter.

There's nothing like a man in uniform, and the stitching on the standard-issue blue smock introduced me to "Wayne Diebold, Manager." "Guess shooting's not allowed, huh? I'm really sorry, Mr. Diebold." I wondered if the emphasis were on the "Die." I made to mosey.

"Not so fast, girl," the man bellowed. "Jus' who you photographin' for?"

I hated pulling the dizzy dame routine but I had to manage with the smidge I had.

"Well, uh, for the guy I came in with. Short, dark hair, raincoat, white. You should talk to him. He's around here somewhere and I'm sure he can explain everything." He'd better. Otherwise I'd been a rube for his Sir Galahad shill.

Diebold put his hooks on my camera and gave more than a gentle tug. "He wasn't explainin' too good when we kicked his ass outta here. You'll find him waitin' on you outside. A nice-lookin' chick like you best get herself a real man next time she pulls shit like this, ya dig? Now you get the fuck outta ma store. And stay the fuck out, ya hear? Else I jus' might do somethin' you'll regret ta that machine 'round your neck. I gotta 'nuf trouble in this place without worryin' 'bout tourists. Now, beat it."

I took a sizable swallow of air and headed to the main exit. I would've run but for a pair of elasticized drumsticks. I should've been worrying about my hide, so what I did next was lunacy. I stopped dead in my tracks, turned, and clicked off a shot of the checkout counters. With peripheral vision I saw Diebold break into a run. Rubbery drumsticks turned into propellers.

"Step on it," I panted as I threw myself into the short. "I'm being followed." Palladino, unruffled, revved the motor and pulled out. Not fast enough. Diebold delivered a drop kick to the rear fender. Obscenities were hurled inside and outside the car. Only after Diebold became a tiny speck in the rearview did my blood pressure dip back to 120/90.

"He take your film?" the sleuth inquired. Not anything sissy like "Are you okay?"

"Nah." I'd show him who was hard-boiled. "He treated me like the fucking Queen of Sheba."

The dick said: "I knew I could trust ya ta take cara yaself." The lightbulb went on in the attic. So this was what he meant by trust. He'd been talking to my Hai Ho fortune macaroon.

"Sometimes, ya know, it's an advantage, yer not bein' a guy. Makes ya less likely ta get bounced around. Unless, a course, ya shoot off your yap, in which case ya'd be askin' for it. Ya get any shotsa tha meat cases?"

"Yeah, I got them before Diebold went on the warpath." I started out nonchalant and built to a brag. "And on the way out, I got one of the checkout. That's why I got chased."

"Hey, hey. Nice goin', babe. Looks ta me like ya actually got some talent for this biz after all. Tell tha boyfriend; ya can quote me." He smiled his first bona fide of the day.

I pixie grinned back. "That's not the kind of talent he's looking for."

"What, he wantsa stay-at-home cook and cleaner ta take cara him? No offense, dollface, but ya ain't exactly tha domestic type. I mean, ya got qualities, but if it's that other stuff he wants, then what he need's a wife."

I hoped not. Though I wouldn't mind having one myself.

Suspicion

Next thing I knew the calendar told me it was September. The time when the art scene starts to cook. Artists, critics, curators, collectors, and groupies race back to the Apple like lemmings in reverse. Appointment books fill up with dates for openings and parties. Cheap wine and hot gossip consumption skyrocket. The flurry continues through October, quiets down with the cold, and flares up in the spring. Summer, the flock migrates back to the sea and the soggy circular motif starts again.

Life on the home front was even-keeled. Hank was caught up reading Mr. B., smoking more dope than usual, and answering the barrage of mail from Winny and the Ohio gang. The letters came covered with odd spidery drawings and often stuffed with peculiar objects that Hank called artwork and I called voodoo craft. The items' effects weren't visible but that didn't mean they were safe. Conceivably they worked like time release cold capsules with a slow whammy. My S.O.P. was to maintain cool while I got my show together, then bring out the big guns when I got to Golgonooza.

My résumé boasted some photos published in a mag or two and a print hung in an alternative space here and there. This to-do, at classy Roseweb Gallery, was my first real break. The show, scheduled to open October 7th, was titled "Slices of Life" and the two other exhibitors were blue-chip. One took documentary pics of suburban S&Mers; the other did color portraits of leftover food. I was showing my Perdues. The exposure meant a great deal to me and I didn't want to blow it. So I spent most of my waking hours killing myself in the darkroom. What little time I had left, I tortured myself reading Blake.

The days flew by like Xeroxes. Until Jean-Pierre threw in a spanner. Two spanners actually.

Disaster #1 concerned the nudes I'd shot of him. They turned me on—in more ways than one—and were definite "musts" for Roseweb. The ruffle was sneaking them by Hank. He might get the wrong—or in this case, right—idea. I hid them under a pile of old work on the desk.

"Hey, c'mon out here a minute," Gallagher shouted through the darkroom door one afternoon.

"What's up, babycakes?" Bright sun shut the retinas down five stops.

Gallagher, barechested, was waving paper around like a semaphore. He stopped signaling long enough for me to take a swivel. The frog prints. Itchy Fingers had gone snooping. "What are these?"

Freudians would insist I'd wanted him to find the skin pics—otherwise I'd have cached them better. If I lived long enough I'd ask my next shrink about that. In the meantime I had some music to face and the tune was the Funeral March.

I feinted: "What do you think they are?" The reverse the charges gambit. Cain used it when God got on his case about Abel. The first murder mystery.

"I think they're close to Inspired." I blinked, not from sunlight but from Golden Boy's dazzling dental display. It was the first time in months he'd been hyped on my work.

"These are definitely Improved Works. Possibly the most interesting stuff you've done."

"I think my other work's pretty interesting too," I countered, not one to let a compliment get off scot-free.

"These somehow have more"—he groped for the right words—"Creative Virtue. Who's the model?"

"Oh, just some French fry on the nude beach who wanted his picture taken." I made it sound like a big yawn.

"Lucky for you he's a good-looking guy." Did Gallagher see Gratified Desire, a.k.a. Opportunity and Inclination, smeared across my pan? I waited for Thunderous Rage, a look of Frantic Pain. Gallagher was calm personified.

"He was certainly cooperative. You couldn't have gotten closer to him if you'd been in bed with him." I couldn't have agreed more but I would've been slitting my own throat.

"I never would have imagined you doing something like this down there." I took that to mean photographically. "I take my hat off to you." He doffed a make-believe snapbrim.

"You can do better than that, sweets," I said, now that the third degree seemed over. "Let's see what else you can take off."

He wound up nude as the nudes. Life imitating art.

The French Connection

One skirmish down but the French Revolution wasn't over yet. The next ordeal happened a week later when the postman rang.

Gallagher went to answer the door. When he came back upstairs, he yelled that I had a package.

"Be out in a sec. I've got one more print to pull. Who's it from?" I hollered back.

"A LeCoq in Paris."

The news knocked me clear into next week. "Sara and her bright ideas," I muttered to the safelight. " 'Hank'll never find out.' Phooey." Well, the jig was up. "We who are about to die salute you," I said to the enlarger as I prepared for the hot squat.

Hank stared at the time bomb lying on the table. "Who's

LeCoq? The nude guy in your photographs?" No flies on Gallagher.

"Uh huh," I said, remembering Rosenblatt's advice at the Scudd trial. Answer all questions yes or no, don't volunteer info, and keep your trap shut.

"Sending you a present, huh? He must've liked you." Saturday night lights shone underneath Golden Boy's moustache.

I couldn't even plead the Fifth: it would've backfired and incriminated me.

"Aren't you going to open it?"

"Oh, yeah, sure. Sure." With my luck it'd be the fancy French underwear I'd said I'd wanted. Or worse yet, a pair of my old underwear. My small intestine half-gainered before jackknifing into my large one. With fingers nimble as salamis, I tore open the wrapping. There was a layer of tissue paper for each of Dante's circles of hell. I excavated two enclosures at the bottom: a French detective comic and a trashy poppit bead necklace and bracelet set. Nothing you could call compromising. Still, better out of sight, out of mind.

"You had to be there," I said by way of explanation, making rapido motions to shut the box.

"Wait, there's a note." Out of the frying pan, into the fire. Hank extracted an envelope the color of J.P.'s sightseers from the tissue.

The note said: "I think these make a laugh for you today. I come to New York in middle *Octobre* for the business. It would give me pleasure to make a visit with you. Maybe I meet your *copain*. Write me a *lettre* to say we see each other this time. I am sad we are not more lying on the beach." There were a bunch of kissy "X" marks above his scrawled *Jean* Hancock.

"He says he thought I'd get a kick out of these, that he's coming to New York soon, and that since he's heard so much about you, he'd like to meet you." I wasn't exactly fibbing, just modifying. "Too bad we'll be in Ohio for most, if not all, of his visit."

"If you don't want to go, you can stay here and see him," Golden Boy volunteered, a strange expression on his phiz.

I admit the suggestion was tempting; fucking J.P. would be more fun than fucking around with a bunch of cowtown cultists. Also less dangerous. But the frog was strictly short run and I was into Gallagher for the long haul.

"Not go? Out of the question, buddy." Was it ever.

"You sure you don't want to stay here?"

Did he think I'd been reading all that Blake for my health? "How come you're so hot to have me stay?" Hank reddened. "Don't worry. I won't embarrass you out there. I'll be 'ready.' Is that what's bugging you?"

"Nooo. It's just that . . . ."

"I know, the Situation." Whatever that meant.

"Forget it." I could see he was suspicious about the frog but wasn't pressing his luck. Instead he drifted over to the couch, lit up a J, and got comfy with *Blake's Apocalypse*, some prof's magnum opus jammed with footnotes. Hank's light reading.

I beat feet for the darkroom with more than dodging and burning on the brain. Third parties—French and fanatic—were messing up the ménage. J.P. and the Blakeans had to be rubbed out. Housecleaning. A woman's work is never done.

Shaft

I was still trying to kick my mystery jones. One afternoon, after a rough printing session, my hand jerked for a private eye fix. I wanted one bad. Hank wasn't around to straighten me out. Not only was he increasingly remote when he was around, he'd taken to hanging out more in Hoboken. He was back into his "Space" trip.

I tried to calm down. I poured myself some bellywash and set myself up with some Willy B. I skimmed the *Songs of Innocence*. Not in the right mood. On to *Songs of Experience*. "The Clod &

the Pebble" caught my eye. I tapped the A-B-A-B rhyme scheme on my gam with an inkstick. Boring.

Ring, ring, ring went the phone. *That* was music to the ears. Likely Hank wanting to know when dinner'd be on the table. No need to ask what: pasta's heaven on a tight budget. And murder on the waistline.

The call wasn't about dinner but its flavor was Italian. "I gotta job," the dick announced.

"Congrats." I beat the Bic on the desk. Dun-dundun-dun duuuun: the theme from *Dragnet*.

"There was this heist at the Chemical up on Broadway and a Hundred Second."

"So?" Bank jobs seemed to be in vogue.

"And tha guy who's up for it, he was supposed ta've had an arsenal up there in Siberia."

"Siberia? We get to travel? I thought we were talking B-job, not espionage."

"Siberia, doll, is tha Bronx."

"I hear it's lovely this time of year."

"Look, insteada me explainin' tha job on tha horn, I'll do it on tha ride up."

"I don't give clearance on short notice. What's the hitch this time?"

"No hitch."

"I remember hearing something along those lines in a supermarket once . . ."

The gumshoe paid that no mind. "I was thinkin' Tuesday, tha seventh."

"Nope. My show opens."

"Sometime this week, then?"

"Impossible. I still have prints to make. And Monday's out; I install."

"Sweetheart, you're puttin' me in another of your squeeze plays, ya know that? Look, I gotta go outta town on a case on tha eighth. What time ya gotta be at this openin' thing?"

"Six thirty. Seven o'clock the latest. Why?"

"Whaddya say we do the job midmorning, early aft, and I getcha back in plentya time for tha meet 'n' greet? C'mon, help out a pal."

I'm basically soft-boiled. I was also two months behind in the rent. "If you swear on a stack of Gideons you'll have me back in time to shower and shave, you got yourself a deal."

"Yer a prince—I mean an angel. Don't think I don't appreciate it."

"Probably not enough. What I want to know, Nick, is how you always manage to pick the world's worst times to employ me?"

"Tha lucka tha Irish? How the fuck do I know? I'll pick ya up Tuesday, say eleven o'clock justa be on tha safe side." And just to be extra safe, he hung up on the sprint.

Big Blonde

The snoop rolled up two hours past the safety limit. To make up for lost time, he drove like a madman. The VW's shocks were shot to hell; for this trip I needed a seat belt *and* a kidney belt.

We headed for a five-story, limestone-trimmed pile, 1940's vintage, that was dying by inches on Stuyvesant. Abandoned buildings flanked it like bookends. Two or three more years and this building's landlord, no diff from his real estate cronies, would walk too.

Nick had a key that let us into apartment 3R. It was no Taj Mahal, but the rooms were spacious. Also empty. What was left were light patches where pictures once gave the walls moral support, mounds of dirty clothes, some empty Buds, and a tower of Rocky's Pizza boxes, a luxury hi-rise for roaches.

"C'mere and meet Blondie," the eye said, ducking into a doorway to his right. Whoever Blondie was, she hadn't made a peep since we arrived.

I followed the sleuth into the bedroom and found him stroking a buxom blond-wood double-doored, freewheeling armoire trying to pass herself off as Queen Anne. She sported gold trim aplenty and an indiscreet amount of scrollwork. She'd once been hitched to a six-piece ensemble that included matching headboard, twin night tables, lamp, and framed seascape. Orphaned when the owners pulled up stakes, she stood sad and alone, desperate for company.

"We gotta take her measurements," Nick chortled.

"Ugh, she's so tacky."

"Well, ain't we hoity-toity. Next time, Miss Interior Decorator, I'll have tha limo take ya direct ta Bloomingdale's."

"I'd prefer the sportscar. Okay, I'm sorry."

"Apologize ta Blondie here, not me. C'mon, let's get ta work. Here's tha poop. After Peter Collins—that's Marvin's client, by tha way—got cuffed, tha law took a look-see up here and said they saw guns sittin' on toppa this thing." Palladino patted the Big Blonde with his palm. "A cute trick, seein' as how our girl's almost seven feet. Bigger 'n' any copper I ever met. So what we do's this. We take that there," he pointed to a three-rung aluminum stepladder leaning against the far wall, "and park it three feet away from her. First ya photograph her standin' on tha floor, then from tha first step, then tha second, then tha third. We move tha ladder back another three; ya do the up and down number again. We move tha ladder another three, do tha same again and then once more."

"There must be an easier way, no?" It sounded like another conceptual piece but I kept my lip buttoned.

"I'm tha brainsa this outfit; yer tha brawn. Get it?" He sounded peeved.

"It's your show, shamus," I conceded. "Mine's tonight."

Going up and down the Jacob, I felt like a mountain goat in training. I was curious whether Blondie was one of those girls who looks better in photos than in real life. How could this baby look worse? I took my last shot, looked at my watch, and said, "Time's up."

"Not so fast, sugar," Nick chided. "One more pic." He got the stepladder and placed it in front of the blonde. He pulled a measuring stick out of his pocket, unfolded it its full six-foot length and propped it up against Blondie's curves. He stood next to her, straight as a flagpole. He said "cheese" but didn't smile. He couldn't have looked more wooden if he'd been sitting for Daguerre.

Vice

"Whaddya say we grabba bite?"

The meatbag said yes, the braincase said no. I had to get home in time to 4F—fuss, fritter, flutter, and fret.

"Tryin' ta worm outta tha resta tha job, huh?"

"What 'rest'? Suddenly this is a doubleheader?"

"Didn't I tell ya?"

"Go ahead, hit me."

"I'm sorry, sweetheart. It's age. The mind don't work tha way it useta."

"You manipulative bastard."

"That ain't no language ta use in fronta a lady." He gave Blondie the eye. "While we're up in this necka tha woods, I thought I'd hava quick chin with Pee Wee Young. He's tha guy givin' Collins a lift."

"Collins is in the jug. He can't go anywhere."

"Not 'lift' like in car. 'Lift' like in alibi. Pee Wee's supposed ta've rodded Collins up with tha sawed-off shotgun that got used in tha heist. But we don't wanna know nuthin' about that. What we're interested in is his sayin' he saw tha client tha morninga tha robbery."

I checked my digital. 3:15:23 P.M. "Where does this character live?"

"Coupla doors down. But before we look for him, I gotta put somethin' in my stomach. I didn't getta chance ta eat this mornin'." Mrs. Dick scored low today in home ec.

A meatball hero, an egg salad on rye, and three quarters of an hour later we rang Young's bell. No answer. A neighbor said try the barber shop; a street punk said the poolhall. The little dip turned out to be at the local bar. Pee Wee sat on a stool, his sinkers barely grazing the floor. He had steel wool for hair, an L-bracket for a snotbox, a siphon for a mouth. The whites of his eyes read like roadmaps and his scent was Colt 45. The way his clothes hung, permanent press was a thing of the past.

He pitched and rolled so much on the way back to his lair that I was convinced we were on the high seas instead of sidewalk. After fumbling with the key, he led us into dark basement digs. The one room was cramped with a couch, galley kitch, and a Formica bar with four barstools. The shrimp barhopped just by coming home.

Young stepped behind the counter and poured some firewater into a dirty tumbler. The stemware was for show. "Yoush wan shoma thish poishon?" he asked, the perfect host. We opted to digest lunch rather than scorch it.

"Sho, wha can I do fer yash?" he asked, settling himself on a stool. His feet dangled.

The hankshaw talked turkey, asking who, what, where, when. I took a bead on the tableau. It would've made a first-rate photo. Even with the Leica's whisper shutter, shooting was problematical. Who knew how the rummy'd react if he caught me mid-snap. He might roll up his flaps on Palladino. Or get p.o.'d enough to pull another sawed-off. A thingamajig like that didn't make neat, minimal holes; it made Jackson Pollock splatter. It made you very dead in a very messy way. A nasty piece of work like that could blow me and my career to smithereens. My Roseweb show would no longer be current work; it'd be a retrospective.

There was also a chance that the film might get subpoenaed. That was always a possibility for dick-job celluloid. If I hit the jackpot, I wouldn't want the fuzz to have the neg. They were already overworked. No need burdening them with art they didn't understand. First off, they'd print it screwy. Worse, they'd twist its meaning.

It's safe to assume that making art involves risks. If I were in Siberia without Palladino, I would've risked the shot. Then again, without the shamus, I wouldn't have risked being up here at all. Catch 22. I put the kibosh on art and tuned back in to the prattle.

Nick was still barbering away with the Q's. "Tell me again, Pee Wee, where were ya that morning, tha tima tha robbery?"

Pee Wee: I told ya, out inna fron', shittin' in my car.

Nick: Howdya know it was ten-a-clock?

Pee Wee: I dunno. I jusht did.

Nick: Think hard. Wasn't there some sorta way ya knew? Like maybe ya were listenin' ta tha radio in tha car. Like tha news comes on and tha newscaster, he tells ya tha time?

Pee Wee's watery ebonies solidified. "Yeah, that mushta been wha happened. Shure, now I remember. Tha radio shez itsh ten-a-clock an right afta that, Petey comesh walkin' down tha shtreet." He gargled more white lightning while Palladino made some notes in a pocket looseleaf.

Nick: Good. Now, can ya think of anybody else round here who mighta seen him 'bout tha same time?

Pee Wee: Ya could try Shalt 'n' Pepper. They'sh out onna shtreet alla time. They'sh whorsh livin' round tha corner. Shalt's tha white one; Pepper'sh black. Guesh that ain't hard ta figure, ish it? You'll recognizhe Pepper eashy cush she's got a bandage on her cheek."

"What happened to her?" Being around Sara I was used to medical chitchat.

"Shtitches. Her mother's boyfriend bit her."

What I knew about bite I'd learned from my orthodontist.

"That dude'sh a ba-a-a-ad motherfucker," Young said and drank to it.

So was my orthodontist.

Shady Ladies

Salt was where Pee Wee said she'd be, strutting her stuff on Stuyvesant and Grant. The doxy was a genuine, straight-from-the-bottle blizzard, with pasty skin, a sleepy expression, and a polyester outfit natty as an unmade bed. Not the Happy Hooker. Not particularly helpful, either. She knew "nuthin' 'bout nuthin' " she said, but that wasn't absolutely true. She knew Pepper was with a john.

I took another nervous glance at my Casio: 5:30:02 P.M. Time to shake a leg. Nick called me a worrywart. I called him an S.O.B. Name calling passed time but it didn't rush Pepper. At 5:50:23 she paraded her wares in our direction. Her open-toed slingbacks stacattoed to the swing of her hips. She was a tall, skinny chick who'd be cuter-looking through a telephoto than a normal. She was roughly the same age as her colleague, only holding up better. She had more smarts; she knew time was money. She turned the meter on when she talked with Palladino.

While Nick put her through her paces, I fixated on the white strip of gauze on the sable's cheek. That somebody would sink masticators into you so deep you'd need catgut—that shocked me more than Pee Wee's sawed-off. A blast furnace in the South Bronx was as everyday as a Cuisinart in Fairfield County. Speaking as a human being, I was more nervous about the gun. I suppose if I were a veggie, I'd have more to fear from the food processor. Nothing—not college credit psych courses, newspaper articles, nor crime novels—prepared me for fang contact. I didn't lead a charmed life, but I did lead a sheltered one.

Nick's fin bought him blue sky. Peter Collins's alibi was pretty shaky. So was I. It was 6:15:46 and time was getting iffier by the second.

Shock

The peeper knew I was sore. He broke the sound barrier but even the SST treatment wouldn't get me home in time to doll. So much for the knock-'em-dead dress I'd Mastercharged. I'd go workaholic chic: jeans, sweater, boots, and expensive camera accessories. If not fashionably dressed, settle for fashionably late.

The trip from Siberia to SoHo, from poverty to posh, made me schizoid.

"Nick, this work ever get to you?" I asked. Compare and contrast.

"Whaddya mean?" He swerved to avoid a jaywalker.

"I don't know, you know, all the violence everywhere, how fucked up the world is, the injustice." I was a hair trigger away from sounding the bleeding heart liberal.

"Pee Wee and Pepper freaked ya out, huh? Things get ta me sometimes, sure. Ya think I got cast iron feelings? They get me down less now than when I started. Now mostly I get like disgusted. Like I seen enuffa tha same kindsa shit over and over. There're times I think ta myself, 'This is crazy. Move ta Florida and go fishin'.'"

"You could be like Travis McGee."

"Who's he?"

"You know, the dick in John D. MacDonald novels, the one who lives in the Keys on a houseboat called the *Busted Flush.*"

"Yeah, I hearda him. I don't read them detective novels much. My kid, he's probably read all of 'em ever published. He's nuts about 'em."

"And you?"

"A buncha baloney."

State of the Art

SoHo's chockablock full of galleries but *the* address downtown is 420 West Broadway. That's where four of the hottest—Roseweb being right up there—roost. That's where we pulled up just after 7:00 P.M.

"As long as you're here, Nick, why don't you come in and see what I do when you're not busting my chops?"

The P.I. was mixed. An art attack had about as much appeal as a short stretch in the stir. On the other hand, he liked me and was curious. "Only for a few minutes, sweetheart, 'cuz I gotta get home."

The art ghetto was out in force; the big, white gallery space was mobbed. The dick and I didn't stay side by side long. Once we stepped inside, it was every man for himself. I was surrounded by people I knew and people I didn't, all saying things I liked to hear. The way it sounded, I had a success on my hands.

Nick picked up speed and elbowed his way to my prints. He cased the images the way he'd double-o a crime site for clues. They didn't look like the Dewinter shots, or the Fifty-first Street nighties, or the supermarket spread. He tilted his upper case this way and that but new slants didn't illuminate. The pics were a mystery to him.

Palladino made to mouse but he couldn't get to the door. Artists kept bugging him. They slotted him as a piece of performance art. That was the downtowners' catchall for strange and unfamiliar behavior. Once they spotted it, they liked to talk it to death. We were both relieved when he made it over the wall.

The crowd swirled like the sea. Flotsam and jetsam bobbed up in front of me and then sunk from view. I thought I was drowning.

Just before I Davy Jonesed, I caught sight of the fam standing off to the side. Mom and Dad were having conniptions; they thought the J.P. nudes were porn. Sara was telling them otherwise. They'd come around. If the work didn't impress them, the prestige of the gallery would.

I spotted my hunk of heaven across the room yammering with Parker and a frail with big cornflower blues. She was early twenties and neo-flower vintage. She had down-to-the-crack-in-the-ass blond hair that guys go apeshit over.

Boyo and I locked headlamps and he fishtailed over with a glass of grape. He looked concerned. "Drink this. Looks like you could use it."

I took a healthy slug. "I know, I look like the 'Sport of Accident.'" I thought that's how Blake would say "underdressed." "But I'll tell you about the accident later. It's too long a story and it doesn't go with the decor." I shifted my weight along with the topic. "How do you think the work looks?" I needed reassurance.

"'Art can never exist without Naked Beauty displayed.'"

"Try that line out on my parents."

"I did."

"And?"

"Perhaps in time they'll find Understanding."

"They'll find a second condo in Miami faster. Who's the skirt with Parker?" I was switching gists the way I switched shutter speeds.

"Her? That's Winny. The bookbinder from Ohio."

So *that* was what She looked like. Definitely Parker's type, all right. Spacey enough. And whistlebait. Soft and sort of sticky sweet feminine. Not sinister and snaky the way I featured her. Still, she wasn't to be trusted, not for one minute. You can't tell a bookbinder by her cover.

"Jesus, everytime I turn around she's in town," I said, meanwhile thinking: If Golgonooza's so great, what the fuck's she doing here all the time. Is she that gaga over Parker? Watching them together, it doesn't look it. "I'm dying to meet her," I continued, wondering if that was an over or under statement. "Invite her to Viv's apartment for the bash afterward, will you?"

Golden Boy fidgeted. "I already have." And then he was gone, swept away by the next wave of well-wishers.

The room buzzed with blab. A few talked about art. More talked art market. A bunch chinned on loft size and high rents. Lots dished up dirt—whodunit with and/or for whom, for how long, and for why. You needed a scorecard for the who's-sleeping-with-who lineup. That was the drift from the Americans. Who knew what the French, Germans, and Italians were yakking about.

Still, compared to my earlier whereabouts, this scene was safe. Nobody in this crowd would dare sink their teeth into you; back-biting was more à la mode. No one in the art world would gun you down; potshotting was the vogue. Physical attacks in artland were rare; character assassinations were the rage. There was no need for weapons—tongues were stilettos.

I poured more vino down the hatch and stopped caring about what was being said behind my back. Good news was being aimed at my front. Cortland Wright, a well-known critic, said he'd write a review to mainstream my career. The gallery director, Barry Webster, *sotto vocce*-ed that collectors were interested in collecting. That sounded right: Their mad money becomes my bank account. My parents had turned the corner and were beaming a second cousin to approval. Sara was in a huddle with a suit who had Young Upscale Professional written all over him. And Hank just looked dreamy.

By the time I arrived at the clambake in my honor, I was feeling no pain. Only when Sara forked a piece of quiche and asked for salt and pepper did I flash on my schizy afternoon. "Down these mean streets a man must go," Chandler wrote. And sometimes a woman.

Crimes of the Art

After the opening, life went back to the quo. With one addition: Winny. She hung around the loft a lot. Hank said they were laying plans for our big Ohio trip. Looked to me like they were smoking lids of Golgonooza homegrown. I kept close tabs on my sweet patootie but Winny's evil didn't stop with dope. She had Gallagher in a spin. Me too; I had to listen to Blake-speak nonstop. I felt out of it. Worried sick. And on the road to frightened to death.

I was also waiting for fame and fortune to give me the high sign. Wright's promised rave came out in a mag that wrapped more fish than reached readers. So much for mainstreaming into the household word department. I sold a few prints but at three hundred fifty bucks a throw—with the dealer skimming fifty percent off the top —my accountant didn't have to find me a quick tax shelter. Success spoil me? Bushwah. I was still worrying per usual about ante-ing up on the bills. Rex Stout's detective Nero Wolfe wasn't joshing when he said "To be broke is not a disgrace, it is a catastrophe."

A lean week went by before Rosenblatt's whiny vocal cords reverbed over the wires. I got a kick from the call. Talking with him was the next best thing to dealing direct with a cash machine.

Marv and I palavered and I waited for him to make his pitch. What he threw was a curve ball. "I thought you'd be interested to know I've taken up art."

I tried imagining Big Marv in front of a canvas instead of a jury but it didn't fly. "How's that?"

"I'm working with Nile Steir."

I didn't know Steir personally—not many people did and most didn't want to—but I certainly knew of him. He was a performance artist who'd come on the scene several years ago, doing a piece where he tattooed himself all over his arms and legs. The videotape he made of that event became a classic in underground film festivals. He also published photos of his "life drawings," as he called them, in an expenso, limited edition. Next he went political and did what he termed "vigilante" art. Others, less poetic, called it defacing property. The law didn't scotch that project: it was a trendy, megabuck foundation that offered to sponsor Nile's illegal art making. Steir protested against its elitist-pig, running-dog, co-opting policies by spray-painting the foundation's brownstone Day-Glo pink, publishing a manifesto, and exhibiting every shred of documentation in a storefront "alternative space" in a Lower East Side rat-infested tenement.

Then he went west to spend time with the Indians. He lasted two documentation-free months before the Native Americans pow-wowed and sent him packing. Right about the time he blew back into the Big Dirty, Monet's *Water Lilies* in the Museum of Modern Art was mysteriously damaged by spray paint. No one was ever charged but Nile was a prime suspect.

Next came his blue period. He stayed in his loft, refused to speak, and lay in bed an entire year, only rotating his position a quarter turn daily. He had a collaborator—alternative titles were slave, masochist, dimwit, and wife—who brought him fresh food and film. Steir was nothing if not a media junkie, so of course the photos were published. He was no looker when he started the piece and looked like a Giacometti when he finished. He was egocentric but you couldn't call him vain.

"He's doing an outdoor work right now," Rosenblatt gossiped.

"More vigilante stuff?"

"That's no longer avant-garde," Rosenblatt carped. "No, what he's doing is refusing to enter any enclosed spaces for six months." Marv rattled off the no-no's like the seven wonders of the world. "No buildings, cars, subways, lobbies, phone booths, restaurants. Even bathrooms."

"I always figured him for an anal retentive."

That slid right by. "He's documenting the whole thing."

"Does a bear shit in the woods?" I sniped.

Marv continued without missing a beat.

"He makes a map every day showing his travels, leaves a stencil mark wherever he eats, a marker where he takes a leak, and takes a Polaroid each place he sleeps."

It sounded more dingbat than imaginative but that's my impression of most things. "So you're collaborating with him on this one?"

"I suppose you could say working with a client is a form of collaboration, yes," Marv speculated. I still didn't get the drift. Scads of artists made bad art but they didn't need to collaborate with lawyers.

"Okay, here's the thing. Last week Nile's sleeping on a loading dock on Warren Street, near Greenwich. He's there with his camera, tape recorder, all the chotchkes, when somebody goes to roll him. Steir's got a baseball bat lying next to his sleeping bag and the next thing the sneak's got stitches in the head and Steir's arrested for assault. The guy's got no money to speak of, so the court assigned me his case.

"They bring him inside the precinct house when they busted him?"

"You think the arresting officer was an art maven? Steir went limp trying to explain his work but the buttons didn't get the concept. Since they had to carry him in, there's an additional charge of resisting arrest."

"He documented that, right?"

"He tried. And for that he's charged with obstructing justice."

"Some artists think the function of art is to be subversive, you know."

"Yeah, and those artists need lawyers to get them out on bail. Which is what I did in Steir's case. We go to trial in a few weeks although I'm working on a stay. Steir doesn't want to come indoors for trial until the piece's finished."

"Where do you meet with this guy? Obviously not in your office."

"On a bench in Foley Square."

"Good thing he didn't get arrested in February."

"You're telling me? That's why I want this business resolved as soon as possible, before it gets cold." In that respect it was easy to sympathize. "So what *you're* gonna do is follow Steir around, photograph him, show what he does and where."

"What the hell for? He already documents his every breath."

"To establish credibility. He's not exactly what you'd call a disinterested party."

And not exactly what you'd call sane. "How'll I know he doesn't go inside when I'm not covering him?" Scouts' honor didn't cut the mustard anymore. If it ever did.

"Because you're gonna stick to him like flypaper for twenty-four hours, that's how."

I gulped. "You think I'm hanging around deserted loading docks all night while our Leonardo gets his beauty rest? Who's covering *my* ass when some maniac goes after my equipment? And I don't just mean photographic, sport."

"Janie, I'm hurt. You know I'm a sensitive guy and you know I know you're a nice girl. Of course, I was planning to send someone out with you."

"Yeah, who? Palladino?"

"If that's who you want, that's who you'll get." You could count my choices on the fingers of a two-toed sloth. "I'll call him and set it up. I'll get hold of Steir somehow and tell him you'll meet him tomorrow, say three-ish, at the corner of—how about Franklin and West Broadway?"

"Swell." The job was bongoland but at least it was in the neighb.

I hung up the phone and walked over to my dirty windows. It was rush hour and the light was fading over Gotham. Wage slaves swam like spawning salmon up Church Street to the IND. That was a lethal scene I was well out of.

Golden Boy breezed in a few minutes later. As I looked up, the clinks tinkled in my sugarfree. "Hi, handsome, what's new?" Staring at his large, golden saucers I had a clue.

"What's this, an interrogation?" Sourpuss flung himself into a chair.

"Ooh, touchy," I said, stung. Something was bugging him or he was more stoned than I thought. I did the only sensible thing under the circumstances; I changed the subject. Hank's attention was limited but when I described Steir's outdoor piece, he drilled me with his dilateds.

"Blake says: 'Folly is an endless maze.' " He looked more pained than even Steir's bad art warranted.

"Speaking of folly," I said, trying to keep conversation bright, "we have tickets tonight for that controversial Armenian flick. I think I'll pass and nod out early. Why don't you call Parker and ask if he wants the pasteboard."

"Parker's busy," Golden Boy snapped like an efficient social secretary. "I'll call Winny."

That got my eyebrows going. Since she hadn't been around in a couple of days I figured her visa'd expired. There's a scene in *Lost Horizon* where a stunner turns into a hag when she leaves Shangrila. I hoped similar happened to Golgonooza frails who strayed from the compound. Sisterhood is powerful, but not across the board.

"Her, uh, plans sort of changed," Gallagher mumbled as he scurried up to the loft bed to make his call.

I tried curling up with *The Book of Los*, another of Willy Boy's I was supposed to have under my belt before Ohio D-day. The giggling I overheard didn't make my Herculean task easier.

Hank returned to floor level fifteen minutes later, working a J around in his maw. He went to the dugout and poured himself a

Rolling Rock. Kitchen cabinets slammed. Dishes clattered. The crepe-hanging mood had passed. Honeybunch was making dinner.

Gallagher cooks cyclone style. Pots and pans whirl; flat surfaces load up with debris. By the time he'd concocted his chef-d'oeuvre, the kitch qualified as a natural disaster area. Except the National Guard wasn't getting called out for a cleanup campaign. I had to dig myself out of the rubble. Don't misread me, though, I think it's neat when men share the domestics. But messy.

I took my dishpan hands off to bed for an early doze-off. My squeeze's being out with the Blakette made it hard to get shut-eye. I tried counting sheep. Sheep made me think "Little lamb, who made thee?" That slush meant I was thinking Blake. Blake made me think about Winny. And Winny made me think about Golgonooza. That made me really nervous. I got up and brought myself a brandy. One splash didn't do the trick. I downed a second. Still no deal. I took out *The Book of Los*. That worked like a charm. I was out for the count in no time flat.

I found a groggy Golden Boy communing with the granola when I came downstairs the next morning. I gave him a pre-toothpaste buss and worried about my breath. "I must've slept like a log. I didn't even hear you get in."

Gallagher's blinkers stayed glued to his spoon as it chased around a raisin. Then he went on a search-and-destroy mission for a nut. Communicative.

"How was the movie?"

"The movie? Not the least Particle of Emanation."

"A bomb, huh? Guess the Armenians didn't stand much chance as filmmakers anyway. Wonder why it's gotten such raves? What did Winny think?"

"She thought it was False, Indulgent, Stupid, Negative, Banal, and totally lacking in Fire, Beauty, and Wisdom."

When the Golgonoozers don't dig you, they *really* don't dig you.

Stink

Nick picked me up and we were heading to Steir-age. "This fella must be some jackoff," the gumshoe grumbled. "You know about this art stuff; tell me, is this guy's stuff tha genuine article or ain't it?"

I shrugged and said, "Beats me."

The dick wasn't satisfied. "C'mon, sweetheart, give it ta me straight. Yes or no?"

"In my personal opinion, it ain't." All art criticism should be so easy.

"So whaddya call it, then?"

"How about false, indulgent, negative, and totally lacking in fire, beauty, and wisdom?" If Winny could pull off that mouthful of marbles, why couldn't I?

"Keep up that kinda talk, sister, and I'll think yer as sicko as this Steir."

Whom we smelled before we spotted. I'd wondered how the dude worked bathing. Now the answer hit me. I'd stopped linking cleanliness with godliness long ago but I still had plenty of ground to cover to catch up with Steir's far-out notions of hygiene. He was well on the way to being an air pollutant. But that was probably part of the concept.

The visuals were less assaultive. Nile had hair like seaweed atop and all around his head. Lopsided black plastic cheaters rode his long, pinched nose. The rest of him was long and reedy to match. The way he was decked out, he looked like a walking army-navy store. I judged him late middle-aged.

"You two can follow me around," Steir consented in a low, surly monotone.

"That ain't no problem," Palladino assured him, his nose puckering in self-defense.

"But not too close."

"Not to worry," I added my two cents, one per nostril.

"I view this piece as guerrilla action."

The P.I.'s head jiggled like a kewpie doll's. "Not g-o-r-i-l-l-a. G-u-e-r-r-i-l-l-a," I whispered. The more I thought about it, though, the more Nick's take seemed right.

"If you interfere, you'll ruin the integrity of the work," Steir patronized.

"Don't worry yer pretty little head about us, pal," Nick said. "We'll stay as far away as possible, believe me." With that his pedals followed his smeller in a pirouette and he sauntered upwind where the Apple's air smelled like a rose garden. Comparatively, that is.

"P.U." Palladino held his schnoz between thumb and index. "Good thing he don't wanna go into court; he'd knock tha jury dead. And Rosenblatt'd be stuck with a murder rap."

We kept a steady block and a half D.M.Z. between us and the urban guerrilla. Nile gave us plenty to do; he had Palladino switching his Sony tape recorder on and off, reporting his every move while I snapped away each time he marked his map or the sidewalk. Four and a half hours into the job, we'd covered a couple of Kentucky Derbies' worth of turf.

It was a good thing I'd wised up about detective fiction lies. On the boredom scale, tailing rated about equal with surveillance. The diff was that tailing made your feet hurt. The hankshaw was in real pain; he'd worn the wrong pair of Florsheims.

"I wonder what makes somebody like that tick," I queried as Steir polished off a legendary Dave's egg cream in two pulls at the outdoor counter. He made his mark on the pavement. There were sixteen similar ones already there, kudos from a true Underground Gourmet.

"A guy like that ticks 'cuz he's a walkin' time bomb, that's what," Palladino assessed as our tailee slipped his stencil kit back into his knapsack. He headed south on Broadway, hung a right on my block, and hurried over to a trash can on the corner. A yellow rivulet followed, then a yellow marker.

I averted my hazels and took a lookaround down the street. A checker pulled up in front of my building and deposited Golden Boy and Winny at the door. Hank was carrying a Velveeta-colored 16 × 20 Kodak box under his arm that he must've brought in from Hoboken.

The street was bathed in yellow light. Steir's yellow marker glowed in the foreground. The scene had all the makings of a terrific color photo. I was in the right place at the right time with the right camera in the wrong company with the wrong film.

I thought about yelling to Hank but he was too far down the block. The way I gazed off into the distance made Palladino suspect. "That tha boyfriend?" he inquired, watching Golden Boy hold open the door for the fairhair.

"Yup, that's my One and Only."

"What's he takin' tha skirt upstairs for? Ta show her his etchings?"

Now *there* was a dated line on boy-girl relations. "Etchings, nah. He's probably showing her pics he took on her commune."

The dick looked skeptical. "Etchings, photos, what'sa difference?"

"She's not a problem," I insisted as Nick continued to scowl. "Hank's cult crazy, not girl crazy."

"If you say so, sweetheart." He looked *and* sounded skeptical.

"Is it an occupational hazard with private eyes? They see sex and sin everywhere?"

"Maybe." The P.I. considered. "Ya tend ta always be suspicious, sure. But I'll tell ya, kid, it's funny but it gets so's ya know, instinct like, when ya smell a rat."

"Speaking of smell," I interrupted, "you and I aren't making it as bloodhounds. The scent we're following is wafting away. We'd better catch up."

"Shit" was Nick's comment.

"No, what he just did was piss," I corrected. "Make a note."

Hot Pursuit

"What's that?" The gumshoe pointed to a hefty slab of curved corten steel parked near the Holland Tunnel entrance. "Wait, don't tell me. I know, it's art, right? Every goddamn thing down here's art."

"You got it, buster. They call it environmental."

"Tha artist, he get paid a bundle for this?"

"Probably a fair amount. But art never *really* pays."

"They say crime don't either but I'll tell ya, it makesa helluva lot more sense ta me."

While we discussed economics, Nile hung a right on Hudson, then diddled in front of an Ethiopian hashery on Vestry. Nothing doing there. He meandered up Desbrosses to Washington, headed south, then east on Harrison to peer into Prescott's and Puffy's, bars where artists tanked up after studio hours. A few waved from their bar stools but kept their butts *in situ*. If Steir's fans were devoted, they were devoted from a distance.

Nile's gait slowed on Duane. His head went down and his feet shuffled. He continued down Hudson to Chambers, then did ten minutes on a bench in the concrete pie-slice at the West Broadway intersection. Nick lit up a cancer stick to pass time. I wished I were home with Hank and Winny. Then I wished Winny would leave.

Steir rallied, roamed some more, then zeroed in on a loading dock on Warren near Greenwich.

"I don't fucking believe it!" It was bolt-out-of-the-blue time. Steir was rolling out his sleeping bag in the exact spot where he'd run into the trouble that'd put us on his tail. "Since when does the victim return to the scene of the crime?" In a previous life the john must have been a kamikaze homing pigeon.

"Tha sucker probably believes lightning doesn't strike tha same place twice. He should go chin with tha Empire State Building."

"You mean something could happen here again?" My vocals tremoloed.

"One thing ya learn in this biz, kid, is take nuthin' for granted. But don't get worked up. Even though this job's cuckoo, odds're against it."

I started to breathe easier until I heard the dick's stomach make a noise I'd heard in Siberia. "Listen, sweetheart," he said midrumble, "I'm gonna go get my car and go get us somethin' ta eat. Yer fellow artist there"—the P.I. handled the words "fellow artist" like rotten mozzarella—"he can live on Sabrett and dig spendin' nights out under tha smog, but I gotta have a Big Mac an' a roof. You hold down tha fort, dollface; I shouldn't be gone more'n a half hour. Whaddya wanna eat?"

"Filet mignon, rare, a side of braised leeks, and a glass of champagne. But I'll settle for a fishwich, some fries, and a vanilla shake."

As soon as the gumshoe split, I felt my teeth curl and my nerve die. Warren Street was quiet and dark as a tomb and as creepy as Halloween. The area was still scummy; artist platoons hadn't moved in yet to renovate. Only a few windows in that art-forsaken area showed the telltale signs of habitation—ferns in macramé holders, air conditioners, curtains. I gave the street a few more years before it became swanky. Steir's artistic judgment might be screwy but his real estate sensibilities were strictly avant-garde.

Time moved like molasses in January. I leaned up against a doorway that gave me a direct visual hit of Steir. He took his Polaroid, crooned into his tape recorder, and collared a nod. It was a drag watching him when he was legworking; now it was a total snore. The minutes ticked by, each more slowly than the last. I had plenty of time to wonder if I was cut out for this private eye shit. My doubts were as deep as the shadows. I could die of boredom.

At first I thought it was just imagination. Then I pegged the quick movement in the dark for a rat. There are loads of big rats in this town and I'd seen a few in my time. But this one wasn't just big. Try man-size. Man-size and slinking steadily toward Sleeping Beauty. Not only slinking but toting a length of pipe. The sap was on a collision course with Steir's thinktank.

I moved in on the action like a sports photographer, raised the camera—the Nikon this time—and popped a shot. The strobe lit up a plug-ugly with crewcut, bulging calf muscles, and Levi jacket ready to beat the crap out of his potential victim.

Seeing the light, the biped wheeled to face me. A second blast showed a face so spectacularly homely that I couldn't pull my eyes off it. Trigger-happy, I hit the shutter again for a portrait. The gesture was sound artistically. And it was effective—like waving red meat in front of a starving lion. Two hundred and some pounds of high octane venom charged me.

My Nikes ate concrete. I'm okay in a sprint but I don't go the distance. I had no idea which way to run, so I headed down Greenwich to Park Place. I had smarts enough to know not to wind up with my back to the river. The pipe gained on me after I took a left on West Broadway. My heart raced along with my running shoes. The streets were deserted and the few cars that passed didn't stop. I ran another block and took a bunch of lefts and rights. I began to have trouble breathing. I took a look over my shoulder; the pipe drew closer and closer to my head. My epitaph flashed before me: "She died for art." Goddammit, this was Steir's art. *He* should die for it.

My legs still worked even if my gray matter didn't. Suddenly headlights muscled in on the street. I heard the screech of brakes but didn't stop. I risked another look-see. No pipe. The only thing moving behind me was air. The action was going on down the street. Palladino'd jumped out of his jalopy, pasted a fist into my pursuer's solar plexus, and put the louse in a full nelson. At that moment, Nick the dick was the most beautiful man I'd ever seen, bar none. And that included Golden Boy. I was even relieved to see —and inhale—Steir. It seemed that I'd run full circle in blind panic.

The artist was up, blinking his myopics. He put on his cheaters, took one look at Nick and the rough trade next to him, and said, "Hey, man, that's the same guy as last time." That made the heavy Larry Fields, an auto mechanic who moonlighted as a pipe wielder.

"You all right, sweetheart?" Nick asked with concern, straining every muscle to hold Fields.

"Oh, yeah, sure," I replied trying to sound blasé and catch my breath simultaneously.

"Good. Now you"—he addressed Nile—"you take tha car and go get tha cops."

"I can't," Steir wailed and by way of apology explained, "I can't get into a car."

"C'mon, fuckhead, this ain't no time ta pull that art shit."

Steir, offended, planted his sinkers into the ground like shrubbery.

"Go find a phone booth then and call 'em," Palladino snarled between gnashing teeth.

"I can't go into a phone booth either, remember?"

The gumshoe tasted bile. "Listen, asshole, and listen good. Ya know tha police precinct on Ericsson Place, near Beach? Go up there and get 'em."

"They'll try to pull me inside again. They'll ruin my piece this time for sure."

"I'll go," I volunteered, seeing how the situation was shaping up. The veins in Nick's neck had begun to bump and grind.

"Okay, take tha car."

"I can't. It's a stick and I only know how to drive an automatic. I'll walk."

"Oh, no, you won't," he growled. "These streets ain't safe." Gears whirled in his noodle. "Tha car's definitely out. So we're all gonna walk." He freed up a hand to reach into his raincoat. He pulled out a .38 Special and jammed the barrel against Fields's spine. "C'mon, move it."

"Hold it," Steir whined. "I can't leave my stuff here. It'll get stolen." He started gathering up his gear like a spazzie spider. That's when Palladino made a mistake: he let his attention wander. Just for a sec but it was long enough for Fields to make a break. Palladino snapped to in a hurry. His eyeballs strafed the road. He located his target and fired a warning shot into Fields's left leg. The runaway crumpled.

Nick pivoted my way. "Your turn, sweetheart. Take a shot." First I thought he meant with his heater. Then it dawned on me he meant the F1. Firearm vocab and photo lingo dovetail and now I understood why. I didn't dig the similarity but I cocked the shutter and fired point-blank. Fields grimaced. It was hard knowing which shot—mine or Palladino's—was more damaging.

"Try any more funny stuff and I'll give ya lead poisoning in tha other leg," the shamus threatened. It was a Hollywood line and sitting in the movies I would've eaten it up along with my buttered popcorn. Such are the differences between the reel and the real. In real life it scared the bejesus out of me.

Fields scrambled awkwardly to his feet. Blood oozed down his pant leg and his mouth screwed the lid on the pain. The wound was just deep enough to make him gimp and manageable. Nick wasn't a half-bad shot. I was impressed. And stomach sick.

"Okay, buddy boy, start walkin'," the hankshaw commanded. "And that goes for you, too, creep," he barked, brandishing the gat in Nile's direction. Me, I didn't need a cold-steel persuader. My feet were dancing.

When you need them, of course, they're not around; when you don't they're everywhere. The streets now teemed with late-nighters and club-goers. Blue- and green-haired punks with safety pins in their ears gave us weirdo stares as we trekked to the police station. The bluecoat outside the First Precinct did the same. "Not you guys again?" was how he greeted Fields and Steir. "Hey, Sarge," he yelled inside. "Guess who's back? I'll give you a hint. It ain't Shaft." Then to us again, "Step right up, fellas. You know the way."

Steir did and balked. He demanded to see his lawyer. The conversation that had to follow had no future. "I'll go in and call Rosenblatt," I said, hoping to avert Steir's harangue about police brutality toward art. Not that Steir's art, and for that matter Steir himself, couldn't use a little brutalizing. Art needn't imitate life but it should never jeopardize it.

The Payoff

Rosenblatt arrived, eyelids at half-mast, circa 2:00 A.M. Fields had already been booked; Palladino and I had been questioned. Steir slouched on the curb droning into his tape recorder. He liked exercising freedom of speech.

Nick greeted the Esq. with a slap on the back. "Next time ya getta job like this, forget ya ever met me, okay? Where d'ya find 'em?" He cocked his bean toward Marv's client. "Ya on somebody's hate list or what?"

"Don't ask. And now, with these complications, *oy vey*. The case'll drag on into winter. I'll have to invest in a down jacket. He'll want to meet me in snowdrifts. With my luck it'll be a winter of blizzards. What did I do to deserve this? That's what I want to know." The lawyer was still muttering as he went down the drab hall to arrange an alfresco affidavit session.

Meanwhile in mediaville, the dailies had sniffed out a scoop.

Reporters began pulling up at the stationhouse. Rumor had it I'd not only stopped a crime but captured it on celluloid. That made me 4H—heroine, hot shot, hot news, and helpful.

"Is it true, Miss Meyers, that you have actual photos of the entire episode?" the *Times* legwoman wanted to know.

"Uh huh," I said, cool as a cuke. On the outside; on the inside I was a mass of quivering protoplasm.

"You got 'em, we'll run 'em," the stringer for the *Daily News* offered.

"Give us the film. We'll process it and print it," the staffer for the *Post* volunteered.

Soup my film gratis? Eastman Kodak, I would've loved somebody doing my grunt work. But these weren't your average, everyday news pics. They were the real McCoy, ipso facto evidence shots. Not to mention bona fide artwork.

"I'm in a pickle, boys," I explained to reporters. They wrote that down in their pads. Pickles make good copy.

"Suit yourself," the *Post* man said, looking up from his notes. "Get us prints first thing in the morning and we'll run the story."

"Send us a set as well," the *Times* lady requested. Ditto for the *Daily News*er and the *Village Voice*r. "Don't forget your friends in the neighb," said the small fry from *The SoHo News.*

One minute I was on Cloud Nine. Then I remembered: I was still on duty for another twelve big ones of tailing. Scratch darkrooming. Bag blowups. So long fame and photo credits, freebee publicity, checks. Hello Ground Zero.

The dick pulled another ass saver. "Don't worry, kid, I'll square things. I ain't gonna let that Nile nerd screw up our chance a makin' headlines. Opportunity like this don't knock every day, ya know. Besides, Steir owes ya.

"I'll just tell Rosenblatt I'll cover solo for a while. It shouldn't be bad; tha twerp ain't goin' nowheres in a hurry. Look."

Steir stood in the middle of a ring—a wide one for olfactory reasons—of legmen. In the sodium vapor he looked happy as an alky on a bender.

"Whaddya say ya meet me and Johnny Carson here, round seven thirty, at tha diner on Leonard Street? That give ya 'nuff time ta make our mugs famous?"

"Sure. Should I meet you outside?"

"Ya pullin' my leg or somethin'? Nile'll be outside. Me, I'll be inside at tha counter. Like a human bein'."

"Okeydoke," I said and made to mosey the few blocks home. The shamus ran interference. He got me put in a prowl car. The cop squirmed when I told her to drop me in front of the Pussy Cat.

"We get lots of complaints about that place," Dickless Tracy said with disgust.

"Yeah, I know. I'm the one who phones them in," I flapped as I climbed out of the whistler.

Looking up I saw lights blazing in my loft. Gallagher having a tough time sleeping without me? Great.

I raced upstairs, the perfect antidote to insomnia. Okay, I admit it. My motives weren't altruistic. After what I'd been through I needed holding and Hank was lined up for the squeeze.

Hitting the top step, I yelled, "Surprise." It was one all right—but on me. The place reeked of whacky weed. Golden Boy's Golgonooza photos were strewn all over the floor. The love of my life lay facedown on the rug. Winny lay next to him. It wasn't a pretty sight.

The squab was up in a jiff. She locked her big blues on me like I was a nasty visual problem that needed solving. "You're not supposed to be here," she said. I was thinking along the same lines about her. "What are you doing back?"

"What are you doing here?" was what I wanted to know. Weren't country bumpkins early-to-bed-early-to-risers? How come this tomato was up past bedtime? Why wasn't she in the crib with Parker instead of here cribbing with my guy?

Hank managed to jackknife into sitting position and added: "I thought you were following that stupid artist around all night and into Dawn's Crepuscular Light?"

"Crepuscular Light? Where did Blake write that?" Winny was impressed. I wasn't.

"He didn't. I made it up," Golden Boy boasted.

She really went for that. She didn't go for the look on my phiz. "Here, have a toke," she recommended, offering me a newly lit joint. Smoke was the Ohio equivalent of chicken soup. "It's really great Golgonooza Gold." The dope sounded like it'd won the Good Housekeeping Seal of Approval. "It'll mellow you right out."

"With you around, sister, mellowing ain't a luxury I can afford," I noted to myself. To the frill I said: "No thanks, Win, Hank-o's the mellower I need." I showed her a full set of shark's teeth and headed over to Gallagher.

"Hug me," I demanded. "You came real close to losing me in the line of duty."

"Huh?" His arms followed orders and his mouth moved. "What are you talking about?"

It was time to give the show away. To compete with the book-binder's evil influence, I punched up the gunplay. Sensationalism's a cheap trick but it gets results. Gallagher hugged harder.

Ms. Ohio, meantime, sucked smoke into her lungs and talked. Her vocals sounded like the soundtrack from *The Exorcist.* "How can you live here? It's a City of such Dark Contraries, such Infernal and Diabolical Enormities. It's so, so Inhuman. So full of Vice. Don't you think?"

Gallagher's head bobbed up and down, so apparently my recent caper got him thinking similar crap.

Sure, Gotham was no paradise. But it was my kind of town. Where else could you go anywhere, anytime, do anything with anybody? Could Golgonooza top that?

So Manhattan had its scumbag side and crime out the kishkas—

didn't I know that from the Steir escapade?—but hell, it had beauty and magic too. You give credit where credit is due, for Chrissake.

I was itching for a fight but it was two against one with me playing the lone hand. I took the diplomat's way out; I cut the rap short with a cute excuse. "Sorry," I said, "I'm a working girl who has to work" and with that I ankled off into the lonely lab.

The exposures and processing were a cinch. As the prints went through the enlarger like butter I thought about George Harmon Coxe's photog detective, Jack "Flashgun" Casey. Not a bad role model. He made a pretty decent living milking this kind of gig. But of course, he was a fiction. So probably was his salary.

I was all right as long as I stayed in the dark. It was the 3-D survey coming out that was the snag. Winny sat close to Golden Boy reading *The Four Zoas* in a hypnotic drone.

But how to bust up this Blake-out? It was 7:15-ish, not much time to come up with a solution. But no time *was* the solution. No, two solutions—with both our best interests in mind. I'd get Hank out of Winny's clutches—that was in his best interest although he didn't know it—and get my prints hand-delivered to the blats in time—which was in mine. I s.o.s.'d. Hank snapped to; he said he'd convey. Winny said she'd be happy to go along. The skirt knew a thing or two about self-interest too. Nuts.

After they split, I took a squint at Golden Boy's floor show. It was new work from his Ohio junket. The stuff looked good. Lots of lush landscapes, a couple of Winny. Too much beauty for my burned-out headlamps. Nitty-gritty was more like it. I swung the F1 over my shoulder, charged downstairs, and went back to work.

I was so wired from a night's worth of caffeine I was afraid I'd get slapped with a speeding ticket on the sidewalk. I braked at the diner and caught sight of Steir catnapping by the door. I didn't wake him; he might talk at me. Instead I barreled into the eatery's shiny green interior and parked my keister next to Nick's. The shamus was working away on cluck and grunts. Red-eyed, blue-jawed, and tightlipped, he looked anything but sunny.

I asked the Greek behind the counter for two poached, no toast, no fries. Girth control. I'd see carbs galore in the Buckeye State. The Blake bunch probably chowed down whole paddies of brown rice and stadiums of homemade bread at a clip. Coffee I needed the way Newcastle needed coal, but I ordered jamoke anyway. It'd put hair on my chest and more spin in my tailing.

Waiting Game

Nero Wolfe vetoed shop talk during meals. He claimed it ruined digestion. He could shoot off his mouth; he had a private cook.

"So tell me what happened already," I hocked as soon as I felt Nick had had enough starch.

"Nuthin' much, mora tha same," Palladino reported with as much animation as dead storage. It was then we heard the tapping on the window. We both sunk our schnozes deeper into our respective cuppas. The tapping persisted.

"You look," the dick ordered.

"Do I have to? It'll spoil my breakfast."

"I already gotta ulcer. It's your turn."

"You're a real prince, you know that?" I twirled my stool in a semicircle. Steir was making ugly faces in the window. I retwirled. "It's bad. He wants us to come out and play. I think he misses us."

"Jesus, ya can't eat in peace no more in this town. Don't tell nobody, but ya know, I wish Fields got ta use tha pipe on our friend here."

"Yeah, I was thinking along the same lines myself. Absence makes the heart grow fonder."

"Some other organs, too. Like tha nose," Nick cracked.

The Greek dropped our checks on the Formica and I made a grab for them. "This one's on me."

A woman picking up the tab made the gumshoe uncomfortable,

but he managed to de-macho. "Thanks, big spender," he said as I stopped at the cash register to fork over a stiff $4.97. The tab set me back two rolls of film. I asked for a receipt. Might as well make it a business expense; Rosenblatt could spring for it.

After going to all the trouble of ruining our breakfasts, you'd think Steir had something important to say. He didn't. Just because we saved his life didn't mean he had to be civil. Maybe he went in for nonverbal communication and we weren't receiving.

He mumbled "morning" but not "good." Next he mumbled "newsstand." We followed him—it was no sweat, he was still no gardenia—to Church and Chambers. He rifled through the *Times* and the *News*. No news in this case didn't mean good news. I panicked. Had Winny and Golden Boy gotten lost and re-Blaked? I wouldn't've put it past the chick to sabotage my delivery to the dailies.

Then it dawned on me: the story broke after the morning rags got put to bed. The first report would be in the afternoon's *Post*. That wasn't fast enough for Nile; he wanted to be a hero now. He went into a bad funk. Bad enough that I had to remind him to leave a stencil mark when he scarfed down a Snickers.

Things picked up around noon. The *Post* ran the story on page eight. I was brought up believing S.P.S.—self-praise stinks—so I usually don't blow my own horn. But I had to hand it to myself, my pics of Fields in action looked bang-up. The pic of me with Nick and Nile didn't. I have a shit-eating grin on my pan and a coif that came out of a windtunnel. Nick has his arm around me buddy-buddy; luckily, Nile doesn't. The *Post*'s legman cleaned up Palladino's slanguage, but the text wasn't half bad:

Photo finish for art attack

Larry Fields learned last night that the camera doesn't lie, only he probably won't thank 27-year-old photographer Jane Meyers for the demonstration.

The lesson occurred around midnight on a loading dock at 92 Warren Street where Nile Steir was sleeping. Steir, who calls himself a performance artist, says his artwork is "concerned with urban survival." Last night's episode certainly bore out his description.

Fields, a 38-year-old burly auto mechanic from Staten Island, was just about to clobber the sleeping Steir with a lead pipe when pretty, petite Meyers foiled the attack with her only weapons—a Nikon and a flash. Within seconds she had taken several incriminating photographs of the assailant.

An enraged Fields then chased Meyers along the deserted streets of Lower Manhattan. The photographer was in turn rescued by Domenic Palladino, a Manhattan-based private investigator patrolling the area at the time. Palladino apprehended the attacker. Gunplay ensued when Fields later attempted to escape.

Oddly enough, this wasn't the first visit Steir and Fields had made together to the First Precinct. An earlier run-in occurred on September 29 when the mechanic attempted to rob Steir—asleep at the same location—of his tape recorder and camera. That time Steir awoke and bashed his attacker with a baseball bat he kept under his sleeping bag. Fields received a head wound and four-teen stitches. Steir was charged with assault, resisting arrest, and obstructing justice when he tried photographing his arresting officer, claiming it was in the interest of art.

Steir's legal problems are complicated by the nature of his artwork. His current project, begun in August, requires he remain outdoors nonstop for six months. His previous arrest has him contesting a court date set for October 18 on the grounds that an appearance at 100 Centre Street will "compromise me and totally jeopardize my integrity in the art community." It is because of this controversy that Steir's court-appointed attorney, Marvin Rosenblatt, Esq., engaged the services of Meyers and Palladino. They were to provide documentation of Steir's whereabouts and commitment.

"Steir was lucky we were both nearby and quick on the draw," Palladino said after Fields had been booked for assault. "I think Jane did an A-1 job, considering she's an artist and new to this kind of work."

Meyers, an artist in her own right, is presently showing her photographs at Roseweb Gallery in SoHo. "Art for art's sake's dead. I'm glad I'm not," the relieved shutterbug added.

Steir, for whom special provisions were made for an outdoor deposition, will continue his art piece—barring any more interruptions—through January 1.

Nile was euphoric. "Uh," he managed to squeeze out, "these shots are kind of okay."

"Gee, thanks," I said. Palladino winked.

"I think I could use a few of them in the book I'm putting out on this piece." Like he was doing me a favor. Like I knew he wanted them freebee.

"Call me when you can go into a phone booth." By that time I'd probably be looking back on the job with nostalgia. By that time Steir would've had a bath. That fact alone would improve our relationship fifty percent.

Knocking Off

Palladino and I were feeling chipper. We'd had a bellyful and now we could knock off. We toodalooed Steir at Duane Street and hopped into the sleuth's crate. Our last shag, Nile stood on the corner, *Post* in hand, waiting for folks on the street to recognize him. Famewise, there are distinct advantages to being in front of the camera rather than behind it. Nobody reads photo credits from a distance. You're lucky if they even bother at close range.

Nick dropped me off at my place. I dragged my ass upstairs. This time there was no Winny. Unfortunately, no Golden Boy either. Ohio was still spread all over the floor, begging to be treated like linoleum.

I had bed on the brain and would've liked company. Hard work deserves hard other things. I dialed 201-555-3779 in Hoboken. A detectivette learns to catch shut-eye when and where she can. I dozed off holding the receiver. ZZZZZ's later the phone was still brrrr-ing. Finally the boy picked up.

"You took a long time to answer," I said drowsily.

"You know how it is. You just get home?"

"Mmmm." My repartee mechanism was on the fritz. "Come

over, okay? I want to thank you personally for delivering my prints."

"I think I'll stay out here for a while."

"Aw, how come?"

"'Without Unceasing Practice nothing can be done. Practice is Art. If you leave off you are Lost.'"

"You won't be lost, you'll only be taking a break."

"Jane, you sound exhausted. After what you've been through you need to sleep. We can talk about this later."

"Uh, uh, sleep. Mmmm." My lids were weighing in like prizefighters. "Okay, tomorrow. I miss you."

"Tomorrow. Pleasant dreams."

Alert

They were more than pleasant. They were big budget technicolor specials. I was being chased through the kinds of places Hank photographed by the kinds of people Rosenblatt hired me to photograph. Suddenly someone named Mr. Mystery stepped out from behind a hill and handed me a camera. It was a Leica-like, rainbow-colored job called a Yes & Know. "Use this," he commanded, and I was just about to when I was interrupted. It was too early in the A.M. for the dingalinging to be any fun. I must be a glutton for punishment. I rolled over and picked up.

"Listen, I had to warn you. They just called me. They know."

"Huh? What?" My noodle was filled with brain fog.

"They saw the piece in the *Times.*"

"What piece in the *Times?*" The fog began to clear. "Oh, *that* piece; it ran?" First I was pleased. Then I kapished: I was in deep trouble. "How'd they see it so fast?"

"They get the paper delivered."

"Aw, shit, Sara. How bad is it?"

"Let's say they've stopped short of cardiac arrest. They're bound to call you so be prepared. I wish I could talk but I've got to run; we're getting our cadavers in anatomy class and I can't afford to be late if I want to get a cute one. Bye. Oh, and good luck. You'll need it."

They were on to me and the trick was getting them off. Nicely. Without a scene. The probability approached zero. Smart money said buy the paper, check out the damage. I went out to Canal Street and bought several. One to read; the extras for my portfolio.

The coverage was less splashy than the *Post's*. In fact, it took some hunting to find it. The two small pictures and the small two-column article was hidden in the back pages of section B. What were they doing, living in Connecticut and mucking around in "Metropolitan News"? Just my luck to be related to busybodies.

There was nothing to do but sit tight, so I sat down to tackle more Willy B. doggerel. The phone kept breaking my concentration. *Performance Artist Gazette, The Journal of Self-Defense, Career Woman's Monthly, Universal Photographer, You, Chat,* and *The Magazine of Forensic Photography,* etc., etc. all wanted interviews and/or material on or about Steir. My appointment book looked as packed as the Brooklyn-Queens Expressway during rush hour. Minor renown takes up major amounts of time. How would I ever get to Blake's *Jerusalem?*

Attempted Bribery

Around dinnertime I picked up the horn hoping Gallagher was on the line. I missed him and was going to propose a nice, quiet dinner in Chinatown. There was a hole in the wall on Catherine Street that served great crabs in black bean sauce.

"Finally you're off the phone. Do you have any idea how many times we tried calling you today?"

"Hi, Mom."

"Are you all right, dear?" Sara'd been right to warn me. The woman sounded upset.

"I'm fine, Ma."

"Julius, are you on the phone?" She yelled in the direction of the condo's den.

"Yes, dear," my father answered on the extension. We were now in battle position. "Jane, your mother and I saw that piece about you in the *Times.*"

Mother: And we almost died. Your regular artist friends aren't bad enough, you have to get mixed up with worse? And working for a detective! God give me strength.

Father: You could have been killed, Janie.

Mother: I took one look at those pictures and it took ten years off my life. Am I right, Julius?

Father: Look, dear, you're an intelligent and talented girl. You've had as good an education as money can buy. You know your mother and I want only the best for you. We want you to have a nice, normal, fulfilling career. Maybe you can get your old job back at that big corporation. You liked that job well enough, didn't you?

Me: No, not especially. It was boring.

Father: Excitement isn't everything, honey, believe me. You pay for it in the end. How about portraits of writers for book jackets? You'd meet interesting people. That would be fun.

Mother: And safe.

What the hand wringers really thought—and probably prayed for—was safer yet: marriage to a lovely young professional with a substantial income who'd make a lovely father to a couple of lovely grandchildren. They might as well ask me to come up with a cure for herpes.

Me: I'll take it under advisement.

Mother: Just remember, dear, your father and I love you and worry.

Me: I didn't mean to upset you.

Not this time anyway; my conscience was clear on that score. I never intended them to know about this number. I silently cursed *The New York Times* for its out-of-state circulation. New York news should stay in New York.

Father: I'm sure you didn't, dear, but the best way to prevent something like this happening is not to get involved in the first place. Tell you what. Why don't we put some money in your bank account so you'll have a little cushion while you go out and look for a job?

Mother: We just want to see you happy, dear.

Me: Then lay off.

They did more than that. They hung up. In perfect unison. The united way.

Secret Rendezvous

He said he was coming to New York and he did. He told me he'd call and he had. I shouldn't have agreed to Monday evening's rendezvous but I did. I'd tried talking my way out of it but I couldn't. LeCoq had a way of wearing down my resistance.

I walked at a brisk clip down Canal to the IRT, goggling over my shoulder every ten feet or so. I wasn't shlepping camera, portfolio, or career paraphernalia. I was dressed to kill. Bumping into Gallagher now would be death.

Hank had answered the phone when Jean-Pierre called from his hotel so he knew the frog was in town. What he didn't know was, I was playing Welcome Wagon Hostess. Why upset him for nothing? The past was past; my fling was a one-time-only affair. I was now a lifer in the true-blue corps.

I got off at Fifty-first. It was the first time in forever that the subway made the run without a breakdown so I was early. I let my high heels click to the Waldorf. I went into Harry's Bar and merged with one of the overstuffed wingchairs. It was the perfect time to dangle a coffin nail from my high glossed lips and blow a smoke ring or two. Except I wasn't a smoker. I began picking at the bowl of nuts on the low table in front of me. It was a nice assortment and it gave me something to do with my hands.

I soaked up the ambiance. The mixologist was shaking the loose ends out of a martini and the waitresses, dressed in safari jackets that just cleared the bush, wiggled around taking orders. Someone behind me was puffing on a pipe: the sweet tobacco smell made me think of a college prof I'd screwed as a sophomore. Nobody in New York City spoke English anymore and nobody was speaking it in Harry's.

It took me a few seconds to recognize Frenchie. I wouldn't have had any prob if he'd been wearing one of his beachy fig leaves, but the three-piece Italian number threw me off. He looked almost as cute in 70%/30% cashmere and wool blend as he did in 98%/2% skin/nylon combo.

He flashed his ivories and gave me the Continental double-cheek treatment. "Jeanne, *chérie*, I am happy you make for me time from your busy *programme*. It is good to see you. You have been waiting long? *Non. Bon.* You will take something to drink with me?"

He signaled for one of the safari jackets to take our order and I gandered how his threads followed his elegant chassis. The man was a plate. Gallagher never managed to look this spiffy. I shifted my gaze to the floor. Some good-looking steer and sheep went to Box Z to make the frog's sleek shoes and soft socks. One pant leg had ridden up and I got hooked on the centimeter of skin that peeked out. The derma was white where it'd once been tan. It looked more vulnerable now and it got me thinking about LeCoq in Guadeloupe. What a neato time we'd had together. How terrif he'd been in bed. It was work making the eyeballs retract. By the time I'd parked myself back in neutral, J.P.'d snatched my hand and was holding it.

"You are looking very beautiful," he said, scanning my map. I extracted my paw and foraged around in the nut bowl.

"How long are you here for?" I asked, calming down with a filbert.

"I am here for one, maybe two days more and then I go to Los Angeles. I stay there, I am not sure. It depends on the business we make there. Then I come back to here. But you say you are leaving *demain*, tomorrow, yes? This news makes me very *triste*. I come with the hope we spend time together."

"Yes, I mean no. I mean yes. I'm leaving with my boyfriend for a quiet week in the country." I just hoped it wasn't quiet like the grave's quiet.

"Ah, *oui*, the boyfriend. He is still around? And you are still in love with him?"

"Of course," I said, avoiding J.P.'s liquid velvets.

Froggie made one of those nasal sounds that only frogs manage to make musical. "And he, of course, is the same?"

"You mean, is he in love with me? I think so."

Luckily the great god of haberdashery made Jean-Pierre's trouser leg drop. That made it easier to concentrate on Gallagher's person than LeCoq's flesh. There was an awkward silence, so I talked up post–Club Med capers. I talked about my show and what a hit his nude pics made. Then I blabbed about the Steir case.

"I like this news of the nude photos very much but this with this gun, *non*. This is no thing for *une femme*. This I do not like, Jeanne. *Pas du tout*. You come to Paris, I find for you better work as a photographer." When English is the second language, "photographer" gets accented on the "photo" and the "grapher" takes a back-seat. "In Paris now they love *les photos américaines*. You come and you will make a success. Of this I am sure."

It was rough getting up the road stake for Ohio; Paris was out of the ballpark. "It's a nice offer, J.P." It'd be even nicer if he sprang for a ticket. "I'll think about it." A success in Gay Paree beat the hell out of my father's corporate lackey idea. "What I'm thinking about right now though is another gimlet with bitters." I'd learned that booze mix from Philip Marlowe.

Round two sloshed into three. I was a pushover by the time LeCoq invited me to dinner. His itinerary wasn't knockabout as it seemed; there was a reservation for two in his name at a swank uptown joint. The cuisine matched the nationality of his suit. I was a little uncomfortable with all this wining and dining but it got easier to take the more wining and dining I did. And I was doing plenty.

The eats were the perfect send-off; I'd remember the *Scaloppine di Vitello al Spada Marsala* and the *Pesce alla Siciliana* fondly while chomping on the rice and sprout fare in Ohio. When we'd finished the pig-out, we poured ourselves into a taxi. J.P. gave the cabby his hotel address and immediately put his bazoo to work on mine. The clinch lasted all the way to Park and Fifty-second, when I blew the whistle. Disentangling was bum as separating Siamese twins, Cheng and Eng.

"J.P., I can't," I said, surfacing for air.

"Again it is the *problème* with the diaphragm? This time I come with, *merde*, I forget now the word."

"Rubbers."

"*Oui, c'est ça.* Rubbers. *Et voilà.*" He pulled a pack out of his pocket. "*Pas de problème.*"

"Wrong. *Voilà*, big problem. Bigger than last time even. See, I don't want to sleep with you. I mean, I do want to but I won't. It'll make things with Hank a mess and it'll drive me bonkers." I sounded as old-fashioned as Miss Marple.

J.P.'s body stiffened. He refiled the eel skins. "Okay, *madame*, it is your choice. I tell the driver to take us to your *appartement.*"

LeCoq put up so little fight I felt rejected. "You don't have to come all the way downtown if you don't want to. I'll be all right."

"*Non, non.* I hear too much New York is dangerous and I do not like the woman going to the home alone."

"It's your time and money," I mumbled, my hormones in a tizzy.

The hack license on the dash read Abdul Shahawi. Shahawi in Arabic must mean "he who delights in giving pain." The guy knew every bad patch of road on the entire island of Manhattan and went for it every chance he got. LeCoq and I were already emotionally battered; now we were black and blue.

The pothole in front of the Pussy Cat was too good to pass up and Shahawi aimed his treads into it. We went flying. When we landed, Monsieur and I were holding on to each other for dear life. Bad driving took the sting out of decision making. The backseat smooching flared up again like a Hollywood Hills brushfire.

The cabbie smiled sadistically through the bulletproof. He pointed to the meter. J.P. dipped a manicured hand into his pocket. I watched him and had a hot flash. I put my hand over his snazzy snakeskin wallet. I longed to invite him up for some Blake-style Gratified Desire but that would've been a Blake-size mistake.

"No," I rasped. "Not tonight. Not ever. I'll think about you, J.P. Could be I'll think about you a lot. But it has to be this way, honest. 'Little crimes lead to big crimes.' " That was a Dick Tracy Crimestopper but the reference would've been lost in translation. "You start cheating on your squeeze and next thing you know, you're cheating on yourself. So I guess this is goodnight. And goodbye."

I was hardboiling fine until the neon from the Pussy Cat threw light on Jean-Pierre's Mick Jagger kisser. My lips responded like iron filings to a magnet. We frenched while the meter jumped from $6.60 to $7.80. My insides were mush when I staggered out of the cab. I stood with my back to the door, listening to Shahawi lay rubber. My heart kaboomed in my chest; I was a hairsbreadth away from waterworks when Razor shot his gorilla head out of the go-go palace door.

"Hey, hey," he leered. "Gettin' a little action on the side, huh, sugar?"

"Aw, go fuck yourself," I spat. "I have."

I told myself I had Moral Fortitude. My throbbing cunt couldn't have cared less. To smooth down I went straight to the liquid fertilizer in the cupboard. I didn't even bother turning on the lights. Being in the dark was nothing new to me. As I poured a stiff one I heard a cough that made me jump halfway to Westchester. A light flared from the loft bed.

"That you?" a husky male voice called.

"What are you doing here? You said you were spending the night in Hoboken." I couldn't believe what a lucky hunch it'd been icing the frog. No trace of trouble and Gratified Desire was still in the running.

"I didn't feel like spending the night alone. I called a bunch of times to tell you I was coming in and ask if you wanted to do dinner. But there was no answer. Where've you been? I began to worry. You haven't even finished packing."

"Out. With Viv." What Golden Boy didn't know wouldn't hurt him. Or me.

"Looking like that?" His blinkers riveted on the high heels.

"Girls like to dress up sometimes." As I said it, I reminded myself to pack hiking boots. Where I was headed, they were *haute couture* and *de rigueur*.

"I see," Hank said but I knew he didn't. "Listen, Jane." He sounded serious. "Are you sure you still want to go tomorrow?"

" 'The apple tree never asks the beech how he shall grow; nor the lion, the horse, how he shall take his prey.' Winny's visit convinced me." Boy did it.

"It did?" Golden Boy seemed startled.

" 'The thankful receiver bears a plentiful harvest.' Right? So now I have a better idea about what Golgonooza's all about." More dangerous and insidious than I imagined. "I got a fix on how much

Winny and the gang want you to participate." They'd go to any length. "I'm a little nervous that they're not going to dig me." Putting it mildly.

"If you're worried, maybe you shouldn't go."

"Hank-o, are you trying to tell me something?"

"Uh, no."

"The deal was I do the reading, right? So I'm ready." Willing and able remained to be seen. "Although I'm more ready right now for bed."

I pulled off my dressy duds. Crawling into the sack, I gave the J.P. scene a final turnaround. I felt guilty and horny. "Expect poison from the standing water," old Willy Boy warned. Better to act. I did. On Gallagher. Most of the night. We could count sheep in the country. If we weren't pushing up daisies.

Alien

Blake verses get lofty but they don't get you where you have to go. Airplanes do that. The U.S. Air flight left La Guardia at the ungodly hour of 7:15 A.M. Golden Boy was beat but raring. He said he felt "Spirits of Creative Force" as soon as we took off. I was feeling spirits, too, but they were the sour kind that come with a hangover.

We stopped over in Pittsburgh at 8:55, then hopped the border into Parkersburg, West Virginia, with the help of the Allegheny Commuter. There was a welcoming committee waiting for us at Woods County Airport: two pals of Hank's—Ken and Louisa Brinsmade—and a human jumping bean. Perpetual motion was Winny's way of saying "hi."

The Brinsmades were deceptively normal-looking for cult crazies. Their eyes focused; they were in their late twenties and passed for twinsies. They dressed identically in frayed flannel shirts, low boots, and faded jeans. Both were square-jawed, thin-lipped, slim-hipped, blond, and blue eyed. Their noses sloped gentle as ski jumps from their fair-skinned faces. My schnoz looked as demure as a shark's fin cutting surf. My hennaed hair as natural as astro turf, my dragon red nails subtle as stoplights in a cornfield, and my designer jeans casual as a Balenciaga. In this land of white bread, I came out pumpernickel.

We ambled to the parking lot. I made a bet with myself that the dented, red-zinger-colored van belonged to the Brinsmades. I won. What tore it was the "Golgonooza or Bust" spray painted in Ye Olde English Calligraphy on the side.

It took an hour to drive the forty-odd miles across the West Virginia/Ohio line to sunny Sparta. It was enough time to see enough trees to last me a lifetime. I perked up when we hit town. It was ultra colleege but at least it had sidewalks. Pavement looked good to me but the Blakeans weren't into it. We drove another ten miles as the crow flies, past scenery that couldn't help being redundant. Eventually Ken turned off onto an unmarked road. Then onto another and another. Cultists always like remote locations. They go hand in glove with cult murders.

Finally Brinsmade cut the motor in front of a cord of wood. And a small graveyard. No markings on any of the tombstones.

A pet cemetery? The family plot? But whose family? The original landowners'? The Brinsmades'? The Manson group called itself a family, didn't it?

"Hey, what's the story with this bone orchard?" I asked. Nobody answered. They were too caught up taking bags—Hank's and mine along with some from the local food coop—out of the van.

All I reconnoitered ahead was a grassy hill. I applied Holmesian deductive reasoning. The solution was elementary. Also organic. "Your crypt, I mean your house, is underground?" The question was directed to Louisa.

"No, no," she corrected. "The underground house belongs to

Shaboo and it's a few miles down the road. Ours is over the ridge there." She pointed a bony finger in the direction of Cleveland.

"Far?" Sherpas would be handy for lugging Gallagher's 4 × 5, heavy tripod, and tons of film holders. Were there Sherpas in Ohio? It was all Tibet to me.

"Nah, a little less than a mile."

Where my legs hailed from a mile = twenty blocks. Even standard measurements turned weirdo on this turf. The mile I scrambled, climbed, slid, scaled, hiked, and tramped was no mere five thousand two hundred and eighty feet. It was the fucking road to Calvary.

Lost in the Shuffle

I was in more grave physical danger in this purported Eden than back home in Baghdad-on-Hudson. The Sparta landscape was a killer. There were nasty ledges for rapid ankle twisting. Poison ivy ready to torment. Ticks and fleas eager to draw blood. At night the peril multiplied: there were no sodium vapors or neon to deter disaster. This bailiwick was so dead you could scream bloody murder—and that was a possibility I had to consider—and the chances of being heard were Zen: about as good as hearing the sound of one hand clapping. Not that screaming in the Big Apple got you much help, but sometimes you could at least draw a crowd.

The first sign of western civ was a small stucco structure with a traditional half moon and a less traditional quote:

> He who Doubts from what he sees
> Will ne'er Believe, do what you Please.
> If the Sun & Moon should doubt,
> They'd immediately Go out.

Quote, endquote, William Blake. Poetry, like a good case of the runs, can strike anytime, anywhere.

The hostile terrain was child's play compared to the Brinsmades' digs. The house rose from a stand of trees, a design collision between Corbusier and Swiss Family Robinson. The confection of slanted roofs, overhangs, cut-outs, bulges, protrusions, and indents teetered on stilts. It looked like a gigantic mutant stork from a distance. Both Ken and Louisa were architects and in this, their maiden voyage, they'd tried every trick in the book and then some. Blake's theory of Harmonious Contraries was pushed to the max.

Inside, Rube Goldberg met Uncle Wiggly. There was a small entryway that acted like a launching pad. From here the pile took off like a rocket.

First you climbed four stairs, hung a fast right and landed, bang, in the kitchen. From there you took a ramp up to the dining area and were smacked with two choices: climb a small ladder to a platform that held, contrary to laws of physics, an upright piano, or go the other route and hit the living room. Off the living room, but raised, was Ken's workroom. There the structure went splayfoot: one leg going off by ladder to the master bedroom and the other stretching, via a small bridge, to Louisa's workroom. Yet another ladder led from there to the guestroom. And to the sundeck. A fireman's pole completed the grand tour. It provided quick reentry to ground level. Where you had another two choices: split or sign up for another go-round. It was a nice place to visit but I wouldn't want to vacuum there.

Unfinished floors flirted with half-painted, overbuilt walls. Closets waited for doors. Insulation leaked out between oak studs. There was no electricity or plumbing. A 3-D version of Chutes and Ladders without utilities.

A big potbelly stove, a Parlor Glow, squatted at the labyrinth's epicenter. The flue airmailed smoke out into the pine-scented wild blue yonder. The gizmo was more than just a quaint touch: it was the whole enchilada as far as the house's heating system went. It ate big logs and probably did a quick turnover in human bones.

Wood did more than raise the temp. A major-league forest had been axed to make tables, chairs, desks, and cabinets. No franchise for molded plastic in this burg.

Weavers in the neighb were doing a bangup biz. The place was texture city, tagged minimum for a hundred and one varieties of homespun, nubby fabric. Paintings and prints, à la Blake, hung on every wall. The artwork looked cloned but all carried different signatures. But what did I know? I still got confused by Braque and Picasso the time they went cubist.

Louisa sprang springwater on us and told us to make ourselves at home. That was as easy as bankrupting Polaroid. The first step was to dump our gear in the guestroom. Golden Boy led the way; I trailed behind him like a wagon train behind the Indian scout. The higher we climbed, the dizzier I got—as much from unaccustomed dependency as height.

I was never so happy to see four walls in my life. Who cared if they were covered with more cultwork? I flung myself down on the foam mattress on the floor and loosened my T-shirt.

"And I thought getting into my loft bed was tricky," I bullshitted.

"Neat, huh?" Hank wasn't kidding. He followed up with a smirk that did something gooey to my erogenous zones. "This place has such mind-blowing Energy."

Mind-blowing was right. "And 'Energy is Eternal Delight.' What Blake didn't say was that it's exhausting. How about testing out the bed." I figured we'd be safe there. Besides, I was terrified of the acrobatic trip downstairs.

Gallagher said: "Too much to do. 'Eternity is in love with the productions of time.' If you need to sleep, go ahead. You look like you can use some."

The mind said "vigilance" but the body said different. It said somebody put something I didn't ask for in the glass of water. How else to explain being so clanked?

"Golgonooza takes getting used to but you'll see, it's a Special Haven for Creative Spirit. In a week's time you'll feel its Power and wonder why we're going back to that City of Assassins. Who knows, maybe we won't."

I shuddered. I didn't know how they did it but the lunatic fringe did fast work. Already they had Gallagher talking funny. He bussed me on my shark's fin and the next thing I remember was the inside of my eyelids.

Blondes, Booze, and Blood

It was a big sleep and I had to fight my way out of it. Nightmares later I slid down the fireman's pole. My spine took a beating when I landed. I was rearranging my vertebrae when I climbed into the kitch. Ken and Louisa sat at opposite sides of the chunky oak table, cleaning the homegrown.

"You sleep all right, Joan?"

"Jane. Fine." Thanks to you and the Mickey Finn.

"Jane." Ken slapped his palm against his forehead. "Jane, please forgive me. I don't have an Aptitude for certain Minute Particulars. Sit down, sit down."

"Guess all this fresh country air sent the old stuffing into shock." I watched closely for a reaction.

Ken looked blank. "Beg your pardon?"

"The air, it must've made me sleepy."

"It can do that sometimes."

"I'll bet." I twisted this way and that in my seat. "Hank around?" I went for the nonchalant tone.

"Winny spirited him away to do some shots of her bindery. 'The busy bee has no time for sorrow.' He said he wanted to get right to work. What Glorious Energy!"

"Yeah, Hank's a real go-getter." Since we blew into the boonies something was revving him up. And winding me down.

"Want something to drink?"

I was up for a belt of something strong but they were pushing herbal brew. Probably Pelican Punch with knockout drops. I passed.

"Last time he was out here," Louisa continued, resettling herself in front of weed and seed, "he was a Source of Great Activity and Inspiration."

"He came home a wreck." Not to say strange, remote, and flippy.

"Golgonooza has a Profound Effect on those who are Receptive to its Light." From the scan he gave me, I registered as much light as a black hole. "Golgonooza needs his special kind of Spirit. What Beauty we would all find if he would stay with us longer. You, too, of course."

"Of course." I felt like the buy-one-get-one-free part of a Rexall two-for-one sale.

"What is your Creative Persuasion?" Louisa inquired.

"Me? I'm a photographer."

"What kind of photographs do you make? Ones like Hank's that capture Sweet Delight and Fine Discriminations?"

"Well, no, uh, not exactly. I'm into what I suppose you'd call 'Dark Recesses.'"

"Negative Imagery, then." This from Louisa.

"No, I wouldn't say that. They're beautiful in a different way from Gallagher's. I just had a show of them at the Roseweb Gallery." Both Brinsmades nodded as if they'd heard of it. Or were being polite. "I showed my body part series."

Ken scowled. "Just Parts? No Wholes? This is what the New York art world perceives as Beauty?"

"Why not? Parts give real clues about wholes."

"No faces?"

"Nope. I'm not much interested in portraits."

"But how can you, if you like Truncation and Fragmentation,

and have so little interest in Individuals, how can you make Images of Wonderment?"

"Wonderment" threw me for a loop. "Would you settle for Fearful Symmetry? They do have that," I said in self-defense. "And my gallery and some pretty influential critics dig them. Besides, 'One law for the Lion and the Ox is oppression,' right?" That Blakean slush shut them up; it carried as much weight here as one of the Ten C's did in the Bible Belt.

"What do you do for money?" The question caught me off guard. I thought money talk was as taboo here as Club Med.

"I scrape by on unemployment like Hank. Sometimes I sell a print and sometimes I work for a private eye."

"I remember Winny saying you saw a great deal of Violence and Destruction. That you were often in the Presence of Evil and Sorrow," Ken interjected.

"Speaking of sorrow," I segued, "who took the earth baths down by the woodpile?"

Louisa and Ken did a double take but neither answered.

"You know, the graves, who's buried in them? There're no inscriptions."

Ken's verbalizer had just started to move when there was a sudden noise from the foyer.

Golgonoozers came in all sizes, and the extra-long model who made his appearance capped off the conversation. Stringbean pinned a swivel my way and glowered. Without saying a word, we were talking insta-hate.

"I brought up some water from the well," the stretch said, plopping a lemon-colored plastic bucket of the natural on the floor. Survival was tough here. Like I needed reminding.

Roughhousing

My admirer was introduced as Patrick Portman, a dual careerist. He was a shepherd and a carpenter. He was also the advance guard for the potluck dinner party Ken and Louisa were throwing in Golden Boy's honor. Other guests were as follows:

Amos and Annie Sherwin: the community's longest extant couple. They'd clocked ten legal big ones together and their splice was considered museum quality. That meant it was open to criticism and in need of restoration. Amos made one-of-a-kind bird callers and Annie supported them both by giving piano lessons to what she called the "Tragically Mundane children of the Foolish Middle Class." The Sherwins didn't like me.

Kimberly Rhodes: miniaturist painter and Alice B. Toklas-quality brownie baker. She didn't cotton to me either.

Beulah McMutt: Kimberly's best friend. She snarled and tried to make a meal out of my leg.

Sativa Pearson: the local drug dealer and answer to the proverbial question "What's in a name?" She was the kind to take you in and sell you stuff to take you out. She warmed to me the way she would to a narc.

Talisman Pearson: Sativa's three-year old nipper. Dad was an anthropologist who'd blown through Sparta long enough to study the Indian burial mounds, the supposed source of the burg's mystical power, and start Talisman's embryo cooking. He liked me but he was too young to know better.

Seth Dubrow: resident Don Juan. He'd been in the pants of almost all Golgonoozettes and presently in Sativa's. Also in Hally Sutton's. Hally, who ran the local antique clothing store, wasn't invited to tonight's feed. She was "fettered by Chains of Jealousy." Romeo hardly looked at me; I wasn't his type.

Martin "Shaboo" Benson: an underground—literally and figuratively—poet who did the best he could teaching Blake's Poeticals to Gatewood U's dumb jocks. He was totally insensitive to my charms.

My fan club assembled in the Brinsmades' aerie, chewing the fat, swilling the grape, and smoking the weed. Baby Talis and I were the only straights. Talis would've gone for the grass but his mom nixed it. My mother would've too—and not so good-naturedly— but that wasn't why I was playing Goody Two Shoes. I'd passed paranoia a long time ago and was speeding down the road to mental breakdown.

Kerosene lanterns took over the light department when the sun went off duty. Privacy wasn't a regional specialty. No book could be read, no piece of pottery thrown, no poem written, no print pulled, no new drug sampled, without the communal once-over. The who did what, where, and to whom got the double dish. When these kids talked seeing "the World in a Grain of Sand," they weren't swallowing camels.

I was new girl in town but a helluva lot of good it did me. All this crew was interested in was Hank. They asked a million questions, but I didn't give them much material to work with. The less they had on us the better. What I needed to know, no one wanted to answer: i.e. where the fuck was my boyfriend, their guest of honor. Panic crept through my skinny body. Something horrible might have already happened to him out there in the woods with Winny the Shrew.

Rolling with the Punches

I was just about to suggest a search party when the man of the hour arrived with the bookbinder in tow. Golden Boy had had another bout with Visions of Eternity. His eyes were as glazed as sugar donuts. Yup, the way to a man's heart was through his stomach and it looked like Winny'd slipped the guy a magic mushroom hors d'oeuvre.

The duo's entrance set off Brownian movement. All around me people collided with each other, backslapping, hugging, teasing, squeezing. Space Cadet Gallagher was a star here. That made me a groupie.

Loverboy lowered his butt between me and Winny. Chow appeared on the table and I went into soy shock. There were more soybean dishes than Arabian nights. They did zip to whet my appetite but they made me think a lot about soybean futures. They were brighter than my own.

The food was harrowing but the conversation was really scary. The Blakeans seemed to be describing past initiation rites, quoting phrases like "All her tender limbs with terror shook"; "Remove away that place of blood"; "Then he rends up his manacles and binds her down for his delight"; and "Some are Born to Endless Night." Ten pair of adult eyeballs focused in my direction on that last one. Then someone added "The girls are mad/I wonder whether they mean to kill."

I wondered about that myself so I slid in a query. "So who's deep-sixed out there in the graveyard?" I tried sounding devil-may-care.

"You mean the Blocks?" Annie Sherwin asked.

"Blocks, tombstones, whatever you call them. Whose are they?"

"They're the Blocks," Amos explicated.

"They *were* the Blocks," Shaboo corrected professorially.

"The Blocks, may they rest in peace," Patrick started to explain, "were . . ."

It was just at that moment that Sativa plugged his yap with tofu. Once plugged, that yap stayed plugged. While everyone else's got busy filling up the silence with Blake-a-tudes.

Which meant I still knew nothing about the Blocks. Ignorance is not always bliss.

Once the crew downed Kimberly's lethal brownies, the evening took off. Amos tweeted out tunes on his bird callers. Shaboo warbled along and Beulah growled—more at me than to the beat. Talis danced in his diapers and almost fell off the living room platform. Baby Blakey had grace but it's hard to dance your way around design flaws.

Gallagher's floor show followed the musical number. It was an easy crowd for him to work. He showed them his prints and went off half-cocked about "the Voice of one crying in the Wilderness." That was a new slant to me but not to the home team. They jumped right on the bandwagon. Kimberly led with "Immensity of Vision." Patrick tackled with "Images of Pure Wonderment." Jack said "Absolute Organical Perception." Annie added "Mazes of Delight." Beulah rated the work three and half bow wows. Winny didn't have to say anything; she'd shot her wad back in Gotham. I didn't know what the cultists' plans were for me; Gallagher they'd kill with kindness.

Sore

Gallagher had to jump-start me the next morning. He was revved for sunrise semester at Shaboo's. It struck me as a wrong number. What good was dawn light when you were shooting underground? Hank could get the same light reading staying in bed, sticking his meter under the covers, and his peter in me. But no, he said something about eternity creating its own internal light. That didn't explain squat but it got me on my feet.

The shoot took time. I'd called it square on the metering and all Hank's exposures were long ones. Plus Shaboo insisted on making us breakfast. A nice offer if you feature being poisoned on brown rice porridge with soy sauce.

Gallagher, however, was into it like an aphrodisiac. Or so I thought at first, when he led me off into a dark patch of forest. Then I found out Golden Boy was taking me to visit Nigel Dawes, certified hermit.

Dawes lived way back in the woods in a log cabin with Blakean decor with a touch of the Jap. We found him in lotus position on his tatami, plugged into his Sony Walkman.

His shtick was sculpting mini animals out of precious metals and semiprecious stones. He got on better with his zoomates than roommates. According to local applesauce, Nigel's old lady recently ran off with an abstract expressionist from New York. Her bad taste left him with a deadly dislike for strangers, women, non-Blakeans, and New Yorkers. A grand slam for me. If Dawes got me alone, he would have soldered me to death.

By the time we breezed Recluseville, the sun was high and so was my boyfriend. My feet throbbed, my back ached, and my feelings were hurt. But did I bellyache? There wasn't time. You can't be a royal pain when you're about to make the royal visit.

Heavy Duty

Balthazar Boucher, né Tom Vernon some fifty years previous in East Orange, New Jersey, was Mr. Big in this realm. He'd originally come to Gatewood U as a grad student in English lit. He married his first queen, fellow grad student Didi Burnham, and sired two kids. While Didi got into heir raising, Tom got into Blake. Heavy. After a knock-down-drag-out tenure fight, he wound up teaching senior seminar PS402A: The True Genius of William Blake. Flowery catalogue copy made it a popular course and Helena Montegomery was a popular coed. So popular that she got extracurricular attention. Lots of it. Long-term. By the time she graduated, the Vernon dynasty had crumbled. Tom took the handle Balthazar Boucher—Boucher being Willy B's wife's maiden name. Didi made a legal switch to a maiden name also—her own. So much for marriages made in college, let alone heaven. Helena chucked "Montegomery" and made "Boucher" her flag at the altar. Prof.

and student bride spent a year honeymooning in Blake archives in England. When they returned to Sparta, Golgonooza was born.

Golden Boy blissed out and I freaked out as we closed in on the Bouchers' two-story log job. I said I had the heebies. "Stop dwelling in the House of Stony Dread" was Gallagher's top-flight advice. "Yeah, and whose fault is that, Space Case," I was tempted to ask.

"Take in the Beauty that Surrounds you," he continued. They probably said similar around Jonestown.

"This is what Balthazar made with his own hands and Firm Persuasion." I was afraid of both.

"He cleared this and the piece of land over the hill where the Meetinghouse is all alone. The man is an Orb of Eccentric Fire." What did that make the rest of them? Flames of normalcy?

"He's up every morning at four thirty to take care of his flock." From the tilt of babycake's head I saw he meant fourlegged variety: little lambs tufted the landscape. Balthazar dealt with his two-legged lambkins later.

"Three days a week he Imparts the Teachings to his Gatewood students. The others he stays in his studio and makes True Works of Art and Literature. He spends an hour each night studying Blake with Helena and he is always Ready to Instruct those of us in Golgonooza. He knows *Everything.* Sometimes I think he *is* Blake." I wished he were even more like him—six feet under.

My knees were shaking—from muscle strain shlepping around Hank's photo equipment and from nerves—by the time we reached the thick oak door. Carved on it was a dupe of the Master's "The Good and Evil Angels Struggle for Possession of a Child." I don't know why the Bouchers bothered. Seemed to me Evil was the hands-down winner.

The latter-day Blakes—if he was William, that made her Catherine—materialized as soon as we rang the cowbell. Right away they looked like trouble. Either they were one and half times life size, or I was hallucinating, or their house was small. And second, Balthazar

was a knockout. His thick blond hair licked the collar of his natty—
for there—flannel shirt. His beard and moustache folded around a
set of flanges as kissable as Jean-Pierre's. The guy was manic-im-
pressive with charisma to burn. He raked me with his beams. Under heavy brows that hung like awnings were laser blues that turned
me to Silly Putty. He was harder to face down than a headwaiter.

The care and feeding of a poetic Charles Manson had to be full-
time occupation. Helena was the backseat type and capable. She
wasn't bad-looking either. Today her tall, thin assembly was draped
in a long flower print skirt and a pair of turquoise shitkickers. In
this circle, the mix made her a racy dresser.

The B's had the kind of retro relationship me and my politically
savvy friends would pooh-pooh back in the Big Apple. In Lincoln
Log territory, it looked a smooth article. I was afraid it'd give Gallagher more crummy ideas.

"Come in, Weary Travelers. Welcome to our Spartan Jerusalem." Balthazar's basso was soothing as a Jacuzzi. He showed us his
ivories. Then he circled my shoulder with a strong, shepherding
arm, swept me inside, sat me down next to him on the couch, and
did a little thigh to thigh. He'd invited me to lunch but did these
moves mean he was planning to have me for dessert?

Natch, the Bouchers went in for Contraries. They paired antique
furniture—mint thrift shop vintage—with modern conveniences.
Unlike the Brinsmades, they'd made peace with plumbing. And
electricity. There were enough lightbulbs, appliances, and stereo
components to make me almost overlook the murals—painted in
the only style going—on walls and ceilings. An additional peek at
the Cuisinart in the kitch gave me hope. Short of pureed soy, lunch
might be all right after all.

"May I offer you Something Restorational?" Helena held up a
good bottle of white wine. The frill had my number and it wasn't
7-Up.

We sozzled the potable and shot what they'd call "the Fiery

Chariots of Contemplative Thought." What we in Babylon called "the Shit." Then the couple trotted out their new fanzine, *The Tyger!*, a monthly hand job filled with Blakaroo. Willy Boy could always use good press. And so, apparently, could Balthazar.

They were sugar and spice as a sales team—Mrs. Persuasive and Calm, Mr. Flamboyant and Emotive. I'm not guru prone but their passion was infectious. If you hold your thumb next to your index, that's how close I came to subscribing. Then they said: sixty smackers annually. Then I thought: not the way to go with extra dough.

"I'm going to Prepare our Repast," Helena announced. She unwound her locomoters from underneath her skirt and stood up.

"Need help with K.P.?" I wanted to hang out with the boys but figured if I were in on the prep, no funny stuff—soy not included—would wind up in the eats.

"I'd love some," she said. "Company always makes for Improved Works." So does a recipe.

Counterattack

I was sitting on a stool by the counter, shaping soybean shamburgers and fantasizing about playing Little Log on the Prairie with my honey, when I caught the chef staring. She had a look on her phiz I couldn't compute.

"We've heard that you don't take True Delight yet in Reading Blake." Now that she had me alone, she'd decided to spill. "The last time Hank was here, he told us you approached the Work with Dread. That instead you read and were influenced by Pulp. Mysteries he said, and in Boundless Number."

"Well, mysteries are faster reads." I felt as shallow as the frying pan Helena used to heat up the sit-down.

"People in Cities often confuse Speed with Content," she sneered. "Such reading is Misguided and Escapist. Before I studied with Balthazar, I read such Nonsense, my Vision limited by Mind Forg'd Manacles."

I stared down at the last patty I'd made and tapped a scarlet fingernail on the butcher block. "But I cleaned up my act; I went wiggy reading Blake." I was sucking up. If she liked me a little, she might convince the others to hurt me less.

"Yes, that report reached us. But We feel it was for Wrong and Insincere Reasons. I hope you don't mind my Speaking Openly with you. That is how we Communicate in Golgonooza."

"Oh, no, not at all" was what I said. *"Oy vey"* was what I didn't.

"You see, I can tell there are Dark Disputes between you and Hank."

Suddenly the person behind the counter was no longer a mere woman. She was Cassandra amid Tupperware. The hair at the nape of my neck bristled like a cat's. Fear clutched at my throat like a claw. It wasn't the shamburgers anymore that scared me.

"Direful Changes will be the Inevitable Result if you don't 'Plant Roses where Thorns grow.' Balthazar taught me that where Love between Man and Woman exists, no Negation must live." I wasn't sure she thought I should live either. Or maybe she was trying to tell me I shouldn't live with Golden Boy.

"Hank is going through a period of Mental Rebellion. He's shaking himself free from the Falsity that's all around him." I wondered if that included me. "It is best to help him through this Transition. You will need all the Delicacy of the Eternal Female." I batted my eyelashes.

"Otherwise, Terrible and Disastrous Things will happen. Bonds may be rent asunder. That's what happened between Balthazar and his first wife when he went through his Transformation. I, of course, am not sorry about what happened; in Golgonooza all things work out for the Best.

"Wake from the Sleep of Error, Jane, and be spared Pain and

Suffering. Open your Doors of Perception and Embrace all of us in Golgonooza who love Hank and want to Help him."

Like they say in the Pulps: Do what we tell ya, sweetheart, and ya won't get hurt. "Then you will be able to take up residence in Golgonooza, the City of Imagination, where Self-Annihilation is the Secret of Art."

City of Art? It sounded like the City of the Dead. Give me Manhattan, where you made art and took your chances going out and getting mugged.

"Trust us and Blake's teachings. Gratify Desire. Share in our Creativity and Love." Roughly translated: Spread your legs and bop till you drop.

"Participate and you will support Hank Wholeheartedly in his Quest."

"Like Nora Charles with Nick." It slipped out.

"What?"

"Oh, nothing."

" 'The most Sublime Act is to set another before you.' "

"I'll give it a whirl, Helena," I said with forked tongue. "Thanks for the tip."

She winked, making all systems "go" for grub.

Dragnet

Willy B. wrote that sex was the Gateway to Eternity. For the moment that seemed the only safe turf for Gallagher and me. But when you're stuck in the Vegetable World, you make do with Eternity's next-door neighbor, Expediency. I rubbed sugarpie's crotch under the table. It was important to stay in touch.

The gab turned to art, with Balthazar doing most of the earbanging.

"Modern Art! A Travesty! Made by Blockheads and Charlatans!

149

Small men with smaller minds have Divorced Art from Talent and Whored it with Commerce.

"Blake spent his Noble Energies fighting the Taste of his Time. And what was he labeled? A Madman! Yet what he advocated was Absolutely Correct. It was Correct then, it's True now, and it will be True in Futurity! Expression cannot exist without Form and Determinate Outline. 'Leave out the line and you leave out life itself,' he said."

Hank was clearly enjoying the meal and the mouth. He sat, cleaning the ends of his tickler with his tongue like a cat.

Balthazar soyed up and jawed on. "And Color! It lulls the Puny Intellect of those who see only the Tint and not the Form of Things. Does a horseman buy a horse for its Color? Of course not! How is it then men use less Sense than horsemen when they buy Paintings? We live in an age of Idiots!"

"Let me get this straight," I said. "Your scoop is that all modern art is bunk?"

"My 'scoop,' as you put it, is Yes Absolutely. All Tricks and Gimmicks, Nonsense and Pretense."

"Boring and Ignorant." Helena wanted her own shot at the jugular.

"What about Impressionism?" Everybody had something positive to say about that.

"With its Soft, Fuddled Boundaries? Its Blots and Blurs? My God, nobody with Sense would credit its contemptible copying of Nature with Imaginative Power."

"Cubism? The cubists certainly used line."

"True, but in Error. For Obfuscation, not for Sublimity."

On and on the list went. By the time the honcho was through, the entire history of modern art was as blitzed as Dresden.

"You agree with all this?" I eyed Golden Boy the way a tightrope walker checks out the net.

" 'The tigers of wrath are wiser than the horses of instruction,' "

Gallagher spouted robotically. Putting me up the proverbial Shit Creek.

I turned back to Boucher. "Your views must make you awfully unpopular some places."

"My dear, innocent, young girl," he riffed, wrong on three counts right off the bat, "Knaves and Fools have blasted my Character endlessly. Slanderous comments have been hurled at me as a Teacher, an Artist, a Husband, and a Man. I have been called Evil, Crazy, and Dangerous. These Insults no longer Sting. I am sustained by Blake's Example and Motto: 'I must Create a System or be enslaved by another Man's/I will not Reason & Compare: my business is to Create.' "

Ray Chandler wrote *Trouble Is My Business;* listening to this Helter Skelter, I began to think it was mine as well. "I have one more question." I almost added "Your Honor," seeing as how this was a kangaroo court. "What's your take on photography?"

"An Infant Art not spared its share of Idiot Practitioners and Impostors. It has yet to Realize its Imaginative Function. It has to Separate itself completely from the Tree of Death which is Science."

"Our Friend here"—he gauged Hank admiringly—"has done the most to Change my Perception. Because he is not a man easily sidetracked by Monetary Gain nor Whims of Style. His Handsome Productions show that it is possible for Photography to depict Beauty. I am Indebted and Grateful to him for this Gift."

Gallagher glowed as if he'd been nuked. Helena asked, "Have you Similar Photographic Vision?"

I covered that waterfront yesterday. Today I couldn't take the hate. I shook my frizz left-right, left-right and stuffed a large piece of shamburger into my smush. I chewed it hard, like Bazooka. Some forms of protein can't betray you.

The Shadow

After the feed we reshlepped into the wilds. Our hosts claimed we were hiking off to see baby baahs. Like a jerk I believed them. Until I saw the sculptures. The landscape was polluted with bigger versions of the creepy voodoo statues Hank used to get in the mail. The closer we got to nowhere, the more there were of them. Plus, I was pretty sure I spotted some more tombstones. More Blocks? I didn't want to know.

We pulled up in a meadow. In the middle was a bizarro circle of stones. With a hefty cement slab center stage. See the sheep, my ass. We'd been led out here like lambs to slaughter.

"What's this layout?" I quaked.

"Our theater," Balthazar explained.

Theater like in operating theater? Sara might like the configuration, but I was scared stiff. The Bouchers, ready to operate, stood behind me, breathing down my neck. Terrified, I glued a grab on Gallagher's flannel shirt. No one home. Somewhere along the line, Hank had been Novocained against danger.

I was waiting for the worst when several little lawnmowers frolicked along. Abraham let Isaac off in the sacrifice department when he saw a ram but I couldn't bank on precedent. Balthazar and Helena probably wouldn't settle for a woolie substitute.

"Their Bleatings are music to my ears," Balthazar said. To mine, they were death rattles.

> Little Lamb,
> Here I am;
> Come and lick
> My white neck;
> Let me pull
> Your soft Wool;

Let me kiss
Your soft face.

Helena recited.

Sodomy *and* murder? When the slaughter was all over, would they celebrate with blood cocktails and Woolite chasers?

I watched Gallagher feed film through his camera like a machine-gunner. That gave me an idea. I could shoot our way out of this mess. I stood where Golden Boy stood; I aimed my camera where he aimed; I shot when he shot. I tried to see what he saw. It all looked like rack of lamb to me.

The way I scammed it, the Bouchers were stuck. They wanted a book out of Hank and they needed his poetic vision intact more than they wanted my prosaic corpus disassembled. It might be only a matter of time before they'd cut me up into bite-size pieces. A neat illustration of Minute Particulars. With Gallagher's name on the photo credit.

We moved off death row and trudged a zillion miles to Balthazar's double-decker *sanctum sanctorum.* Where I was held captive and bludgeoned with artwork.

If imitation is the sincerest form of flattery, then Balthazar was proving it by the square inch. His studio held an airplane hangar's worth of Blake knockoffs. The dude was a big producer. Not a big seller.

Who'd want his "Loom of Death," "Murderous Providence," "Furnaces of Affliction," "Hate Eternal," "The Bloody Deluge," and "Upon the Verge of Non-Existence" hanging over the living room couch? These weren't works of art, they were threats. The soy curdled in my meatbag when Balthazar asked me to pose.

High command was topside. From this roost Golgonooza's main man wrote his poems and tracts. What must have been hit lists, brainwashing programs, and torture tactics were stacked up on a large rolltop. The piles were held in place by paperweights that bore an uncanny resemblance to human bones. Okay, he found them along with some arrowheads when he was clearing his property. Or maybe he bought them to sketch from. Sure there was a simple explanation. Every weird-ass thing up here *could* have a simple explanation. The problem was I didn't buy them. Doubts multiplied when I studied the strange diagrams, S&M with an Anglophile twist, that were pushpinned to the wall. Pen and ink were mightier than the sword, but Balthazar wasn't leaving anything to Murky Chance. Bet he used the sword, ax, garrote, noose, whip, knife, and gun as backup.

Next on the torture trail we suffered through a tour of Helena's workspace. It was smaller and so was her output. The style was no surprise. William B. liked keeping his art and wife under his thumb so he taught Cathy how to make art like his. Ditto for the Bouchers. Plagiarism begins at home.

Cult Queen's artwork had titles like "They Plow'd in Tears," "A Woe & a Horror," and "Judge Then, of thine own Self." Big deal they were less scary than her hubby's. I wouldn't sit for her either.

Still figuring the duo had designs on me, I gave Hank the clings while he 4 × 5'd the two studios. It's harder to hit a moving target, and Gallagher was on fever burn; film flew in and out of the Calumet. I'd seen Boyo work before but never like this. They must've been slipping him uppers for sure. But where and when? I hadn't a clue.

We made our escape when the sun started to fancy park for the night. Everything in this godforsaken was out for blood. The sky here turned crimson. Backlit by the last rays, the gruesome twosome stood by their door, arms around each other's waists, smiling and waving. They looked as hospitable as a pair of piranhas.

There was unexpected good news when we arrived back at the Brinsmades. Ken had brought Chinese takeout. The tragedy was, all he'd bought was bean curd.

We chowed down and went to bed early. I thought about storming the Gates of Eternity. Eternity would wait till tomorrow. Instead Gallagher was giving me an earful. He sounded like an ad exec. doing pillowtalk, a Mad. Ave. hard sell on the Bouchers. I tabbed them like cigarettes: okay from a distance; hazardous to the health up close.

In the Woods

When you get The Call, you answer It. Mine came at eighteen minutes past two. I wanted to get out of bed the way Corpus Christi wants to leave Texas. Besides, I was afraid of the dark. Several shrinks ago, one told me that most photogs were afraid of the dark and compensated by working in darkrooms. What a crock of psychobabble; there were plenty of times I was afraid of the darkroom too.

Hank, I figured, would help. I went to wake him and patted air. He'd lammed, along with the flashlight. He'd gotten a Call also. Either Nature's or Balthazar's. Either he was taking a leak or taking a fall.

There was no time to lose. Gallagher's inner—and maybe outer —life was at stake. I pulled out my old Barnard sweatshirt, the one with the pic of the honeybear in front, and covered my butt. This was no daytrip in the Sun Belt.

The firepole was out. No way was I doing a direct drop into the Void. I opted for the inchworm technique. I picked my way down the first ladder, cursing my kidneys. I crept down the ramp, cussing my ureters. I stubbed my toe on a stair, swearing at the Blakeans like a sailor on leave. Decades passed before I palmed the front door open. Finding the path was hairy. My bare feet cha-cha'd through every patch of poison ivy this side of the outhouse. Branches slapped my face and shoulders the way abstract expressionists flung paint on canvas.

By the time I reached the privy, my sphincters were screaming and my pores were oozing fear. Down the beaten path a sound and light show went on full swing. I heard high-pitched, animallike noises and saw brights.

"Babycakes?" I whispered, double-jointed with terror. "Are you there?"

The lights went out. Blackness ate me. Crickets played backup to the moaning and rustling.

I imagined my One and Only tied down, smeared with paint, or worse. With Blake-like designs all over his hunky body. Surrounded by a bunch of nude Daughters of Albion dry-humping to a primitive beat. Or being gang-banged by all the Blakeans on the block. Or going one on one with Balthazar, losing his virtue, his will, and his mind.

I knew if Gallagher signed on with the cult he'd never be quite the same again and I'd be out a boyfriend. I wasn't crazy for that idea and the idea made me crazy. Love might be murder but I loved the guy too much to let any or all of the above happen to him.

Besides, once they rubberstamped him, they might rub me out. If they recruited a new member, they'd need new blood to celebrate. I was type O, the universal donor.

I didn't know if I was coming or going. Ditto for the footsteps. One set went away and one set didn't. A blast of light hit me right between the eyes.

"Haaaaank," I bleated.

He emerged from the bush looking moony but unmarked. More investigation was necessary. Real damage, like real beauty, is more than skin deep.

"Hank, honey, are you all right?" I toned down the four-alarm. I was his girlfriend, not his mother.

He let his upstairs debate team toss that around for a while. "Why?"

"I thought maybe something was the matter."

He got a little wild-eyed but no noise came from the mouth.

Q: Is there?

A: No.

Q: Are you sure?

A: Yes.

Q: Really?

Nod.

Q: Is there something you're not telling me?

A: No.

I slanted it different this time.

Q: What got you up?

A: My feet felt a Pressure.

So did my bladder, but that wasn't the same story.

Q: And so?

A: And so nothing.

His attention wandered. The flash lit up the "He who doubts from what he sees" quote on the john door. I was tempted to turn the beam on loverboy, interrogation style.

Q: What did you come down here for?

A: To See.

Q: See what?

Or was it whom?

Shrug.

Maybe they'd made him swear a vow of secrecy. Maybe there were threats if he talked. Suddenly there were more rustling noises in the bushes.

Q: What's that?

It sounded big. Like giant economy cult-size.

A: Nothing.

I went from asking to telling. "Hank, I'm scared. Really scared. Something is very, very wrong here."

"What?"

It was back to Twenty Questions.

Q: You don't feel it?

A: I don't feel a thing.

Q: But don't you see, that's one of the things that scares the shit out of me?

A: There's nothing to worry about.

That sounded as convincing as a campaign promise.

Q: Are you positive?

A: Jane!

Q: You think I'm overreacting, don't you?

A: Yes.

Q: But you have to admit you've been weird?

A: I'm not weird.

"Oh, yes, you are."

"Okay, you're right. I am."

"Now you're humoring me."

"Have it whatever way you want."

Q: Are you sure there's nothing to worry about?

A: As sure as I can be.

I aboutfaced from factfinding to peacemaking. The hormonal balance shifted too, from adrenaline to estrogen.

"Okay. Enough. Since we're both up, how about a walk over to the clearing?"

"A walk? Now?" His feet seemed to have depressurized.

It's never too late to storm the Gates of Eternity. "Well, I had more than a walk in mind." The great out-of-doors had to be good for something.

"Do you know what time it is?"

"What's that got to do with anything? We're on vacation." Sara'd used that line in Guadeloupe and the results were very satisfying.

"I need Repose. I've had a busy night, I mean day."

"Aw, reconsider." Rubbing up against him had the persuasive

power of a baloney sandwich. "Okay, big boy," I conceded. "Take me to bed." Which was exactly what he did. Literally. Dammit.

Discovery

"Oh no" was the first thing my mind registered when I woke up Friday morning. Suspicion had begun gnawing at me by the crapper and now it was full-bloom. "What is proved was only once imagin'd" was the Willy B-ism. Having him be right didn't jack me up any.

I right-angled on the bed. Gallagher was lying on his back, rubbing sleep out of his sockets. The pillowcase had intaglioed a wrinkle on his cheek. He was up enough for the squeal.

"Hank-o, we've got a problem."

"We do." Pre-coffee, there was no affect.

"Yeah, we do. It's bad and getting worse by the second." Gutturals came from the other side of the foam. "I can't take it much longer."

He turned toward me. He looked pale, lying there between the sheets, white on white.

"*You* may not think something's wrong but something for sure stinks."

He looked pained.

"And I think it's us." I pointed to my armpit with my left, held my smeller with my right, and let some B.O. mix with the air. "We have to do something about it immediately." Provided it didn't mean a lather in an ice-cold creek. "Before we asphyxiate each other."

"Is that all?" Gallagher asked, jumpy.

"Yeah, and what do you intend to do about it?"

He grinned a big one. "I'll borrow a couple of I.D.'s and we can go shower at the gym." He leapt out of bed like a broad jumper.

"Old Charlie Chan proverb," I cracked. "No tickie, no washie."

Washout

The Ethel and Stanley Lowenbacher Gymnasium, home of the Gatewood Grizzlies and their showerstalls—was a brick box flung into a pancake of a landscape. The setup was molecular: it sat, like a proton surrounded by electrons, in the middle of football fields, baseball diamonds, tennis courts, and tracks.

Gyms were never my scene. The closest I got during my college days was the time I played defense against a bulldozer during a demo. I was throwing around rhetoric against Columbia's proposed sports complex; Morningside Heights needed better housing, not bodybuilding. In art school I got involved with physical beauty by dating a male model. Now I just jump to conclusions and the only things I run up are bills.

Stan and Ethel—or rather two lifesize oils of same—helloed you at the portals. They looked midwestern and civic minded. "Stan, dear," Eth seemed to be saying, "those kids need a nice place to play." Stan probably shook his crewcut and said, "Good thinking, hon. We can use the tax deduction." A call to the lawyer, another to the accountant, and the rest was athletic history.

The Grizzlies were proud and showed their appreciation by spiffing up the place. Trophies—displayed like the Treasures of Tutankhamen—gleamed in cases lining the cinderblock walls. The glare was so bad you needed Ray Bans.

Hank and I parted company at the fancy lacrosse cup. He went left to the men's locker room; I headed right. I go for a good coed hosedown myself but Stan and Ethel disagreed. Teamwork was okay as long as it stopped shy of unisex.

To get to the shower I cut a swath through clean-cut collegians the way Sherman marched to the sea. I spotted a familiar face deep in yakkity yak with an unfamiliar one. I walked up to the familiar and said "Hi."

"Hi," Winny said, her best features widening. "I didn't expect to see you here."

"You said something like that the last time I saw you in New York," I said. "It makes a person feel unwanted."

Winny didn't fall all over herself to convince me contrarywise.

Her dirty-blond companion was introduced as Hally Sutton. The girl who didn't come to dinner. That made an opener easy. "I hope I wasn't interrupting important boy-talk," I asked.

Five will get you ten that all locker room talk is the same. Guys talk about girls, girls talk about guys, and everybody talks about getting laid. It was a safe bet that the two twists were dishing up the latest in the Sativa-Seth-Hally isosceles. Threesomes give one person two choices too many. I could see why Seth was having trouble. Both picks were headturners. Hally was better-looking and smarter but Sativa had sass and chemistry going for her.

" 'Love to faults is always blind,/Always is to joy inclin'd,/Lawless, wing'd, & unconfin'd,/And breaks all chains from every mind,' " Hally recited. Whether to console or aggravate herself was up for grabs.

Winny rolled her cornflowers. There were bags under them that good clean living didn't put there.

"Love's a bitch, huh, Win?" I was trying to pry her jaw loose and get her talking about the cult's sex rites. Or her own. Maybe she'd at least open up and chin about Parker. Or lack thereof. Were they on the rocks or was she getting her rocks off in Blakeland? The raccoon markings under the optics pointed to a local. I wondered who. The only guy I'd seen her with, come to think of it, was mine.

Ambush

" 'Sooner murder an infant in its cradle than nurse unacted desires,' " Winny countered.

Hally looked nonplussed, but what's a little infanticide among slaymates?

"Is Hank here?" Winny asked.

"He's in the men's." I gave her a sidelong. "Why?"

"Just curious." That wasn't reassuring. Curiosity's been known to have lethal side effects.

Hally said: "Guess it's time for us to go."

The two fumbled with their coats.

Winny said: "See you this afternoon."

I said: "You will?"

"Sure. Hank's coming out to take more pictures of my work."

"He is? He didn't say anything to me about it."

This was beginning to sound awfully palsy-walsy and I didn't like it. When Cathy B. had a similar problem with Willy she put her foot down. He'd been chumming around with Mary Wollstonecraft and shooting his pen off about free love. Mrs. B. made a stink and hubby shaped up. Mary went on to become a feminist, wrote *A Vindication of the Rights of Women,* got married, and gave birth to the author of *Frankenstein.* The Blakes lived—if not happily—devotedly, ever after.

I went for that story. Balthazar's first wife was a sucker for it, too, and banked on a similar finale to the Helena saga. Look what that got her. Erratic alimony payments.

History repeats itself but not her story if I could help it. My snag was that I'd gone in for some extracurriculars myself. Catting around was okeydoke for me but Hank shouldn't hang out with other women? The double standard reared its ugly head. How could I be so unfair? The answer was, "Easy."

"When did you set that up?" I was suspicious.

"Yesterday."

I racked what was left of my brain. How'd he schedule it, seeing as he hadn't been near a phone all day and Winny didn't have one? They hadn't seen one another to discuss it. Or had they? Did it have something to do with Gallagher's strange stroll into the night rite? Or was the answer kidstuff. Where adults lived in treehouses and Tinkertoys, they probably played telephone. Golden Boy told Ken who told Louisa who told Patrick who told Hally who set up the date with Winny.

"Looks like I'm the last to know."

"Looks like it," Winny said and was gone.

Out to Lunch

It took twenty minutes under the nozzle to blow the grime. I came clean enough to squeak and the change of clothes improved my outlook.

Whoever said females were the vainer sex deserved a knuckle sandwich. I took my time fussing with my puss, but Hank's toilette was taking a year and a day. I parked my sitter on a wooden bench in the entryway. Even scrubbed I didn't pass as a Grizzly; the Lowenbachers still looked down at me.

There was nothing to do but boywatch. I always liked staring at jocks but never gave them a lot of house. I figured them for no brains and they figured me for too many.

Hunks bounded, loped, and lunged into the locker room. I passed time matching sport to stride. Big Shoulders was a swimmer; Bounce-to-the-Ounce was a basketball star; Meatloaf played football. The game occasionally got sidelined by a handsome kisser, a good set of gams, or cute buns. Those got the Leica treatment. Making pics of these animals was a helluva lot more satisfying than making them of Boucher's lambchops on legs.

I was having a friendly chitchat with a swell kid from Cinci when Hank came around the corner. Loverboy was still the hunkiest of them all.

I gave the kid the brush and Gallagher threw his arm around me.

We brushed jibs and then he said " 'Hunger clouds swag on the deep.' "

"I'm starving, too."

"C'mon, I'll take you to lunch."

I did a double take. "You will?" He looked snappy and alert.

"Sure." He gave me a broad first-date smile.

"Look, I know Blake says 'All Wholesome food is caught without a net or a trap,' but no health food." When it comes to survival, you look a gift horse in the mouth.

"No, no. None of that shit. Real food."

It was the first healthy thing he'd said since we got here.

The Stratfordshire was a colonial-baronial joint but had martinis that were the real thing. The drinks were Gallagher's idea and at noontime they slid down smooth and sinful. We tied on the feed-bag and pushed red meat over the t-buds. We also got sloshed, took a trip down memory lane, and got sentimental.

Later, driving down the road in the Golgonooza or Bustmobile, Hank started jabbering about buying land, building a log cabin, setting up a photo studio in town, and getting a big dog. He'd just gotten to the part where I wore dresses and baked pies when we pulled up at Winny's.

Double Whammy

Booze and "Determinate Outline" don't mix. I had trouble peg-ging Winny's hideaway for style. Early Cutism? It looked like an overblown dollhouse and the doll had built it herself. Goes to show you. Win looked weak but she was a powerhouse with a chain saw.

We went inside, and that's when the hooch started backfiring. Not that I got gauche and puked. Something about the place made me queasy. I couldn't quite put my finger on it. Maybe it was the perfectly lined-up, metallic and mean bookbinding tools that made me think of murder weapons. Maybe it was seeing six of Golden

Boy's prints on the wall above the big brass bed. That threw a spanner. Aside from the *artiste* himself, I thought I owned the biggest collection of Golden Boys this *and* that side of the Ohio River. A fast count showed I was now one shy of the title. The update pissed me off.

It also ticked me that Sweetie Pie had clammed about selling prints. That is, assuming he'd sold them. Maybe she got him in a mind meld and he let her have them for a song. Until I knew the tune, though, I was whistling in the dark.

The Deal

Hank and Winny started trading Will-isms. Fearing another Blake-out, I pulled Golden Boy aside. While we confabbed, the trim went over to her worktable and tested her tools for sharpness.

"Aren't you going to photograph?" I used the Protestant work ethic the way they used the cross in vampire movies.

" 'Damn braces. Bless relaxes,' " Gallagher snapped.

"Isn't that what you came here for?"

" 'The man who never alters his opinion is like standing water and breeds reptiles of the mind.' "

"Hank, we can't stay here."

" 'Listen to the fool's reproach.' "

"Fuck you." He wasn't himself but I wasn't taking abuse from his look-alike. Out of the corner of my eye I was pretty sure I saw Winny smirking.

"I'm sorry, Jane." He looked upset. I certainly was.

"Look, Hank, we have to split. It's too dangerous here."

"Dangerous? Are you nuts?"

We'd traded in reptiles of the mind for bats in the belfry. "Not me, heartthrob, but maybe some of your friends. Aren't the bones and graves and sharp tools plenty of evidence?"

"You're just being paranoid."

"Better safe than sorry," I said, pushing Gallagher toward the door. "Looks like we have to blow, Win."

The frail came to the door holding a pointy object in her hand. "Leaving? How come? You've hardly smoked anything yet."

Gallagher looked uncomfortable. I played the heavy. "I don't feel good."

If looks could kill, hers would've put a quick end to my misery. I told Hank to get in the van. He did.

"Drive," I said, and he did.

"Where're we going?" he asked.

"Shopping."

The Bargain

Wits and wiles. That's what desperate women survived on and I'd joined their ranks. Helena'd squawked something about using the Delicacy of the Eternal Female to keep Hank. I sneered then but I wasn't sneering now.

I had Gallagher head up Route 52 toward the Divine Image. The Brinsmades had gotten some of their multilevel design stunts out of their system by the time they'd T-squared Hally Sutton's antique shoppe. The barn's exterior was bumpkin chic with an inside that was farmhouse flavor. The walls were painted Blake, the goods were good if you go for fussy, and the prices were slightly lower than Lower Manhattan's.

"More! More!" says Mr. B., "is the cry of the Mistaken Soul." "Less! Less!" is the cry of the Bargain Hunter. When Hally asked me what I had in mind, I described it more and less. Gallagher's jaw had to rebound off the floor before he could grin ear to ear.

Hally brought out a frilly, femme thing and I gave it a tumble in the dressing room. I wasn't convinced, but Golden Boy gave it the green light. Hally backed him up with a dukes-up salespitch. "An Immediate Affinity! The Detailing is the Foundation of the Sublime on you." She followed that up with a spiel about the heavens rejoicing, meadows blooming, and wolves howling. Who knew so little material could do so much? And for only $55.98. Then she insisted I buy a vintage flannel shirt to go with the long skirt that was a wardrobe "Must." The additionals jacked up the tab to $108.53 and left $26.71 in my estate. I felt woozy writing out the check.

"They're a lifetime investment," Hally said, pocketing the paper fast as a fingersmith. Her smile scored in the minus numbers on the convincing scale. What she likely meant was I'd be lucky if I got to wear them at all.

The Tumble

To ensure at least one wear, I wore the frock back to the Brinsmades. Ken and Louisa were still at the office. Could be we both had the same idea at the same time but I like to think Gallagher started it. My new wearable may've had something to do with it. If it did, I hadn't pissed away $55.98 for zilch.

My boyfriend used to be a four-star lover but lately service was slow and erratic. There were days when his ratings dipped to two or even one. Recently he'd closed up shop altogether and gone fishing. That made me a very dissatisfied customer. Today, however, he was back in tiptop form.

One thing to be said for dresses is that they give your honey's hand a clear, clean shot at the crotch. Gallagher took aim and scored. The panties came down, the dress came off. Pretty soon we were both in the Morocco. Once we got horizontally situated, we began making music, playing each other like instruments. Winds, strings, percussion, the whole orchestral kit and caboodle. We adagioed in missionary and allegroed symphonically from there. Presto, I was on top for the finale. It was fortunate nobody was home. We made an atonal racket when we crescendoed into the Big O together.

There wasn't much time for afterglow. The Brinsmades' return worked like the sirens' call. My Ulysses, no longer lashed to my fuselage, wiggled into his jeans and made to split.

"Hey, wait," I called. "Give me a sec to slip into something less comfortable and I'll go downstairs with you."

"I'll meet you there," he said and slid away.

I hung up the dress with a sigh. I put on my new flannel shirt and my Calvins. By the time I landed in the living room it was too late. Hank was there all right. In body. But not in spirit.

Ken and Louisa ignored me. Patrick stopped by and avoided me. Winny came over and treated me like a leper. Lance Carroll, an auto mechanic/dancer, said hello and nothing thereafter. It was lousy being cold-shouldered by the gang but worse being shut out by your man. That night in bed I explained the difference to Hank. The words went in one ear, passed through a vacuum, and out the other.

Marking Time

The following is a report of the events that occurred during the approximately thirty-nine-hour period between Friday morning, October 24th and Saturday evening, October 25th.

Friday, 5:30 A.M.: Alarm. Not the clock but Hank going off. But where? Answer vague. I tag along. Wind up at Meetinghouse. Find Winny wandering around. En route home from a late night rendezvous with her current beau? Or maybe it was an orgy. She looks wrung out. She sees me and scrams.

Friday, 6:46–11:27 A.M.: Meetinghouse: one-story log affair. Handmade everything. Attention to details rivals art nouveau. Meant as a compliment. But, oops, nouveau on Balthazar's shit list. Mum's the word. Again. Gallagher photographs like a fiend. I write postcard to Sara as sun comes up. "Greetings from CLUB MEDita-tion. Wish you were here, though I wouldn't wish it on anyone. I'm going out of my mind and Hank's lost or misplaced his. The Golgo-noozers have BIG plans for us. They say here, 'What can be Created Can be Annihilated.' It could mean yours truly. If you don't hear from me by Wednesday, October 29th, send help. Don't breathe a word of this to Mom and Dad or I'll kill you. XXXXXXXX, Jane."

Friday, 11:28 A.M.–*12:17* P.M.: Balthazar gives me a pat on the ass and a bone-crunching squeeze. Refers to Hank as the Prince of Light. Informs Prince that he's throwing a party Saturday night in His Majesty's honor. Hank's coming-out party.

Friday, 12:58–3:46 P.M.: Lunch and lecture at Brinsmades' ar-chitectural office, converted gas station. More multilevel mania. At least there's indoor plumbing. Talk to the nth on Mr. B.'s impact on architectural philo and practice. "An Outside spread Without & an Outside Spread Within." Sounds like instructions for making a peanut butter and marshmallow fluff sandwich more than a basis for building.

Friday, 4:18–7:37 P.M.: Another photo session. Sally Riggins, candlemaker. Wax figurines à la Mr. Big. Price tags carry slogan "Fight the Darkness with Eternal Radiance." Night lights with a message.

Friday, 8:23 P.M.–*Saturday, 12:42* A.M.: Dinner at converted creamery owned by lesbos Babs Taylor and Patsy Wortheimer. Tay-lor designs smocks for Little Bo Peeps. Wortheimer etches like you know who. Guest list includes: Bouchers, Brinsmades, Seth—this time with Hally; Raymond Rainbow, a freelance and freewheeling philosopher; the ubiquitous Winny; K. D. Sawyers, a potter; and Max Richter, papermaker. Conversation: Rah, rah, sis boom bah, yeah Golgonooza. Menu: as varied as the art.

Saturday, 1:18–1:48 A.M.: I'd hoped to get laid but instead Hank laid into me. He said I wasn't making it as a Daughter of Albion. I said, "What does that mean?" He said his friends didn't like me. I said he wasn't helping any by being such a zombie. He said his friends said I was Negative. I said his friends were Hostile. I said I was scared. He said I was being ridiculous. I said he was being impossible. He started quoting Blake. There were more I saids and he saids that got us nowhere but angrier.

Saturday, 2:02–2:14 A.M.: We fuck and make up. The earth doesn't move so much as wobble.

Saturday, 2:15–7:48 A.M.: Over and out.

Saturday, 7:50 A.M.: Alarm. Gallagher not going off but returning. Find him undressing and crawling back into bed. Yesterday's story backwards. Dyslexia meets déjà vu. Where's loverboy been and for how long? Answer vague. I complain. Gallagher conks out.

Hank	*Jane*
Saturday, 7:51–11:59 A.M.: zzzzzzzzzzzzzzzzzzzzzzzzzzzzzzzz	*Saturday, 7:51–8:19* A.M.: Listen to Hank snore; hyperventilate.
	Saturday, 8:20–8:43 A.M.: Pace.
	Saturday, 8:44–8:48 A.M.: Try to wake Hank.
	Saturday, 8:49–9:34 A.M.: Attempt to read *The Visions of the Daughters of Albion.*
	Saturday, 9:35–10:39 A.M.: Sneak copy of Horace McCoy's *No Pockets in a Shroud* out of suitcase.
	Saturday, 9:40–10:45 A.M.: Read contraband material.
	Saturday, 10:46–10:55 A.M.:

Hank	Jane
	Stare at Hank, who continues zzzzzz-ing.

Saturday, 10:56–11:01 A.M.:
Try again to wake Hank.

Saturday, 11:02–11:13 A.M.:
Stare and bite nails.

Saturday, 11:14–11:23 A.M.:
Stare and hyperventilate.

Saturday, 11:24–11:44 A.M.:
Pace.

Saturday, 11:45 A.M.*–12:10*
P.M.: Answer call of the wild and take trip to the outhouse.

Saturday, 12:00 noon:
Hank gets up.
Saturday, 12:08 P.M.:
Hank vanishes.

Saturday, 12:11–12:13 P.M.:
Pound pillow with tiny fists of fury.

Saturday, 12:14–12:18 P.M.:
Bawl.

Saturday, 12:19–12:21 P.M.:
Breathe deeply.

Saturday, 12:22–1:10 P.M.:
Search house and grounds. Scream Hank's name repeatedly.

Saturday, 1:11 P.M.: Discover van is missing.

Hank	*Jane*
	Saturday, 1:12–1:30 P.M.: Monsoon waterworks.
	Saturday, 1:31–1:39 P.M.: Bite remaining nails and begin work on cuticles.
	Saturday, 1:40 P.M.: Head back to jungle gym.
	Saturday, 2:01 P.M.: Head back to bedroom.
	Saturday, 2:04 P.M.: Head straight for bed.
	Saturday, 2:05 P.M.: Curl up in fetal position.
	Saturday, 2:06 P.M.: Pull covers over head.
	Saturday, 7:34 P.M.: Signs of life downstairs.
	Saturday, 7:35–7:43 P.M.: Signs of life upstairs. Fly out of bed and slide downstairs.
	Saturday, 7:44–7:55 P.M.: Find Ken and Louisa. No sign or word of Gallagher.
	Saturday, 7:56 P.M.: Head back upstairs.
	Saturday, 8:05–8:09 P.M.: Put on dress.
	Saturday, 8:10–8:21 P.M.: Put on warpaint.
	Saturday, 8:22 P.M.: Put on act.

Rite and Wrong

The view out the van's windshield was dark and the view out the rear wasn't any brighter. Ken was behind the wheel, pointing the car bash-ward. The silence was as thick as lentil soup.

"Okay, what've you done with Hank?" I nerved up to ask.

"Done with him?" Louisa's laugh bubbled up from deep down in her throat.

"Why, nothing," Ken snorted, finishing up the conversation. We were in front of the Bouchers now and he sent the Golgo-noozamobile into "Park." It joined the handpainted VW's, beatup vans, pickups, weathered Volvos and—I shuddered to note—an old hearse already stationed there. When Ken and Louisa got out and hotheeled it for the meadow path, I knew this was no houseparty.

The trail had been a pisser by day. I didn't have a flashlight, I wasn't blessed like the Blakeans with Eternal Vision, and my night vision wasn't so terrif either. At least that spared me a second gawk at the path's grotesque Kon Tikis while I fell, scraped my knees, twisted my ankles, and stubbed my toe on a headstone.

I was making turtle's progress when suddenly there was a deafening boom. It came from the top of the hill. I had to hike a bit farther to discover the source of the blast: Spectre and Imagination. The band probably called this earsplitting, glass-shattering din Music of the Spheres. Just more proof that I was traveling in the wrong circles.

The second assault was on the nose. Even at a distance, the smell of pine had lost out to dream weed. Of course, the cultees never claimed they got high on life alone.

Next came an explosion of harsh light. A humongo bonfire burst into view in the middle of the clearing. The fire revealed swarms of Golgonoozers; their ranks seemed to have tripled overnight. Maybe they *did* fuck like bunnies.

The bird's eye scared me all the way to my root canals. I kept my lasers skinned for Golden Boy and I forced myself to creep closer. I stuck to the side of the trail, not wanting to be seen. This was one party where it paid to be a wallflower.

I had a better bead on the food orgy going on over to the left. The crackpots were hitting the eats heavy. Vice is nice, liquor is quicker, and soy is joy. Blakean Soul Food with the Harmonious Thunderings of Spanish Fly.

Those who were already lit wriggled and writhed around the fire in response to the band's primitive window rattlings. They made the crazed Club Med hokey-pokey look sedate as a waltz. Art-historically, the scene looked more like a Bosch painting than a Blake etching.

There was still zero sign of my boyfriend. But then again, you're not supposed to see the bride before the ceremony. I did spot Big Daddy though. Balthazar moved like a tiger on the prowl. He was stalking something. He passed up the grub, so that wasn't it. Someone? He barely letched the beazels. That could mean he was hunting for me. I huddled further into the bush for protection. Better a case of poison ivy than a dose of Boucher venom. Poison ivy at least wasn't fatal.

Still nosing around, the Leader of the Pack headed for the back of the strange concrete altar. That put him temporarily out of my field of vision. Out of sight in his case didn't mean out of mind. A few minutes later he jumped up out of the blackness and up onto the slab. The dude knew from Hollywood. He'd copped his entry from *West Side Story*. He could've sung "When You're a Jet" and Lenny Bernstein could've collected royalties.

Instead he raised his arms. The music stopped. The dancing didn't. The beat went on. Blacks weren't the only ones with natural rhythm.

It was necessary to creep still closer to the fire. Not to be nearer the warmth but closer to all the hot air.

" 'Arise, and drink your bliss, for every thing that lives is holy!' "
The crowd cheered. "Tonight we are here not only to Gratify Desire as usual"—more huzzahs—"but to Initiate the Newest Member of our Family." Hurrays galore. "To Shed the Mundane Shell is
a Terrible Struggle." A collective groan. "Our initiate cursed and
wept but Dared to Aspire." Yelps of encouragement. "And now
Open to Sweet Delight and Desire"—more cheering—"he joins
Golgonooza, the City of Imagination, where Self-Annihilation is
the Secret of Art." Yells and whoops. "We are Privileged and we
Rejoice. We must Welcome him with happy Love free as the
mountain wind." Lots of Yays and Yippees. "Love him as we have
Loved one another." Yays and hurrays, screams and yells. Speech
finished, Balthazar raised his flippers again and the eardrum de-
stroyers went back to the blast business. Shake it up, baby, tryst and
shout.

The master of ceremonies jumped down and reappeared a minute later leading the convert. Applause filled the air. It made me
sick to hear it. Boucher, smug in triumph, did another disappearing
act. That left the new recruit to go it solo. This wasn't a rite of
passage; it was an audition.

The crowd wanted entertainment. Hank knew how to please and
went to work doing it. He began a bump and grind routine that'd
knock the g-strings off the Pussy Cats back home.

He was still on the lewds when he ripped off his shirt. His pecs,
glistening with sweat, looked great by pyrelight, only I wished he'd
repack them in flannel. They were a private eyeful and shouldn't be
available for public consumption.

Meanwhile Balthazar'd come back on stage. This time he'd
brought along Helena and Winny, the Blakettes. No show's complete without a chorus line.

The crowd went apeshit. Now they were really getting down.
The increase in body heat blew the merc sky high in the sexometer.

Balthazar decided it was time to up the ante. He started getting it on with Winny. Then he switched and started going down on Helena. That was the go-ahead. Golgonoozers began shedding clothes as fast as inhibitions. It was group grope full tilt boogie.

It was one thing for Winny to play Ginger to my Fred but no way was she going to play Eve to my Adam. Faster than a syncing strobe, I raced to the rear of the slab, crouched low behind it, and waited for Hank to wiggle his tush close to the edge. He was dry-humping the air and going for his zipper when I hooked a hinder. He tripped and fell off the stage. Balthazar was too deep into Helena to notice and Winny was doing a tarantella in outer space.

Golden Boy was about to call me a party pooper when I clamped my hand over his yap. "Remember," I screamed over the heavy metal and heavy breathing, " 'Opposition is true Friendship.' " Willy B., like Hallmark, had a sentiment for every occasion. I looked into Hank's eyes. He wasn't stoned; he was bouldered.

The meadow was the arena for a no-holds-barred Blakenalia, an everythingathon where everybody had more than his or her hands full. We had to make a quick getaway before Boucher and his henchpeople stopped coming and came after us.

I was planning our escape route when Golden Boy suction-cupped a bazonga, hiked up my dress, and started murmuring Blake nothings I didn't find sweet in my ear. He whipped out his shlong and said, " 'Joys impregnate.' "

I can't say I wasn't tempted but I pulled myself together. "Not here. I know a better place not far as the crow flies. Put that away," I pleaded, "and let's go."

" 'The eagle never lost so much time as when he submitted to learn of the crow.' "

Outcited, I tried another tactic. "Arise!" I commanded in my best Balthazarian mode.

When that didn't work, I pulled him to his feet. All the years of hauling around camera equipment finally paid off.

"Now, let's breeze." Not even a twitch. Apparently he responded best to the rough stuff. I gave him a shove. "Move it!" I muscled him again. "This hurts me more than it hurts you," I insisted, weeping as I brought my foot down hard on his tootsies. That gained my team some yardage. " 'Rouze up, rouze up! Eternal Death is abroad!' " That got even better results. Hank left-righted along with me as we picked our way through the fucking crowd.

It was sticky going. Arms like tentacles wrapped around our gams, trying to suck us into the action. A Blakette I'd never seen before glommed onto Golden Boy so tight I was afraid she'd have to be surgically removed. One bozo hurled himself on me, so I kneed him out of commission. A frill did a bisexual come-on. I spanked her and sent her packing.

We finally made it to the parking lot. "Hand over the keys," I demanded but Gallagher wouldn't. I rummaged around in his pocket until I found them. I opened the passenger door. "Get in." I two-fisted. "Wrap this around you." I shoved a blanket at him. Still bare-chested, he was shivering now that he was away from the bonfire.

I peeled out. We were deep in enemy territory and all roads led to nowhere. Hank had nodded out and was useless as a navigator. I nosed the van into a small clearing off a short dirt road off another short dirt road. We'd spend the night in the car. This was hell. On wheels.

I had lots of trouble falling asleep. The snappy fall weather made my teeth chatter. I tried not to think about the Blakeans, so I thought about the Manson gang. Helter Skelter had one thing going for it: location. Southern Cal was warm.

Blowup

I woke with a jolt. Gallagher was leaning over the gear box and giving my tonsils a quick swab. "Wake up," he cooed. As if everything were hunky-dory. "The light's absolutely beautiful. It's an incredible day to photograph."

I blinked in disbelief. "You turn traitor, you disappear for a whole day, star in an orgy, wake up in the middle of God knows where, and you want to talk f8 at 1/250th of a second?"

"You're wrong. It's more like f45 at eight seconds." Hank was straight now but still unconscious.

"No, I'm not. I'm talking thirty-five millimeter film and you're talking sheet. Cut the techno crap, Hank-o, and talk to me."

"What do you want me to say?"

"Explain what's going on, for Chrissake!"

" 'Why wilt thou Examine every little fiber of my soul, Spreading them out before the sun like stalks of flax to dry?' "

"Tell me in English, you bastard. Not Ye Olde variety."

" 'O'er my Soul thou sit and moan. Hast thou no sins of thine own?' "

"What is this, kiss and tell? Look, I asked you first. And besides, you're changing the subject." And besides, I didn't want to talk about my sins, small as they now seemed in comparison.

"Okay, Jane, you want to know what's happening? You're blocking my Emanations. You're turning into a Negation rather than a Contrary. With Contraries there's Progression. But lately you're full of Malice and Jealousy."

"And you're full of shit. Let me put you wise. Mostly I'm full of Concern. You know, that funny little emotion that goes hand in glove with Love, Interest, Devotion, and Fear? All this Blake-a-rama is bending you all out of shape, sweetie. You're turning into a Golgonooza clone and it hurts to watch. And I can't stand your cutting me off every which way when I try talking to you about it."

" 'Improvement makes straight roads; but the crooked roads without Improvement are roads of Genius.' "

That cut it. "Can't you take the goddamn soybeans out of your ears just once," I screamed. "I've had it!" I stabbed the key into the ignition. The motor turned over along with my stomach. I pulled out and drove as badly as my old cabbie, Shahawi. Daylight made it easier to decode the landscape. In no time flat I screeched the car to a halt beside the Brinsmades' wood pile. I was so p.o.'d, I almost ran over the Blocks. Not that they would've noticed. Gallagher split open his mouth so his dominoes could twinkle. Charm.

"This is your stop, Genius," I snarled.

"Jane, don't be so difficult. If you weren't so consumed by Envy and Jealousy, there'd be Improvement. Balthazar thinks your Doors of Perception are closed for futurity but I keep telling him there's Hope."

"Get out."

"Where are you going?"

"Into town."

"Town?" Golden Boy made a face. "It's Abominable."

"Maybe I'll meet the Snowman."

"The light's too spectacular to squander on parking lots, cinderblocks, and aluminum siding. Come and shoot with me."

"Go shoot yourself," I snapped and drove off.

I carried the mail as far as Marshall Street. I was still fermenting as I spudged around the main drag.

Store windows were cluttered with lumber jack and jill wear that passed here for à la mode. There wasn't much street action; Spartans were either hymn slingers or late risers. My pedals escorted me to the local ptomaine palace. My nostrils craved some grease and I needed to wrap my beams around some Formica. They'd seen enough wood grain to last till Kingdom Come.

I was a few feet from the door when I shagged the car. "Nah, couldn't be," Left Brain transmitted to Right Brain. "You sure?" Rightie relayed back. They were so busy arguing that I smacked into a gee.

"Excuse me, I'm sorry," I mumbled to the Florsheims. My sights rose. I was staring up at the last person on earth I expected to find in the Buckeye State.

Private Investigations

"Holy Toledo! What the fuck are you doing here?" I shrieked. "Don't tell me you're interested in William Blake, too?" That would be the acme, the absolute acme.

"Blake? Never hearda him. Fella I was huntin' was named Brown, Curtis A."

"Who's he? He board around here?"

"He's tha guy Rosenblatt sent me ta find out in Muncie. Marv thought he might be a witness in a case he's workin' on. I found Brown easy enough but tha mouthpiece ain't gonna want him stayin' found. 'Cuz what he knows could do lotsa damage ta Marv's client."

"So what's the lay?"

"He'll probably take a long trip somewheres and forget ta leave a forwardin' address."

"None of that explains what you're doing out here in the boonies, gumshoe."

"I'm drivin' back ta tha city. Look, ya wanna cuppa coffee or somethin' or ya wanna stand here blockin' traffic?"

I opted for in and I wasn't disappointed. The guts of the Debly Luncheonette was just what the ophthalmologist ordered—trashy fifties with countertops of gray Formica, the kind with the pink and white boomerang pattern. The lighting was as flattering as the Lincoln Tunnel's. Fake ferns mulched in the dust by the window. The earliest layer of grease on the grill dated from the Paleozoic era. A bastion of sleaze nestling deep in the heart of America the Beautiful.

The peeper and I sat down in a booth by a pane. We gave our order to a prune in an apron. The only thing to say for the brew when she brought it was that it was hot. Not good and hot. Just hot.

"How come you didn't fly to Indy and back?" The buzz continued.

"I'm afraida flyin'." Nick twirled his pack of Luckies around the ketchup. You don't expect fear of flying from a danger chaser. Yet another demo that real life P.I.'s aren't cut from the same metal as the made-up ones. Nuts.

"So you just happened to be in the sticks and thought you'd drop in."

"It's on tha scenic route, ya know, so's I figure ta take in some a tha scenics. That way I got somethin' nice ta tell tha missus for a change when I get home."

"Quit conning me, Nick."

"Ya can't take a joke? Tha air here, it doin' somethin' bad ta yer humor glands or what? Whadda I know from scenics? An' whadda I care? Burgs like this here give me tha creeps.

"Look, kid, I'll level with ya. I come here 'cuz I gotta job back in tha urb and I want ya in on it. I figure I'm out here, I'll drive a little outta my way, pick ya up, take ya back, have somebody in the car ta talk ta, and save ya some change in airfare. A good deal all round, no?"

I put my coffee cup down on the paper placemat, covering one of its "What's Wrong with This Picture" puzzles. The set of Palladino's flytrap told me he was calling it square.

I played for time. "How did you know where to find me?"

"Whaddya think I do for a livin'? Sit on my arse all day and make art? Ya got amnesia? Lemme refresh your memory, dollface. Parta my lina work's skip chasin', remember? Findin' ya, sweetheart, was a snap."

"Oh, yeah? Tell me about it." I hoped it would sound Grimm.

"It's like this. I'm about ta split Indy when Marv calls and sez he's gotta job that needs pics. We know ya got this boyfriend inta communes in Ohio and Marv's hip ya got a kid sister in med school in Philly. I let my fingers do tha walkin' and sis sez call yer friend Whazzerface, she knows where you guys are cultivatin' and tha name a tha folks yer stayin' with. I call tha broad—Vi? Viv? Something—and had a helluva time wanglin' info outta her. Finally she comes across with tha name 'Brinsmade' and sez they got no plumbin' or phone. Sparta's gotta be Podunk so how hard can it be tracin' a coupla Brinsmades, right? So's I drive down, decide ta hava cuppa, and bingo. Ya plow right inta me and save me all tha legwork."

"Anything to help out a pal."

"Anything?" the dick leered.

"Well . . ."

"Tell ya what. I'll settle for ya takin' tha job. How fast can ya pack?"

"Look, Nick, I'm flattered you went to all this trouble and all . . ."

"Dollface, how much straight time ya got left in this jerkwater?"

"The E.T.A.'s Tuesday."

"So ya leave a coupla days aheada schedule. Big deal."

"It's just that if . . ."

That "if" was slippery. The conditional came with a string of "ands" and "buts." Say I take the job; the "ands" were considerable:

The Ands

1. I'd make a fair piece of change on the caper.
2. I'd be quits with soybeans.
3. I wouldn't die—of boredom or otherwise—listening to Sunday's sermon on the Meetinghouse Mount (Bro Boucher was presenting Willy B's blockbuster, *Jerusalem*, a tale of Passion, Lust and Atonement).

4.   I'd leave with my ass intact.

There was, however, Hank to consider. I'd be leaving him at the mercy of

The Buts

1.   The Bouchers
2.   The Brinsmades
3.   Winny
4.   Hally, Seth, and Sativa
5.   Patrick
6.   Shaboo
7.   The Sherwins
8.   Nigel Dawes
9.   Etc.
10.   Etc.

"So? Ya take me up on tha offer, what happens?"

"I'd be out of here and happy. I'd send Mr. Pevsner, my land-lord, a rent check and he'd be happy. But Hank would be a goner."

"Sounds ta me, honey, like he's a goner already. But if it'd make ya feel better, we could squeeze him inta tha crate and take him back with us."

That was no car trip he was offering; it was a jaunt in a four-wheel pressure cooker. But so what? You take help where you find it and I needed all the help that came down the pike.

"He'll probably put up a fight. You might have to prod him a little with your .38 caliber persuader." Ray Chandler wrote that when you didn't know how to handle a scene, have someone enter with a gun. Ray was full of sound advice.

"No can do, sweetheart. I forgot ta bring it."

My mother was full of advice too. She said good help was hard to find. "What? No roscoe?"

"I had it out ta pack back in tha city but I got inta a huddle with Junior and got so worked up I took off without tha damn thing."

"Great. Now what do you suggest?"

"Gun 'im down with that machinegunner moutha yours."

"And if that doesn't work?"

"Screw 'im."

My headlights read "high beams."

"Sorry, sugar. Screw'm like in leave'm."

The lights went out.

Showdown

Nick followed me out to the Brinsmades' spread. His plan was to wait in the short while I t.c.b.'d. "These tha rejects or tha welcomin' committee?" he asked when he spied the Blocks' rest camp.

"Nobody here's talking. Take your pick."

"Ain't worth usin' up valuable brain cells decidin', sweetheart. Tha net result's tha same. Go get your boyfriend and let's get tha hell outta here."

I found them in the living room in a fifty-minute configuration. Gallagher was on his back on the couch. Someone I didn't want to see was sitting in a chair slightly behind Golden Boy's golden thinktank.

I hadn't disturbed the conversation because there wasn't any. They were broadcasting on the Cosmic Station. It was a higher frequency than my flaps could pick up.

Boucher looked up at me and transmitted thoroughbred hate. Hank just looked fuzzy.

I thought about humming a few bars of "I Could Have Danced All Night," but then thought better of it. Instead I opted for the caj. "What time did the party break up, Dick Clark?"

"The 'party' "—Balthazar sounded like he'd been gargling vinegar—"is Perpetual. Obviously, you don't Understand its True Nature. As your Absurd and Disruptive behavior only proves. What you did last night was Tantamount to Murder."

"Excuse me but are *you* calling *me* a murderer?"

" 'Murder is Hindering another.' "

"Sorry. I'll try to behave better at the next shindig."

I shifted attention to my supposed victim. "Hey, Hank, you'll never guess who I ran into on the way to the luncheonette." This was finessing into a strong-arm play.

Gallagher shrugged. "Your French friend, LeCoq."

It was a low and unexpected blow. Similar charges had been dropped in New York. Now I was under indictment in Ohio. I revved up enough sangfroid to say "No, not him. But you're close."

Balthazar continued to glower and Hank regarded me funny. "I give up. Who?"

"Palladino." I hurled his handle like a pitcher throwing a spitball.

Gallagher's expression grew greasy. "What's that Vice Monger doing here?" Nick was to Golgonooza what the snake was to Eden. "Don't tell me it's pure Coincidence." The tone was snide.

"No, uh, not exactly. Listen, can I talk to you in private for a minute?"

"You can say whatever you have to say in front of Balthazar."

"Hank, I really need to talk with you alone."

"Golgonooza thrives on Openness," Balthazar intoned.

"Secrecy's unnecessary, Jane," Gallagher said after an optic transfer with his guru.

"I'm not talking secrecy. I'm talking Torment, capital T, and *that* I'd rather discuss in private. If *you* don't mind." The barb was aimed at Boucher's solar plexus.

Hank made motions to rise but Balthazar shot out a hand to push him back into supine. I ran interference, pushed his meathook aside, and said: "C'mon, sport." I palmed Gallagher's hand, got him on his sinkers, and played chutes and ladders up to the guest room.

I laid my cards on the table.

"How he got here's a long story. The 'why' is short: Nick the dick's got me a gig. The poop is that he wants to split quick. One of the perks is a one-way trip for two to New York, the Art Capital of the World."

"New York is the Capital of Corruption."

"Well, that too," I conceded. "But we do happen to live there, remember?" Although I knew he was trying to forget.

"Okay, try this on. I'm broke and you're broke. We leave a couple of days early, we take the drive, we cash in our airline ticks and save the bucks."

"Money is a Curse that has nothing to do with Anything of Significance. Blake suffered Poverty and he Conquered."

Me, I just suffered. On all fronts. "All right, scrap the moolah angle. Forget I even brought it up. Hank, *please* come home with me."

"Hank will leave when he's Ready to leave." I heard the sonic boom before I sighted the missile.

"Be missing, huh?" I snapped when all of Balthazar entered the room. "This doesn't concern you."

The guru set like epoxy. "Every Occurrence in Golgonooza concerns me." That meant he was nosy. "May I remind you that Hank has Important Work to Complete here. That he is collaborating with Me on a most Serious and Necessary Project. That the Community here—in which he is now a member despite your Selfish and Shortsighted Antics—needs and wants him."

"May I remind you that I need and want him too?"

The Big Cheese threw his arm around my patootie. Buddy-buddy. "You see, My Friend, it is as I warned. She wishes to Deter you from your Bright Future."

"That's a lot of far fetch. You don't believe *that* malarkey, do you

186

Hank-o? Hank? Ha-aaaank?" Dreamboat was making a close study of the wood grain pattern on the floor.

I clipped a silencer on my larynx before I slid my jib altogether. "Skip the thousand words, babycakes; I get the picture."

I glared at Balthazar. "Your brand of voodoo sucks, you know that? Go peddle it someplace else while I pack." Actually I was already packing, dunking clothes in my bag like a basketball player sinking layup shots. The Grizzlies would've been proud.

Balthazar broomed, leaving me and my squeeze in emotional gridlock.

"I'm sorry, Jane," Golden Boy said, mealymouthed.

I said: "You should be."

"What do you want me to say?"

I could've gone for something classical along the lines of "Don't-leave-me-I'll-die" or "I'll-do-anything to keep you." I would've even settled for the standard "I love you." But if he couldn't come up with the lines himself, I'd be goddamned if I was going to feed them to him.

"Promise me something."

"What?" His slightly glazed eyes looked a bit filmier than usual.

"That you'll definitely take the 7:30 P.M. flight back on Tuesday."

"Okay."

"Better yet, take an earlier one."

"Well . . ."

"Think about it."

"Okay."

"I act with benevolence and Virtue," Willy Boy wrote. "& get murder'd time after time." Blake was jake on that score. The smell of slaughter filled my nozzle.

Hank looked down at my bags.

"You need help?"

187

That was the understatement of the century. "Yeah. Let's get this show on the road."

Farewell, My Lovely

Palladino was slumped over the wheel asleep. His satchel mouth hung slack. I figured Hank for a few cutting remarks, but knock on oak, he scotched the criticals.

He tapped lightly on the windshield. Rip Van Winkle slept on. I banged on the hood. That brought results. The hankshaw's eyelids rolled up like windowshades. He blinked and rallied. He jerked his compact body out of the Beetle and shot a stubby hand out in Gallagher's direction. "Domenic Palladino. Nice ta meetchya." The sleuth was on good behavior. "No luggage? Ya ain't comin' with us?"

"No, I'm staying."

"Sorry ta hear that." Nick shot me a squint of sympathy.

"Your girlfriend here's top drawer. Ya know that, buddy?" He slapped Hank on the back for added oomph. Hank flinched.

"Yes, she's pretty nice, thanks," Hank concurred, making what should have been a wrong number turn into a meeting of the minds. I'm partial, however, to chinfests where my virtues get banner headlines. I would've liked the guys to keep it up but unfortunately we didn't have all day to kill.

Golden Boy pushed the top of his boot into the dirt. Nick said: "I'm real sorry ta butt inta yer vacation like this. I wouldn'ta if me and Rosenblatt didn't think it was important. I'll tell ya, I appreciate yer loanin' me Jane here. She's tha right girl for tha job." Palladino was making a bid for male bonding.

"She's not mine to lend," Hank countered, trotting out his women's lib consciousness. "She's her own person. She has her own life and she makes her own decisions."

Nick scowled at Hank, as if Golden Boy'd said something complicated. "Sorry, buddy boy. Didn't mean ta rile ya. A course I know she leads her own life. Ya both do, don'tchya? It's easier that way, ain't it? That way ya get ta do yer thing out here." He displayed his snappers in a sarcastic smile. "Well, I guess we should step on it; we gotta long drive aheada us."

I put my holders around Gallagher and slapped a buss on him. He held me tight and then went serious, gazing into my daylights. I was close to watering.

"Hurry home," I said and meant it. "Well, guess I should go." I stayed anchored.

Nick broke up the osculation. He pushed a paw out to Gallagher, pumphandled a second time, and mumbled: "Nice meetin' ya." This was his Emily Post routine. "I'll take good care a tha little lady, I mean woman, don'tchya worry."

Hank wasn't. "Bye," he said, rumpling my frizz. I climbed into Nick's heap. My last glimpse of my One and Only was at the end of the Brinsmades' road. He stood by the woodpile, looking his usual to-die gorgeous and shaking the moonrocks around in his head.

Highway Patrol

While Nick tore up asphalt, my gastrics made inroads into my stomach lining. Not that I was carsick. It was just that leaving Hank took more toll than the turnpikes.

To get my mind off Golgonooza I thought back to the time, not so long ago, when I still believed in detective novels. How I'd dreamt of a long road trip with a glam gumshoe. The itinerary promised romance, adventure, excitement, strange towns with stranger people, shabby gas stations, motels with magic fingers, truck stops with mom's apple pie. Boy, I'd had some flippy notions before I'd met Palladino. He'd been setting the record straight ever since. This trip was a real eye-opener.

For one thing, real private eyes don't pay much attention to the public sector if there's no money in it. Palladino's idea of a roadside attraction was a McDonald's or a Burger King. He wasn't even an adventurous eater.

A few times I asked him to stop.

"Waita coupla more minutes, okay, and I'll pull inta a gas station."

"No, stop right here."

"Here? Ya gotta weak bladder or somethin', ya can't hold it another five? Or did ya get hooked back there pissin' in tha wind with tha natureboys?"

"I'm not talking bathroom, Nick. I'm talking photographs. I want to photograph something."

"I swear ta God yer fuckin' crazy. There ain't nuthin' ta photograph. All there was was some scummy, rundown mini golf, fa Chrissake."

"That's right. That's what I want to shoot."

The peeper tamped a cancer stick on the steeringwheel. "It's yer film, kid. Ya got it ta burn? Then go ahead and waste it."

I tried explaining my photo m.o. but it was hard sledding. Enough penetrated so Nick stopped asking questions when I asked to stop. He even tried being helpful. "Hey, angel, there's some more art," he'd cry, pointing to trash along the highway and smiling all the way down to his tonsils. "How much ya think ya'll get for a pic a that crap?"

The Verdict

Seeing as how the P.I. had an opinion on almost everything, he was curiously tightlipped about Hank. "So what did you think?" We were zipping through Mechanicsville, Pennsy, when I asked.

" 'Bout what?" Nick swore under his breath at the beige Pontiac that was passing him in the right lane. The teen behind the wheel waved.

"About Gallagher."

"Nice-lookin' guy."

"Yeah, and?"

"And nuthin'. I don't like him."

"Because?"

"Don't trust 'im."

"You going to tell me why?" Not that I gave a damn what Nick thought. He was no expert in the interpersonals.

"He ain't my type. I dunno. Vibes. Like I told ya tha time we was workin' tha Steir job and we seen him and that twist headin' upta yer place. I get impressions. Somethin' with tha guy ain't on the up 'n' up.

"Like that hoopla he spouted about yer bein' independent and—what was it? Oh, yeah—bein' yer own person. That goes down smooth with dames like you but it ain't on the level, honey. That's jive from pretty boys like him. He's talkin' both sidesa his mouth."

"Man, if you think that's jive talk, you should've heard the Blakean mumbo jumbo. Nick, you think I did the right thing leaving him out there?"

"Sweetheart, it ain't him I'm worried about. Ya don't know it yet but I did ya a big favor. Ya don't belong with a buncha sex-crazed fruitcakes and a dude who don't take good enuff care a ya. But ya don't wanna hear this shit, right? Besides, it ain't my place ta go stickin' my schnoz in yer lovelife. So let's drop it, okay?"

And that was that on that score all the miles and burgers back to the parking space across the street from the Pussy Cat Lounge.

Nick helped me carry my gear upstairs. He didn't want the trip to end on a sour note. Palladino's physical condition was like Hammett's Continental Op's—"fat and forty." "This place is all right," he panted after the two-flight climb. He took a load off his pedals in one of the director chairs by the kitchen table and gave the layout a frisk. According to his formula, all artists lived in cramped, cruddy garrets and I threw a monkey wrench into the equation. I lived seminormal. The pink plastic flamingos flanking the couch accounted for the "semi."

"You want a drink?" I asked and got a negative.

"Nah, gotta get home ta tha wife." Even though it was late, he was hoping to find a big Italian dinner waiting for him. Hearing him salivate was the first clue I had that he ever tasted what he shoveled down his muzzle.

"If she's such a good cook, how come you don't ask me over for dinner some night?" I liked home cooking, especially in someone else's home.

"The wife, she's been buggin' me ta bring ya over."

"I'm portable."

"I'll talk ta tha boss."

Screw Jobs

When the investigator left to face down his hot lasagna, I took a long soak in a hot tub. Never again would I take indoor plumbing for granted. Seems I'd been taking lots of things for granted that I shouldn't. Like the Dewinter case being sewn up. Last report Jack Price had mysteriously disappeared. Troy and Paula were shacking up again in the penthouse. I go merrily along, thinking that's a marriage patched up and whammo, Palladino falls out of the sky and blows the lid off that notion. We'd come back to town to go back on the case. Opportunity and Inclination Revisited.

This go-round the troubs were Troy's. He gotten himself inclined and entwined with Bettina Baldwin, a foxy doxy up in Syracuse. The tomato wasn't the problem; it was her two older bros, Michael and Murray. Versatile guys, they'd loansharked a little, tried armed robbery, dabbled in assault, and messed around as hired guns. But now they were interested in taking care of baby and had taken up singing. They had a special performance planned for Paula. Troy spent twenty-five hundred clams chilling their repertoire and continued shtupping Bettina whenever he went upstate. The boys worked up new lyrics. They'd blow into town, they said, and try them out on Troy first; if he liked them, he could buy them to the tune of three thou.

The beat could go on like this forever, but Troy's dough-re-mi couldn't. He knew, though, that if Lady Lavender got wind of the hanky-panky, she'd Reno-vate him for all he was worth. And this time she'd probably get it. As for Bettina, Mr. T. was having doubts. She was an expensive habit. Her maintenance payments were going up faster than those on his Riverside Drive apartment.

Opportunity and Inclination had more heads than a hydra. Troy baby had it and was trying to hide it; Paula'd had it and lost it. The Baldwin brothers were using it and Bettina was supplying it. Palladino was detecting it and yours truly was back into documenting it.

I shut the cranium on the Dewinter headache for the night. I'd have plenty of opportunity and inclination to think about them on the job Tuesday. Better to use the present opportunity to incline my thoughts toward Golden Boy. There was plenty to worry about. I couldn't shake what the dick had said to me in the car. It was enough to drive me to the bottle. The Valium bottle. I popped 5 mg.

At 3:30 A.M. the mental machinery went on down time, where I planned to keep it until noon. It was a nice plan until a berserk mosquito buzzed my ear. I swatted at it with my hand but the little bastard wouldn't quit. It turned out to be the phone, and it was 6:30 A.M.

Panic

"Jane?"

It was too disgusto to be true. "Nick?"

"Sorry ta wake ya, baby doll, but we gotta update. Troy just heard from Syracuse. The Baldwins're comin' in taday insteada tamarra. They're gonna be on the U.S. Air that gets in at 8:02. Those bastards *would* pick tha early flight. I'm drivin' outta tha airport after I hang up ta get a look at tha terminal. Ya been ta U.S. Air before, right?"

"Yeah, to go to Ohio," I said, groggy.

"Good. So ya know what ta do and what ta bring, right? Meet me at tha ticket counner atta quarter past eight." Slam.

There's nothing like a good dawn rush of pure panic. You fight open the lids and presto, you feel fat and ugly. You're breathing double time and the ticker's beating triple. Every shred of wearable clothes is dirty or locked up at the cleaners. Every hole on the golf course is the nineteenth. From there the rest of the day is a crapshoot.

Most women go into a tizzy about men. Me, I go mental about equipment. Today I was stirred up because of my 90mm. It was all I had and it was a pipsqueak as telephotos go. That magnifier wouldn't give me a running start if the boys from Syracuse got hip to me. And there was a decent chance they'd spot me, seeing as how the 90mm made up in size what it lacked in power. It wasn't the shy, retiring type; it built out the little Leica body like Jayne Mansfield.

Big deal I had vision. Parker had the goods. I knew that from the first Dewinter job on the Seymour roof. The right item, a 200mm bruiser, was probably looking for work in Parker's closet only blocks away. But with Gallagher in Ohio, the sucker might as well be on Mars.

My situation was desperate. With no way on earth to be unobtrusive, the only way to play it was fast and loose. Go for baroque. Be obtrusive and then some. That was the technique Nick's two-ton operative Ferrara used. It worked for that hippo, it might work for a skinny kid like me. Then again, it might not. Russian roulette isn't a game with complicated rules.

I listened to my mother's voice inside my head: "Make sure to wear decent underwear in case you're in an accident, dear." She could have added "in case you're gunned down, taken hostage, beaten to a pulp, or arrested" had she known where her Number One daughter was heading. Better she shouldn't know. On went a pair of black lace scanties Gallagher'd given me last Valentine's Day. Anything goes with basic black.

Next I slipped into a pair of faded jeans, my beatup Nikes, and a moth-eaten crewneck. I futzed two hanks of hair into pigtails. I stuck a few barrettes into the mop for color, went light on the makeup. I checked myself out in the mirror. Forget the fairest-of-them-all-Snow White malarkey. As long as nobody looked too closely and I kept my trap shut, I passed for an art school bimbo.

Tailing Away

Palladino was standing by the ticket counter. In disguise. Instead of his wrinkled mac, he was wearing a wrinkled gray benny. Plus loud checked leg-bags, a plaid cap pulled low over the Wildroot, and shades. His lummox from Trenton look. But who was I to throw stones? I looked like a dip from Teaneck.

His buzzer was buried in a *Daily News* and he hardly glanced up when I waltzed in. According to instructions, I was to tail him until he found a place to confab. I thought I knew a thing or two about shadowing from the whodunits. I was doing just fine on the congoleum circuit until I got cocky. I tried to tail and finagle Dentyne

out of my purse at the same time. By the time I'd untangled pock-
etbook strap from camera strap, the gumshoe was gone.

I could (A) have a nervous breakdown, (B) have Nick paged and
blow our cover, or (C) go with the Laws of Inertia. C was in the
lead when Nick came out of the men's room and continued his
terminal tour. We hit the gift shop and the shamus cocked his
headgear. I sidled up to him at the mag rack. I scooped a *Vogue*.
Might as well pick up a quick fashion tip along with my photo
assignment. Nick spoke to me through a *Playboy*.

"Dewinter's in tha coffee shop with tha baboons. They're big,
mean, and ugly, so watch it, will ya? I don't want 'em makin' sidesa
slaw outta ya, okay? All we needs're some head shots so we can
identify tha dudes later. If I ain't in tha cookshop while yer
shootin', don't panic. I'll be around if ya need me."

"Like you were in the Harlem caper?" I said, controlling the
voice quake.

"Try like on Warren Street, sweetheart," Nick retorted, making
me feel a heel.

"I deserved that."

Nick scowled. "Yeah, ya did, but forget it. Now, look. As soon as
ya got what ya need, scram. I'll meet ya back at tha ticket counner
—say round quarter ta ten—after tha creeps board tha plane back
ta Syracuse. I'll give ya a lift back inta town."

"What happens to Troy?"

"He takesa cab outta Kennedy and meets tha little woman and
flies down ta some island in tha Bahamas. Get this, ta celebrate
their sixth anniversary." Nick snorted but I couldn't tell whether it
was a comment on the Playmate of the Month or Dewinter's playboy behavior.

"Six years of marital bliss, huh? Time flies when you're having
fun." I admired a high-style Avedon photo of a not-so-bad Halston.

"Speakin' a fun," the P.I. said, slapping his slick shut. "Let's go.
I'll show ya tha clowns."

Tough Customers

The snack bar was spiffed up with Styrofoam wood beams on the ceiling, stucco on the walls, pseud family crests, mahogany manqué Formica, and dungeon lighting. The food counter ran parallel to the door; the booths ran perpendicular; and the tables clogged the middle. The ambiance was as charming as the inside of a refrigerator.

"Ya see tha second booth in there?" the sleuth asked as we stood outside by the window. My index finger squirmed but I knew better than to point. I stuck the twitcher deep into my pocket and nodded the braincase.

"Tha guy facin' us, that's Troy." I blinked once, twice, and let it go at thrice. Paula Dewinter sure knew what cut of meat she liked. She was as consistent about men as she was about color.

Which is to say Troy was a duplicate of Mrs. D.'s sailor Jack Price. Actually vice versa. The summer issue was a reprint of the earlier edition. Mr. D. was a little broader and a little older and a lot dressier. Though the latter was no trick, since I'd only seen Price in cut-offs or birthday suit. According to Dun & Bradstreet, Troy was better endowed than Price. But was he as well hung? That was the question. Kudos to Paula if her consistency extended to what the Golgonoozers would call "Minute Particulars." Only in this case, the particulars were anything but minute.

Dewinter, I'd been told, wasn't born with a silver spoon in his yap. He'd worked his way up to his cutlery. And bought himself some class along with it, judging from the elegant wrist action he used lifting his coffee cup and buttering his danish. His good taste lapsed only when it came to tarts.

About the two bohunks, I could tell little. They sat with their backs to me. Mike, on the right, was the one with the rat's nest for a coif. Murray, on the left, had the Henry Moore do. Every hair on his head had been lacquered into sculptural curves. Smoke from their cheap, fat stogies hung over the table like smog in L.A.

Nick said: "Remember, kid, make it short 'n' sweet. No heroics. Ya got that?"

I replied: "Check. Shoot and give the Bronx cheer." I planned to hang around those beefcakes the way I planned to drive a car without brakes.

I saluted the hankshaw gladiator fashion, ducked inside, and nosed into the food line. I ordered a large Tab on the rocks with a twist. The booth in front of Dewinter's was vacant. Dead ahead and bearing down on it was a young hippie couple. I sideswiped them with my tray. I pearlied apologetically as I plopped tush and soft drink down simultaneously.

From where I hunkered, I now got a rear view of Troy and a frontal of the huskies. Their kissers were thick and doughy. They smacked and slurped their way through eggs, fries, toast, and bacon. They took shortcuts. Rather than hoist their forks all the way up and in, they brought their mouths down and around. They liked moving their lips. They probably moved them when they read. *If* they could read.

Nick had said Bettina was a stunner. If beauty—inner and/or outer—is a genetic trait, the Baldwin clan passed it through X chromosomes only. The double-Y-ers got the ugly genes. Nobody in the fam inherited brains. The males had unfurnished rooms upstairs and the female thought gray matter was gravy. Perfume did the same work for her, if not better. And a damn sight quicker.

I'd brought along a *New York Times*—not to read all the news fit to print but to cut a hole in and poke a lens through. Standard issue peeper trick but a flivver for a rookie like me. I was too jittery. The paper'd shake and rattle, and the spuds' heads next door might roll. I reverted to Plan A, the one where I go obnoxiously obvious. When you're on the *Titanic*, go first class.

Target Practice

I was wasting time when there wasn't time to waste. There was no way to know exactly how long this coffee klatch would stick around to sip and chew. I took a long swallow of sugarfree and took Jayne Mansfield out for a stroll. We ambled over to the flower children so I could apologize for my bad karma. They said "far out," which I took for forgiveness. Then I bullhorned "Can I take your picture?" They said "far out," which I took as "yes." I made such a production out of shooting even a blind person could see me. Then I did a busboy holding some plasticware. Next I trained my lens on an old crone dottering down the aisle with a soggy tuna on rye.

I shuffled back to my booth, passing close enough to the Baldwins that I could hear them masticate. I sat down and sweated bullets.

So much for the limbering-up exercises; it was time to tackle the extortionists. Dewinter'd been warned to ignore me as if his life depended on it. Which it did. Mine did too. The baddies were engrossed in playing Let's Make a Deal. A Leica's built like a Rolls. I said a silent thanks to Ernst Leitz for designing it with a whisper shutter. It was making life a lot easier. And hopefully a lot longer.

I took my first shot and then, feeling gutsy, took another. A right hook, a left jab. Life went on.

I tried a feint. I pointed the M2 at the skid top, crater face sitting slightly behind and to the right of Brers Baldwin. Golden Years saw me aim, got up, and charged. His jaw was set like a steel trap and his eyes, behind his cheaters, were molten lava. He was old enough to have a heart condition and my only hope for survival was that he'd suffer a touch of angina before he reached my table. Between this and the earlier tray episode with the hippies, write me off as a humanitarian.

Paralyzed with fear, I sat my ground. The firecracker stood over me. "You an agent?" His raspy voice cut through me like a hot knife through butter. He didn't whisper like the Leica. Troy, Mike, and Murray turned and stared.

My luck the Big Waiter in the Sky bollixed up the orders. "The heart attack was for the geriatric, not for me," I wanted to yell. "And that customer there"—I meant Dewinter—"didn't ask for heart trouble either." Nick had gotten me into this jam; he was supposed to get me out. He was nowhere in sight.

Things got worse instead of better. Murray sprang up from his seat like the Colossus of Rhodes. You bet *that* changed the rhythm of my EKG.

He had a murderous expression planked on his puss. It read: one way ticket to the ultimo *camera obscura.* So what I was a woman. That didn't mean I'd get treated like a lady. I was about to wind up like chivalry: dead.

Murray's hand dipped into his pocket. I held my breath and waited for the icy metal of his barker to press slowly against my temple. After that there'd be the flash of fire, the smell of scorched skin mingling with the smell of cheap stogie, the sound of fleeing footsteps, and I'd be beyond pain. My saucer-size hazels were hypnotized by Murray's digits inching their way like earthworms out of his jacket. A lump of cold, hard cash caught the light. The stakes changed from death and dying to buying and selling. I wondered what the going rate was for that kind of silence that's this side short of the grave. I didn't have to wait long. Murray opened a Philadelphia bankroll and peeled off a finif. "What a cheapskate," I thought angrily. Until I copped a view of him heading for the Mr. Coffee. He armed himself with two cups of hot brew. Was his plan to scald me? Scar my pretty face beyond recognition? He came closer. And then he slipped back into his seat. The trio resumed negotiations. I was relieved. Spell that with a capital R and while you're at it, underline and italicize it.

Lies

But I wasn't out of the woods yet. I still had the aged firebreather to deal with. A voice came out of my mouth; it sounded like my voice only it came from far away and was high-pitched with terror. It said: "Who, me? An agent? What a dumb idea." I built my lips into my coyest smile. "I'm a photo major at the School of Visual Arts." I figured he'd go for the higher education angle.

His facial topography didn't shift. I fabricated on. "It's in Manhattan. I'm doing a senior project on fast food in airports. Documenting how people eat in transit. It says a lot about our culture, don't you think?" I poured on the schoolgirl charm thick as motor oil.

"I like a goil mit pep." He spoke with an Eastern European accent. "I ken sit a liddle?" My answer was irrelevant. He'd already made himself at home on the bench facing me, his back to the plug uglies. He flipped a card out from his wallet. The fancy blue script with more spit curls than Betty Boop read "Limousines by Mr. Phil, Orlando, Florida" and a phone number.

"You got mebbe a card?" Mr. Phil wanted to know.

"Uh uh." Freelance pros carried cards but students didn't. My card stayed in my wallet.

"You godda name?"

"Of course I have a name. It's Jane."

"Jane vhat?"

I hesitated. Intuition told me the creature from Disney World wasn't mixed up in the Baldwin caper but he might yet show a dirty deuce. You're not supposed to talk to strangers but if you do, you might as well lie. "Jane Glenn."

"A nice name for a nice goil. So tell me, Miss Jane Glenn, how old are you? Vait, don't tell me. Let me make ah guess. Eighteen."

"I'm flattered." It was the first honest statement I'd made. "But really, I'm twenty-one." Truth only played a bit part in this drama.

"Vell, ya don't look it." Mr. Phil's thick glasses needed to be thicker. "How old ya tink I yam?" Late sixties but I knocked off ten; that made us even-steven in the flattery department.

"I'm sixty-fife as of June. And ya know vhat? I've been married six times." He held up his left hand with all his feelers extended and his right with just the thumb up. The right was spruced up with a sapphire ring on his third finger. The left was bare. Mr. Phil was between wives.

Complications

The irony hit me over the head like a sledgehammer. What we had going here was a marriage junkie teaming up with a person who might never make it to the matrimonials, who was on assignment photographing a third party's extramarital *mishegaas*.

"Since you like being married so much, how come you haven't proposed to me yet? You've known me for a whole five minutes. I mean, what's wrong with me?" I was playing Mr. Phil because I *had* to keep him in his seat. While the poor bastard was talking, I was pretending to photograph him. My sights, however, were on the booth next door. The Floridian was a better protective shield than Colgate's Gardol.

"*Oy*, a smartess. I vas a smartess vhen I vas your age." While I wondered which of my ages we were talking about, I took a snap of Michael Baldwin.

"So, *nu*, ya vanna get married?" The matrimony maven delivered the line pokerfaced. Hank always burst into nervous laughter when he said anything vaguely similar.

"I have to finish school." I played along.

"How much ya got left?"

"Another semester," I answered, popping off a pic of Murray.

"So vhen you're through, ya come down ta Orlando. Ya ever been ta Disney Voild? It's febulous. End mit your pep, ve'd have a lodda fun. And down dere ve got loadsa fest food places ta photograph. Bedder den here, believe me." He dismissed our present surroundings with a sweep of his plainer hand.

"I know from young goils taday. Ya vant vhat ya call space end ya vant to make mit a career." At that moment I wanted another shot of Murray. Wanted it and got it. "End ya vant somebody should be supportive mit your voik. Mine fourth vife, she vas the same vay. So ya see, I know vhat's vhat. Vhat's modern." He slapped his concave chest. My shutter went off when his hand made a thud. "See, Mr. Phil's no macho pig." But Michael Baldwin was and I got a good, clean shot of him putting a wad of scrambled in his smush.

It sunk in slow because I was giving the visuals my full attention and Golden Oldie only a half eardrum's worth. "Hey, wait a minute. You really are proposing, aren't you? Listen, I was only kidding, honest." Why was it these sleuth jobs always got so damn complicated?

"Ya vorried I'm too old? Mit age comes visdom. I'm in good healt. Dr. Goldstein in Orlando, he's da best der is; he tells me I got da constitution of a forty-year-old. And if ya got your healt, *tateleh*, ya got everyting. Besides, I got money. Vhat more ya vant? Da moon? Dat, I'm afraid, I kent give."

What I wanted was my last shots on the roll to be of Dewinter sliding a chunky envelope over toward the Syracuse end of the table and then of Murray's thick fingers around same.

"Is this how you courted all the other Mrs. Phils? Are you always so impetuous?"

"Impetuous shmetuous. Yer a nice goil. Ettractiv. I'm a nice man. Life is short. Tink it over. It's da best offer ya'll get all day. Sit, I'll buy ya another Coke."

"Make it a Tab." I shouldn't sit, I should split.

"*Oy vey,* don't tell me you're vorried from da vaistline. Yer too young ta vorry."

"I vorry." About everything.

"Vait." The limo king left and returned with my soda and his coffee. "So, *nu?* Now det ya took so many pictures of mine hendsome *punim,* ya gonna send me vun et least?"

What could I say but "sure"? I dropped a new roll of black and white in the camera and blew off a few frames. I promised myself that as soon as I'd printed up Rosenblatt's photos, I'd glossy Mr. Phil's portrait and mail it to him c/o Mickey Mouse.

"Well, I'm afraid I have to beat feet." There was no sense tempting fate or Mr. Phil more than I already had. "It's been a real pleasure."

"Ya von't forget vhat I sed about Florida? Tink it over. Just giv a call—collect—and let me know vhen ya vanna come. I'll send a limo ta pick ya up at da airport."

"Will do." I kissed one of the Grand Canyons on his cheek. "Thanks."

"Tanks for vhat? A soda? Vhat's a soda?"

"Just thanks for everything. For just being here. Have a safe trip back."

It wasn't till I reached the door that I spotted Palladino. I hadn't seen him earlier because he'd changed costume. He was wearing a woolen watch cap and an orange parka and looked like a Hoosier on holiday. He'd been sitting in the caf the whole time. He knew I could handle trouble so he let me handle it. As I walked past him, neither of us made a sign. I took a squint at my watch. Nine seventeen A.M. The upstaters weren't due to leave for another half. That was more than enough time for me to get in hot water.

Voyeur

I had nothing special to do and nowhere special to be so I followed my feet to the flight gates. Wanderlust. My trip to Ohio hadn't put a crimp in the "wander." Or, as I stopped to think about Gallagher, in the "lust" either.

It's no news that photographers are voyeurs. I wasn't going anywhere so I might as well get some kicks making pics of people who were. No harm done; no souls stolen; nothing splashy to report.

A 747 dumped a load of Corn Huskers; another wind flapper left for Johnstown, Pa.; a group of nuns in penguin getups waited patiently for a connecting flight to Houston; some jawsmiths left for a dental convention in St. Lou. A typical day in the tourist trade.

I sat down by the window to pop another b&w in the Leica. A stratoliner—coming in from who-knew-where—coasted to a stop. A portable gangway fastened itself to the fuselage like a lamprey and then a man, small as a carrot, carrying a large briefcase, led the parade out of the aircraft. Next came a fat lady who used magic markers as makeup. A small herd of yokels waddled out, uncomfortable in newly starched shirts and tight Sunday shoes. They were followed by comedians, clowns, geeks, and dummies. Followed by what appeared to be—from my twenty-foot vantage point and through bloodshot eyeballs—a two-headed blonde. This was no ordinary passenger list. This was the sideshow shuttle. Nonstop. Direct.

Partners in Crime

Personally, freaks aren't my photo bag. Diane Arbus had milked that territory dry long before I came on the scene. But this I had to go for. I raised the M2, P.D.Q., to eyelevel, and spun the focusing ring. Siamese twins didn't show up in the viewfinder. Sandwiched between the frame lines were two separate organisms, so closely intertwined and similarly dressed that it was hard to tell where one started and the other began. I *still* couldn't believe what I was seeing. As soon as the shutter clicked I wanted to shoot myself. And not with a camera. One of the fairhairs was Golden Boy. The other was Winny.

It was a toss-up whether to throw myself in front of the next plane, sob hysterically, give a primal scream, puke my guts out, or hide in the ladies'. A part of me—creative, masochistic, or vindictive, I wasn't sure which—went on autopilot, and that part continued photographing. The rest of me fought to keep my head while war was being waged in my chest. I drew the Maginot Line at my neck.

I tailed the two to the baggage claim. A piece of cake. Their lips got as much workout as their feet and their progress was slow. Painfully slow.

"Be rational," I repeated over and over, the way I'd practice foreign phrases in language lab. Sherlock Holmes said: "It is of the highest importance in the art of detection to be able to recognize, out of a number of facts, which are incidental and which are vital." So maybe what I saw wasn't as serious as it seemed? Maybe Hank's thing with Winny was incidental while what we had was vital? This fling wasn't the real thing, wouldn't last, meant nothing? The hell it wasn't, wouldn't, didn't!

But what about that crime of passion on my own record? Shit, I deserved a pardon. I had the decency to cheat with a sam who lived a zillion miles away, whom I saw almost never, and whose charms I had learned to resist.

Blake, pushing "Gratified Desire," would have pooh-poohed my whole defense. And I had to remember Hank was into Blake. And into Winny who was into Blake. That made a nice tight circle. Compared to that, what I had with LeCoq was a short dotted line.

The lovebirds smooched until the conveyor belt burped out their

luggage. Me and the Leica noticed Winny'd brought a bag too big
for a short visit. She'd be hard to send packing.

I complimented myself on being such a crackerjack. I could photograph Opportunity and Inclination blindfolded, with one hand
tied behind my back. I had the Dewinters to thank for the profes-
sionalism. Who knew their photo assignments would be dress re-
hearsals for a full-scale personal tragedy?

Waterworks fogged the M2's eyepiece as I took my parting shot
of the duo hopping into a cab I knew they couldn't afford.

Wounded

I had another five before I met up with the shamus. It wasn't
minutes I wanted to kill, it was Gallagher. No, better yet, Winny
the Worm. I wanted vengeance, Mickey Spillane style. Except I
was a softie, more Ross Macdonald/Lew Archer-ish—understanding and compassionate—than Mike Hammer-like. The only other
route was suicide. That solution had the added benefit of bringing
posthumous photographic fame. That would really stick it to Hank.

Short of insta-death, what was I going to do? That depended on
Golden Boy. Would he have the balls to show up at Walker Street?
If so, when? If not, why not? What would he, could he, say?
Where were the bill-and-cooers now? Joining giblets in Hoboken?
When had they started shtupping? Had they ever lumped up in my
bed? An ugly bunch of questions; the last one almost made me
heave Mr. Phil's Tab.

I called myself a visual artist? Revoke my artistic license. I
couldn't see what was going down right in front of my face. I
claimed savvy in the detecto department? I missed every clue. And
now that I knew what I knew, saw what I saw, shot what I'd shot,
all I wanted to do was turn candy-ass.

When I finally made it to Checkpoint Charlie, Nick was leaning
against the counter, smiling his razor blade smile that signaled all'd

been aces. "Hiya, sweetheart," he said cheerfully. Then his brows began to crochet. "Whatsa matta? Ya look like ya lost yer best friend or somethin'."

I burst into tears.

"Jesus H. Christ, whad I say? I was just makin' a joke. Ya know, ha ha, joke?" The shamus didn't know what to do with his arms, whether to use them to comfort me or to push me outside before I made a scene inside. Handling hysterical broads wasn't his forte.

Playing Dirty

"What's got inta ya? Back in tha coffee shop yer fine. Ya handle yaself like a real pro. That business with that old guy, that was terrif. I leave ya alone for a coupla minutes and tha next thing I know yer a fuckin' hydrant. Women, I tell ya, if I live ta be a hundred, I'll never understand 'em. C'mon," he said in his gentlest twang. "Ya can tell Uncle Nickie all about it in tha car."

Everything looked underwater to me as he led me to the parking lot and coaxed me into his jalopy. He got in, pulled out a smoke, and lit one. He settled in behind the wheel, took off his cap, ran his mitt through his slicked shag, and blew tar and nicotine in and out of his lungs. "Okay, what's with tha boohooin'."

I put my knob on his shoulder and bawled. He put his arm around me and stroked my sleeve. If ever there was a time when he should have been wearing his raincoat, this was it.

It took a while for me to wail myself out. I must have been a pretty sight, all puffy and pigtailed. It wasn't Beauty that interested me; it was the Beast. I blurted out my tale of romantic and photographic woe. I don't recall exactly what I said but it included stocks like "how could he," "I hate him," "how could I have been such a chump," and "where did I go wrong." What I lacked in originality, I made up for in angst.

"I'm sorry, toots."

"Me, too," I sniffled.

"Whadda fuckin' asshole."

"Go ahead, hit me when I'm down."

"Not you, dollface. Yer boyfriend. I mean yer ex."

"Ex?" The term was hard to swallow.

"See, angel, I tried ta see what ya saw in tha shmuck but I'll tell ya, after tha pretty face, tha guy was a zero. I tried ta warn ya. Remember I said that farewell number back there in Podunk was bad news?

"But, ya know, I kept hopin' for yer sake my radar wasn't workin' its usual hundred percent. That you was right about tha guy and I was cockeyed. For what it's worth, sweetheart, tha way I see it, yer a helluva lot better off without tha jerk. Forget tha other dame; she ain't tha problem. Whaddya wanna be mixed up forever with a airhead with a crush on a commune?"

That started the lachrymals up. Saline lubed my contacts and slopped over my cheeks. "Oh, God, what am I going to do?"

"For one," Palladino insisted, "yer gonna pull yerself tagether. Actually, babe, ya don't have mucho choice in tha matter. I meant ta tell ya earlier but I forgot. Rosenblatt wants tha job in tamarra. No fail. And then"—he paused thoughtfully and blew a smoke ring —"I gotta plan. . . ."

The Plot Sickens

First thing I did when I got home was water the pillow. I would've continued, too, if I hadn't had so much to do for Marv. Better to work and weep simultaneously. I headed into the darkroom to duke it out with the film. My eyewash didn't screw up the D76 dilution any. Just because I was overagitated didn't mean the same for the Kodak. The negs came up technical knockouts. The culprits—the Esq.'s and mine—were perfectly exposed.

Phase I completed, I hung up the telltale Tri-X in the drying cabinet and picked up the phone. I dialed 215-555-5046. I needed sisterly sympathy, support, and suggestions.

"What's wrong?" Sara asked after my aquatic "hello." I reran my sob story.

"What are you doing for it?" Sis made it seem like a medical problem. I outlined Palladino's plan. "Sounds good but you know what I'd do if I were you?" She almost never did what I would do so I didn't. "I'd go out first thing tomorrow and buy some new clothes. And I'd try to find out if Jean-Pierre is back in town from the Coast. He's just what this doctor ordered."

I sounded sick.

"What do you want me to suggest?" Sara shucked her nice bedside manner. "Ashes and sackcloth? Widow's weeds? Tell you to sit *shiva?* I'm trying to be consoling, Jane, but you don't make it easy, you know.

"I think what Hank did was the pits, and I'd love to do a little radical surgery on the fucker—without anesthesia. Fortunately for him, I won't see him. Unfortunately for you, he'll probably survive just fine. Men usually do; they have it easy. But it's you I'm worried about. The best cure for your kind of heart disease is finding somebody else. Pronto. Fight fire with fire."

"Yeah, and get burned again? What kind of sadist are you, for Chrissake? What's your lovelife like that you can suggest such torture?"

"What lovelife? All I do is study. The closest I come to another body is my cadaver in anatomy lab."

"Be grateful. Necrophiliacs don't die from broken hearts."

The Consequences

The long-distance shmooze got me thinking about Hank-less living. What exactly would I miss? The dufus way he lit his cig? The triangle of freckles on his portside? His winking and tapping when he focused the 4×5? The food caught in his handlebar? His forever wrinkled wardrobe? The way he smelled (and I don't mean stank the way he had in Ohio)? Those things weren't so significant; they just dissolved my heart like sugar in water. With luck, I'd get over those toss-offs by the time I turned fifty.

But what about those long, lonely days and longer, lonelier nights? Fill them with other studs and mashers? Yuk. Hang out with my pals? That'd help. There was also workaholism, alcoholism, and drug abuse. Or how about the ultimate pain killer, a lobotomy? Maybe I could find a sympathetic surgeon who'd trade work for services. The snag there would be that my photos would appreciate in value over time and the sawbones' work would depreciate.

Bachelor life had *some* benefits. There'd be more room in the closet. More space in the bookshelves. My detective novels could come out of hiding. Not to mention more wallspace. Hank's prints would come down. Sometimes photos fade along with their photographer.

Murder

Palladino's scheme was growing on me. I set up the darkroom to print. I mixed a tray of Dektol, a tray of stop, and one of fixer. My snotbox twitched getting accustomed to the smelly chemicals. I got out a box of 8×10 Poly RC. I popped a neg under the condenser and sized the print on the easel.

First I blew up a head shot of Mike Baldwin, then played follow the leader with one of Murray. The pair made a slimy-looking diptych. Next I did the pugs together and finally one of them with Dewinter. Troy looked as carefree as a gee going into oral surgery. He could afford to relax now; he'd gotten his money's worth, at least as far as photos were concerned.

Feeling peppy, I did a quick blowup of Mr. Phil. Like the song says, "Make Someone Happy." The photo was enough to blow the Supp-Hose off the Mrs. Phils of the future.

Then I died by half inches. I put the first neg in my two-timer series in the carrier and threw on the Omega. It killed me to print it. The exposure felt ten years long—one year per every second the Time-O-Lite ticked off. I had gray hair, wrinkles, and varicose veins by the time it was over.

The second blowup didn't tear me up quite so bad. By the sixth I was a trouper; by the tenth, I cranked them out blasé as a Xerox machine. The whole array was printed by 8:30 P.M.

While they dried, I went for a soak. I wasn't good for much else. I positioned a bottle of Rémy on the rim of the tub, near my head. I dawdled over the first glass. The bartender built me a second. That went down in a gulp. I ordered a third. Three strikes and you're out.

Setting the Trap

I toweled off and slipped into my pj's. The night air was nippy so I let Gallagher's bathrobe hug me. Following the dick's instructions, I put the photos of Abelard and Heloise in chronological order. I got out the pushpins and tacked the evidence up, making sure to mount them on a wall where Hank couldn't miss them. "He's inta Art? Make it look like an art gallery, sweetheart; then throw tha book at 'im" was how Nick put it.

It was now 10:45 on the shnoz. I got under the covers with more firewater. I tossed down a glass. Another slid down after it. Then I had one for a chaser. Then I passed out. Not for long, however, because around midnight I got up to be sick. Drowning your sorrows in drink is okay; redrowning isn't. I slapped toothpaste around the oral cavity and staggered back to bed. My feet didn't hit the floor again until 9:30 A.M. A pile driver had taken up residency in my head; sandpaper did a guest spot for my tongue; and a cement mixer was pinch hitting for my stomach.

Tasteless Conversation

The toast had as much flavor as corrugated and the perc tasted like sludge. So much for the breakfast of champions. I tidied up the darkroom and put Mr. Phil's present in an envelope marked PHOTO-GRAPHS—DO NOT BEND. Not that the warning meant much to the P.O. goons; those were the packages they liked mangling best. I stuck in a short, friendly note. I wasn't interested in a husband, but you never know when a limo in Orlando might come in handy.

Rosenblatt's bill got typed up and went in the manila with the Baldwin glossies. I kept my hands busy as windmills to keep my optics off the prints on the wall.

I bent my steps down Broadway. It was autumn in Gotham but it was hard to tell. Concrete doesn't turn colors like leaves. When I arrived at his office, Clarence Darrow was sitting at his desk with his shirtsleeves rolled, guzzling his first java of the day and munching a bagel with shmeer. His legal mind was working the *Times* crossword.

"Well, well, if it isn't my favorite shutterbug. Come on in." Rosenblatt, to his credit, was happy to see me. "Have a seat, Janie. Just dump that pile of papers there on the floor." Even with paper piles wall to wall, Marv could put his hands on a necessary legalese quicker than a magistrate could say "Blind Justice."

The mouthpiece had gotten stuck on 31A, a five letterer meaning "Hotbeds." I couldn't help; the days when I knew about hotbeds were over. I plopped the envelope right over the Will Weng.

Marv flipped through the prints and gave the top one a kiss in tribute. "Another bang-up job." He wasn't so nuts about the invoice. "Uh, about this"—he jabbed his pencil into my letterhead—"I'll have my girl put a check in the mail in a couple of weeks."

"I'm afraid Mr. Pevsner won't like that."

"Who?"

"The man who's threatening me with loss of loft, liberty, and the pursuit of happiness. A.k.a. my landlord." Guilt, like a well-placed electrode, can modify behavior and Marv wasn't Miriam Rosenblatt's boychik for nothing.

Marv jumped. "He's telling you he's going to evict you?"

"He's not talking the Bill of Rights. You want to represent me in landlord-tenant court?"

"You'll have your check by the end of the week." He wrote himself a note on his calendar and lined up his pens. "Palladino tells me you had a rough time out at the airport. I was sorry to hear that."

I wrapped and twirled a strand of hair around my index. "I don't much want to talk about it, if you don't mind."

"Mind? I understand completely. Who knows, maybe things will work out. You never know how a trial's going to end until the jury comes in with the verdict. Sometimes there are unexpected happy endings." He sounded less than convinced.

"Sometimes." I sounded even less than his less.

"If there's anything I can do, you let me know, okay? You don't have to be shy with me. How about letting me take you out for a fancy dinner sometime this week? In fact, what're you doing tonight? I promise no kosher Chinese. I learned my lesson."

"Thanks, Marv, but I've lost my appetite. Tell you what, though, I'll call you post mortem."

"Whatever's best for you, Janie. I don't want to push. But call soon. I won't eat until I hear from you." Marv knew from guilt.

Hoofing it home, I replayed Mr. Phil's marriage proposal and Marv's starvation threat. Some lovelife I had in store for me. Well, I had my work. And when I went upstairs I realized I always had my oven. Con Ed says cooking with gas is fast and efficient. It doesn't tell you what temp to set the thermostat if it's your head you're baking. Probably 350°, the same as for chicken.

Manslaughter

I dialed 976-1616. "Eastern Daylight Time: 7:22 and twenty seconds." The telephone voice needed a nasal decongestant. It was dinnertime U.S.A. I wasn't hungry. One thing to be said for heartache, it's dietetic. Lose your lover and unsightly extra pounds. Eat your heart out and turn those pelvic bones into daggers.

I was as twitchy as a junkie gone cold turkey. Reading was out. I rang Viv. She had a nerve not being home. Where the hell was she when the chips were down? Out somewhere having a good time, the creep. I didn't bother trying Sara; she was probably making it with her cadaver. I tried Palladino to talk strategy but all I got was his machine. Growl, beep, hang up.

I knew what to do when the time came only I was convinced it never would. I dialed 976-1616 again and found time standing still. The voice with the clogged nozzle told me it was only 8:02 and forty seconds. I was so bonkers I went into a cleaning focus. I vacuumed, cleaned the toaster oven, alphabetized the spices, even dusted. The let's-pretend-things-are-in-order gambit.

I started hitting the diet drink, then switched to the harder stuff. I tried Viv again. She was still out having a swell time. The traitor. I called Dial-a-Joke, Horoscopes-by-Phone, and Weather. The jokes were pure Catskills. The horoscope for Scorpio was cheerful and full of crap. The weather was rain.

At 9:40 and sixteen seconds the key turned in the lock, size twelve and a half desert boots pitter-pattered up the stairs, two at a time. I composed my face and scarfed down a tranq. Gallagher put his grips down by the table and flung his Levi's jacket over a chair.

First I gazed into his eyes. Only mini-stoned. Golden Boy wasn't just a doper; he was a dope. He was wearing a hand-knit I knew hadn't gone west to Buckeye territory. Proof positive he'd been back in Hoboken. If he'd been bright and read some of my dick lit, he might have pulled off his scam. He'd have known the big picture meant zip without fine tuning. That the little details are the little murderers. Still, he had *some* imagination. Shlepping the bags was a nice touch. Playful. They had to be empty. Charades.

"Welcome Weary Traveler," I gave the official Golgonooza greeting.

Loverboy's response was kissy, huggy, and clutchy.

The dick's tactics were play the scene cool as a cuke and give the kid plenty of rope to hang himself. "How was your flight?" I asked, as if duplicity were the farthest thing from my mind.

"Uh, okay. Got any coffee? I need a cup." He was lucky to get instant. And in a cup, not in his lap. "I didn't get much sleep last night."

"Oh, no? How come?" I could afford to play the mark a little longer.

"Lots of loose ends to tie up," he flimflammed.

"Like what?" I was feeding him enough noose material for a lifetime.

"I had things to go over with Balthazar." He was driving with the gas pedal to the floor on a tank that read "empty."

"Yeah, what?"

"Our project, plans for Futurity, that kind of thing."

Swiss cheese had fewer holes than his wheeze. What I didn't get was why he was bothering to string me. After the test drive, why didn't he just trade me in for the new model. After all, that's what he'd done with the frail before me.

Golden Boy was antsy, so he threw the rap my way. "How'd your job with Palladino go?"

"The plans changed so we wound up at U.S. Air yesterday morning." If Hank was putting two and two together, he wasn't letting on about four. "The job was much tougher than I ever imagined."

"Get what you wanted?" He fumbled around in his jacket pocket for the makings of a joint. His digits had trouble rolling. Nerves of steel under pressure, buckling.

"I wouldn't say that, no."

"Anything you can use?" He sucked in on the blaster and slurped some java.

"They're pretty heavy on the Truth end, low scorers on Beauty."

"Are those the shots tacked up on the wall?"

I squeezed out a "yes" between my crockery and watched my spoony trot over to the photo show. My legs had turned to aspic and my keister'd shellacked itself to the campstool. My pump beat a tattoo in the brisket and my sprinkler system was ready to Niagara.

Hank's Mr. Gorgeous bod puffed up and collapsed like a soufflé. His temp dropped to glacial and his beams spun like fruits in a Vegas slot. A noise like a disabled subway came from his throat. When he faced me dead on, his mug was a delicatessen of emotions.

The Long Goodbye

"Did you suspect all along?" he rasped.

"A couple of times I thought maybe something was going on but this was the first time I really 'knew' knew. I've had some time to put it together since. I figure it started the minute Parker introduced you."

"Not exactly the . . ."

"That got followed up by that magic mushroom session. The one where you had a Myriad of Visions. Visions, my ass. What you had was a shitload of sexual fantasies."

"Uh . . ."

"Then you went off to Guyana West and that clinched it. Now

that I think about it, you must've brought her home with you that time, too."

"Er . . ."

"That's why you showed late and 'needed space,' huh?"

"Well . . ."

"After that, Whistlebait was in and out of the city every minute."

"Not every . . ."

"Like a bozo, I thought she was here to see Parker. You let me think that natch. My being a chucklehead worked in your favor."

"I didn't . . ."

"Let's see, what else? You made sure to invite her to my opening. But of course you would. For you she was the life of my party."

"Jane, you don't . . ."

"And then there was the time you allegedly went to see the Armenian flick at the film festival. 'No Emanation, No Fire,' you guys said. 'No go' was more like it."

"We . . ."

"Mustn't leave out the rendezvous the night I was out on the Steir case, either. That was a high-risk night for both of us. I almost got offed and you almost got caught."

"You don't . . ."

"And I don't even want to think about all that went down in Helter Skelterville. I was a nervous wreck, worrying about your thinktank, not your chassis. What a joke." I made a noise in my windpipe, a laugh cut with sulfuric acid. It hurt. "Macabre cult rites! Brainwashings!"

"It was never . . ."

"Jeeesus. All the time it was just teeny weeny Winny. I could throw up." And almost did.

"I went out to that goddamn cultural wasteland and busted my fucking rump trying to be a goddamn Daughter of Albion. Your friends threatened me and all you did was act like a heel."

"I, I . . ."

"How convenient for you Palladino showed up. It made things very nice for you and your little friend. You know, the shamus was on to you from the beginning. He said something was fishy right from the start, but I wouldn't listen. 'The eye sees more than the heart knows,' according to your boy Blake. In this case, make it Eye as in P.I. and you'd be calling it square."

Hank opened and closed his gills and then went to work chewing his lip.

"Explain, dammit!" The peeper warned me that the minute I went soft, I was a goner. "And spare me the mystical mumbo jumbo, okay?"

"Jane, I . . . I, uh, wanted to tell you. But you didn't like Blake and his idea of Gratified Desire." I was stuck with the lingo whether I liked it or not. "I didn't know what was going to happen and I wanted to keep things between us the way they were but not have to deal with the Chain of Jealousy.

" 'I sought for a joy without pain.' You have Boundless Energy; Winny has Purity and Spirituality. With the two of you being such Contraries, I hoped to get the kind of Harmony Blake believed possible. Can you understand that?"

I was nothing if not understanding. And heartsick because of it. "It's called 'having your cake and eating it, too,' pal. How serious is this thing with her?" Sherlock Holmes wanted to ascertain.

"I don't know."

"So you parked her at your digs to find out? What were you planning to do? Give the PATH tubes a real workout, shuttling back and forth between us until you figured it out?"

"Something like that."

"And Winny was willing to go along with that?"

"She has Cultivated her Understandings."

"Well, consider me barren soil, buddy."

"Jane, believe me, I didn't want this to happen."

"I'll bet you didn't. But you saw your chance to have us both and you went for it. You even lugged me to Ohio to rub my nose in it."

"I tried to tell you not to go. I tried not to hurt you."

"Trying wasn't good enough. I can't trust you, Hank, not after this."

"If you're going to talk about Trust, what about that guy LeCoq?"

I was waiting for that one, and this time I was ready. "What about him?"

"Well, what about him?"

"Nothing about him. He's not worth discussing. I mean he was a mistake, okay? But he was never a threat. I can't say the same for Winny. As long as we're being upfront, if you were so suspish about the frog, how come you never said anything?"

"Because, I, uh . . ."

"I'll tell you why. Because it took the heat off. If I had a lover, you didn't have to feel guilty. Right?"

Gallagher looked lousy. He was dragging on the doobie double time.

"There's no choice, Hank. We have to make a break." I finished my sentence through tight labials.

"You're not . . ."

"It's the only way to go." Up until now I hadn't been so sure. And hormonally I still wasn't. "Don't you see the way it is? We don't ride the same track. I can't live your kind of life and you can't live mine. . . . It's just the way the cards are stacked." I copped some of the tough guy talk from pulpster David Goodis.

"Jane, can't we . . ."

"No, we can't." I twisted my mouth into a Bogie sneer. "Look, Hank-o, let me level with you. It was easy to be nuts about you. I love you and you love me. What of it? I could let the situation go on like this—a week, a month, a year. Maybe you'd get tired of her, maybe you'd get tired of me. If I put up with this arrangement, I'd

220

be playing the sap for you. And if you wound up with her, I'd *know* I was a sap. I can't buy your terms, though a lot of me wants to. Part of me wants to say to hell with the consequences, just go along with this Blakean drek. But I can't. And I won't because you counted on me to go along with it the way the Golgonoozers go along with it. But I'm no Blakette, though I tried. I'll miss you and I'll have some rotten nights, but that'll pass."

It was lucky Hank wasn't familiar with *The Maltese Falcon* since I lifted most of my lines from Sam Spade's windup with Brigit O'Shaughnessy. Hammett's dialogue got me over the rocky spots.

"The only thing left for you to do is pack your stuff and go back to Gingham Girl."

"In the morning."

"Uh uh."

Golden Boy got up and took me by the shoulders. "Tell me the truth, is this really what you want me to do? Leave?" He planted a lip lock on me that took my breath and some of my resolve away.

"Uh huh," I whispered. "That's what I want you to do."

"All right. I'll come back tomorrow and do it."

"Uh uh. Put your things in those two empty bags you dragged here for show and take everything back to Jersey tonight."

Gallagher was pissed. "Okay, if that's how you want to be about it." Not "wanted to," had to. Before my insides turned to mush.

He took his Mr. B.'s from the bookshelves one by one and stacked them à la Brinsmades. He paid a visit to the closet and pulled out wrinkled shirts and pants as well as a duffel full of dirty laundry. He disappeared into the can and came out with tooth-brush, comb, razor, and shaving cream. He unzipped a suitcase slo-mo and looked sick. There was nothing inside but air. He divvied up his possessions by weight, half going into the valise, the rest going into the equally empty camera case. The luggage at least was well balanced. More than I could say for its owner. And certainly more than I could say for yours truly.

We stood at the top of the stairs. Eyes swam. There was nothing and everything to say. We said nothing—he because he was chickenshit, me because I was a dishrag. Memories went to the cleaners —all the dirty spots and stains washed out. What came back looked white and bright. Reason defended its title and punched its way back into the limelight. I wasn't sure the fight was worth it.

"I guess you want your keys back," Hank murmured softly.

"Guess so." My larynx was tangled in my throat like a Slinky.

"Sorry I never got around to fixing the leak in the darkroom sink. I know I promised."

"Don't worry," I blubbered. "I'll manage somehow." There were no end of repairs I'd have to make once he'd split.

Gallagher put his arms around me and I buried my squash in his chest. He gave me another Golden Boy special on the flanges. " 'I have Erred, & my Error remains with me.' " And with that as his swan song, the Love of My Life put on his jacket, picked up his gear, and walked his to-die hunk away forever.

Pulp

No matter how I sliced it, Gallagher'd done me dirt. "He made his bed, now he can lie in it," Sara said. Lying in it with Winny, I pointed out. Viv, the lawyer, said: "Criminal." Golden Boy beat the rap and I took the punishment. So much for justice. Change my name to Patsy.

"I was just one tight knot of muscle, bunched together by a rage that wanted to rip and tear." Check, Mike Hammer. If I couldn't tear Hank from my heart, at least I could rip him from the wall. Swearing like a marine, I shredded the pics to smithereens and hurled the confetti out the window to its shabby death. I stopped short of celluloid slaughter; I'm a pacifist when it comes to negatives.

After the mayhem, I ran for covers. Last night's torrent was a drizzle by tonight's standards. Don't let the suckers kid you—the good, clean break exists like Santa Claus and the tooth fairy.

Sentenced to life in solitary, I began serving time. In bed. I hurt less horizontal. One morning I dragged ball and chain, ass and Ohio film, into the darkroom. I developed the rolls and as soon as I did wished I hadn't. The ones of Hank with the woolies almost killed me. I thought about putting the whole shoot in the circular file. I nixed it when I spotted some aces. I put the film on hold. The world had waited twenty-seven years for me to produce a masterpiece; fuck it, it could wait a little longer.

Two communiqués arrived from the Outside. LeCoq wrote he was *très* sorry but he'd non-stopped from Le Coast to La Belle France. Why didn't I come to Gay Paree, he wrote. Why didn't he put his money where his pen was, I wondered. Aw, hell, who cared? I was off men forever.

Parker sent a yellow. Bad news travels as fast as good, if not faster. The trust fund kid was spending his latest dividend check on *ganga* in Jamaica. He knew, he wired, just how I felt. I knew he was feeling no pain now and wished I had the drugs to not feel similarly. Maybe he'd console me with some when he got back. Or loan me some of his lenses. Nah, what for? I'd never do detective work again as long as I lived.

Trial and Error

I was moistening the linen when the phone yowled. Hank with the scoop that the honeymoon was over and he'd come to his pre-Blake senses? You'd think I'd know better than to think that. I did, but I thought it anyway. I put some wind in my chest so as not to sound overeager when I said "Hello—I didn't mean it—All's forgiven—Come back—I love you."

I got the "hello" out fine. Then the voice cut me off. "Hey, kiddo, how's tricks?"

"Oh, it's you."

The P.I. wasn't fazed by my enthusiasm. "Not so hot, huh? Must mean tha boyfriend gave tha photos a fave rave. Nuthin' ta say in his own defense, huh? Ya wanna tell tha old mastermind here what happened?"

I gave it to him verbatim, the way Archie Goodwin reported to Nero Wolfe.

"So he wanted ya ta stick, huh? But ya gave'm tha gate. Atta girl! Good riddens ta bad rubbish."

"Nick, cut it, okay? Even if it is true."

"Sorry, sweetheart. How 'bout outta sight, outta mind? Onta bigger 'n' better? Speakin' a which, I gotta offer."

"Ugh." I stuck my tongue out at the receiver. I'd detected more than I ever bargained for and the whole dick shtick—novels, movies, and jobs—got the big kiss-off. No more evidence-chasing in my future. There were less disastrous ways to make a buck. It was time to get some mileage out of the classy M.F.A. I kept stashed in the closet. "Thanks, gumshoe, but I'll pass."

"Mothera Mary, already with tha mouth and ya ain't even heard tha proposition yet."

"The answer's 'Forget it.' "

"Will ya shaddup for a sec and listen? Whaddya givin' me a hard time for? It ain't my fault tha two-timer lammed."

Bull's-eye Palladino. His plan only put the two-timing in perspective. "Okay, what's the skinny?"

"That's better. Now what I been tryin' ta tell ya ain't even work related. It's a invite ta dinner Friday. Even if ya don't wanna come, yer comin'. Gina, that's tha wife, she got her thumper set on this dinner party, see, and yer tha guesta honor. If ya don't show, I'll never hear tha enda it."

"Look, Nick, I'd love to really but, I mean, I'm the next best thing to anorexic."

"Don't worry, babe, tha appetite'll come back when ya see what tha little woman's got planned. So come by tha apartment, say round eighta clock. Right? Right."

There are any number of ways to end a conversation. Nick's was surgical. With a simple flick of the wrist, he severed the connection.

Busting Out

By six o'clock Friday I'd lived three days, seventeen hours, and fifty-three minutes without my squeeze—if you call moping around living. I had to pull myself together for my dinner date. Not that I needed much time to dress or put on my face. Who cared about minutiae when mere legwork was a minor miracle? I left enough time to get to a florist. Marv's check had come in, Mr. Pevsner'd been stalled off for another month, and Masterchange knew where it could stick my $35.00 minimum payment. I still had a little jack to spring for posies.

I passed by Roseweb Gallery. The Levelor blinds were drawn, the art tucked in bed for the night. The director'd scheduled me for a solo show next season. Which meant getting new work together. The Ohio stuff for starters. Well, I suppose I could pull some workprints as prelims. I was tough, I could take it. Pure bunk. I wasn't tough but I'd manage.

The Palladinos lived on Mott Street, between Prince and Houston. The block was safe and well protected—and I don't mean by New York's Finest. Big, bosomy mamas yelled out their windows *"È ora di mangiare"* like a war cry and their Marios, Tonys, Sabinas, and Marias would scream back, "Aw, Ma" and obey.

Number two eighty-five was a bruised but clean six-story. The names on the buzzers shared a certain ethnic persuasion. Floor after floor, the creaky elevator made me feel it was doing me a favor taking me to five. From the smell of things, Signora Palladino wasn't the only good cook on the floor. My snoot told me there was serious competition in B18, B20, and B23. The aromas sent my unemployed tastebuds back to work. Nick said I'd be hungry when I got there. I had to hand it to the guy, he knew about appetites. All kinds.

Homebodies

I rang the bell at B22. The shamus and a blast of garlic greeted me at the door. Palladino looked relaxed. His outfit was sporty. The canary shirt with floppy collar, the navy sweatshirt, and the powder blue staypresseds toned down the glare from his gold chain and diamond pinky ring. His hair'd gone from the wet to the dry look. Not dry exactly, but drier.

I expected the place to look like the inside of his VW, only bigger. It didn't and the reason blew into the living room like a tornado, wiping her hands on her apron. Gina Palladino was a short woman built for stamina, not speed. Otherwise, how would she have stayed married to the gumshoe for thirty-two years? She radiated warmth like a pizza oven. She had a backbone chiseled from Carrara but ruled the roost with a sceptre of spaghetti. I liked her immediately.

She held me at arm's length and brown-eyed me. "Too skinny. No meat on the bones. Not good." Gina was a Jewish mother in Italian drag.

"I'm really glad to meet you, Mrs. P. I've wanted to for a long time." I shoved the florals at her.

That earned me a peck on the cheek. "What're we standin' around for? Siddown, honey, and take a load off your feet. Make yourself at home. Nick, make Jane here a drink while I do a coupla last minute things inna kitchen."

Her pink scuffies made a "chchchchch" sound on the floor. Their color didn't quite match the housedress but the concept was there. The apartment, a tight four-roomer, was a noise box. The fridge door slammed. Pots and pans rattled. Gina hummed and was happy.

Spending time in a short or on a roof or in a greasy spoon isn't the same as sitting with the king in his castle. Surrounded by bric-a-brac, wedding pics, a framed reproduction of *The Last Supper*, and needlepoint pillows, the king and I were a little uneasy.

"Name your poison, sweetheart."

I asked for a Scotch and soda on the rocks and got one heavy on the clinks, stiff on the booze, and light on the soft stuff.

"I gotta tell ya, dollface, I ain't happy ta see ya goin' ta tha dogs over some shmuck. Ya look pretty crappy, angel."

"Are you trying to tell me I'm falling apart? Look, Palladino, ol' buddy, they don't call me Bite the Bullet for nothing, you know." The lip reassured him I hadn't gone completely off the deep end. "So tell me, who else is coming for dinner?"

Double Take

"It's a surprise."

"My system's too weak to take any more. I'm a delicate flower."

"Try some mora tha liquid therapy and ya'll feel stronger in no time."

"Aw, c'mon, fess up."

There was more hustle bustle with the pots. Gina yelled "Jane, shuddup and stop worryin' will ya, fa Chrissake."

"Okay, Gina," I hollered back, getting into the decibel swing of things. "My life's in your hands."

The oven door slammed. The doorbell rang. Enter the first guest. He was an enormous surprise. If you measure surprises by weight.

"Hey, Jane, how ya been?" Flash Ferrara smiled his endearing toothless grin.

I heard two other voices but Fatso impacted the scan. Once he squeezed his bulk through the living room door—a Herculean feat that made him look blotchy—I got a gander of guest number two. Something had happened to him since I last saw him. There was no trace of the world-weary, disinterested witness about Sal Martino now. Nope, he was anything but. Sal was in love.

The Trim Man

One squint at his date and my wiring shorted. My jaw booked a tour of my knees. Air whistled out of my lungs and the floor looped the loop. The third, and most potent, shocker was none other than the rooftop Romeo, Jack Price.

He was a new twist in the tortellini. As far as Nick and I knew he'd dusted the Dewinter scene and disappeared. Now we pieced together the whole boiling. Somehow from Seymourside, Sal had pegged Jack a switch-hitter. It was only a matter of time before Price switched from AC back to DC and when he did, likely he'd drop in at the Cosmo Baths. Sal was willing to wait. One night it happened. In the steamroom. Sal saw his opportunity and grabbed it. Price had inclination and let himself be grabbed. Paula got the brushoff. She made nice again with Troy, who had Bettina, etc., etc. There are a million stories here in the Naked City and this was one with more kinks than the Edsel.

Some people know what they want and go after him. Sal was one of them. Winny was another. Sal I admired. Winny I wished would drop dead. The Palladinos' was no place to boohoo over spilt moo juice. I sniffled a little over my Scotch.

The regrouping of forces got us flummoxed. The silence got to be hairy. "Relax, you two," Sal finally said. "It's cool. He knows all about the roof."

"I hear you got some great photos." Price's laugh cleared the air like Lysol. To me he added: "I'd love to see them sometime."

I gave a quick replay of the boudoir scene in my upstairs screening room. The footage was strictly X-rated. Thank God Gina appeared. Otherwise, I still might be standing there, staring at Price's crotch.

The hostess kissed Ferrara on the top of his cranium. Years of experience had taught her the aerial approach was easier than fighting the Battle of the Bulge. Sal she knew "from when he was this high" which, when she demonstrated, wasn't very high at all, and she gave him a hug. Price wasn't exactly what she had in mind when Martino said he was bringing a date, but she wasn't fazed. She looked more put out when she glanced at her watch.

Treading Water

Nick gave the boozers something to lap up and Gina rekitched. I heard her hoist the phone, dial, hang up hard, and curse. Fifteen minutes went by approx. She looked at her Bulova and then she looked pissed. "Another ten and we eat," she announced. That sounded great to my gastric juices.

The guys spent the ten talking football. I ambled to the cookroom.

"Can I do anything to help?" Gina was spicing up the feed.

"That's sweeta ya ta offer, honey, but there's nuthin' for ya ta do. I got it all under control. You're a guest. Go siddown."

She stood in the doorway and yelled into the living room: "Dinner!"

Stranger

With the leaves pulled out, the table was almost the size of the dining room. Eat or else.

Gina did the honors. The seating arrangement stacked up like this:

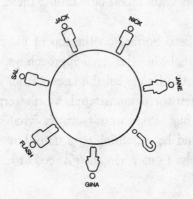

That left a mysteriously empty chair between me and Mrs. P.

Somebody leaned on the bell. The hankshaw padded to the door to answer it. He came back with a dessert on legs.

Whoever the sam was, he was breathing like he'd run the three-minute mile. He got Gina in a bear hug. She smiled up at him and gave him a light smack. "What's the matter with you? I tell ya eighta clock; ya tell me 'sure, sure.' Eighta clock comes, an' nuthin'; eight thirty, nuthin'. It's after nine now, mister. And if tha food's ruined, it's onna counta you." She sounded fierce as a kitten.

"I'm sorry. I got stuck on the phone with my agent."

"Skip the creative excuses."

"It's the God's honest. I can't do any better than that, can I?"

"This here's Nick Junior," Nick Senior said, coming in to ref before the soup got cold. "This here's Jane Meyers"—he head-cocked my way—"and that guy there's Jack Price. Everybody else ya know. Even if ya don't wanna admit it."

Baby Nick showed his uppers to Price and sat down between me and mom. "You must be the photographer Dad works with." Gina watched him taste the minestrone. He gave it the thumbs up. Mama beamed.

"Yeah," I said, making less than brilliant repartee. I was too kayo'd to speak. The gumshoe'd mentioned he had a kid but I just assumed "like father, like son" and passed. Who said breeding shows?

Sonny was a genetic conglom. He had his mother's smile and olive skin. The beams were seal brown like hers, topped by Dad's heavy lids—the perfect bedroom set. Hair he'd inherited from Nick —the color, not the sheen. His vocals were a blip lower than the dick's but had the family twang. Gina's cooking had bulked his six-foot-two frame to one hundred eighty but none of it was flab. I put him somewhere around thirty and his aftershave smelled great.

Dynamite

During the main course I kept my mush in motion and my blinkers trained on Nicklette. He said he was an inkslinger so I asked just what kind of ink he slung.

"Fiction some, mysteries mainly." My ears turned into antennae. "My first one's being published this spring."

I asked him to tell me about it. He did, all the way through the arugula salad. He discussed mysteries in general over the manicotti. The Italian stallion sounded like he'd read everything ever written on or about detective fiction. He even taught a course on the topic at the New School. I couldn't afford the tuition but I had hopes of becoming teacher's pet.

Multo vino later, I queried: "Get much material from Pop?"

"Yup. And from Flash. Maybe I'll get some from you."

"Maybe."

"Suppose I can?" His come-on smacked of Fred MacMurray's in *Double Indemnity.*

"Suppose I don't?" I did my best to sound feline, à la Barbara Stanwyck.

"Suppose you change your mind?"

"Suppose I won't?"

"Suppose I make it worth your while?"

"Suppose you can't?"

"Suppose you're wrong?"

"Suppose you convince me?"

We left it up in the air. Dessert took up all our attention. Stomach linings were stretched to the max but we did right by the cheesecake. Make that plural; Flash had one all to himself. After espresso, Ferrara gyrated his adipose and made the bye-byes. He had a job as bouncer at an after-hours club on the Lower East Side. He'd be trouble tonight; after the hi-cal intake he had more bounce per ounce than ever.

Sal and Jack split next. They were hot to get home. They'd been hot for a while. I could tell. After the second round of pasta, something more than kneesies was going on under the table.

Before I scrammed I had a question to put to Palladino Jr. I tried to make it sound normal and everyday. "Out of curiosity, Nick, what do you think of William Blake?"

"Come again?"

"William Blake. You know, the writer? The guy who did etchings? The, uh, mystic?"

"He wrote 'Tyger, Tyger,' right?"

"You got it."

"Tell you the truth, I haven't thought about him since he was required reading at Columbia and even then I didn't think much of him. How come you want to know?"

"It's a long story. Maybe someday I'll tell you about it. Maybe it's raw material." I wiggled my brows. "It's certainly raw."

"Okay, but tell me, was that some sort of test?"

"Sort of, I suppose." So much for sliding one over.

"Did I pass?"

"Keep this up and you'll go straight to the head of the class." At the speed of light.

Up for Grabs

"How're ya gettin' home, toots?" Nick Sr. wanted to know.

"Walk."

"Oh, no ya ain't, sister." Since the downtown shootout, the sleuth didn't cotton to my walking around at night solo. "I'll drive ya."

"Nickie, honey, you walk her," Gina screamed to her baby boy from command headquarters.

Under normal circumstances, this prima bigmouth and lame-brain would've yammered hardboiled stuff about being able to take care of herself, thank you. Or gotten huffy and cited statistics on exactly how many cabs were cruising around with itchy meters just waiting to take her home. Or gone the martyr route and said something sugary like "Oh, but it's so far out of his way, he needn't bother." Tonight I shut up tight like a cherrystone. I told Gina earlier that I put myself in her hands. It was the only right decision I'd made in weeks.

Kid P. yelled back, "Jesus, Ma, you just went and blew my big play. I planned to walk her home hours ago."

We were almost out the door when the P.I. said, "Hey, dollface, I almost forgot. I think I gotta job for us next week. Ya interested?"

"Sure, what the hell." This frail was back in business.

"Good, I'll give ya a call in tha next coupla days."

Outside it was misty and looked like Frisco. We took the long way back to my place. Much as I wanted to, I didn't invite Nick up. Since the Gallagher fiasco, the joint looked like the Collier mansion. The sink was filled with dirty dishes, the counters were covered with empty cans of sugarfree, clothes littered the floor, the bed was unmade, the linen was soggy, and the bathtub was full of hair. The mood wouldn't have been right.

"How about your coming over to my place next week?" Nickie asked. "I've got something I bet you'd love to look at."

I'll bet he had. "You mean, come up and look at what your old man still calls etchings?"

Just then Razor poked his dome out of the Pussy Cat and sniffed the air. "Etchings?" He shook his bean in disbelief. "Ya gotta be kidding with a line like that." He laughed an oily one and slipped back into the go-go's stale atmo.

Baby Nick laughed too. "No, better than etchings."

"Better?" The stakes for this no-limit poker game were high and getting higher.

"Oh, yeah, much. I'll show you my pulp collection. Which, I might add, boasts"—he paused suspensefully—"a complete set of *Black Masks*."

"Wow," I gasped. This was hardboiled heaven. *Black Mask* was the famous mystery mag that launched guys like Hammett, Gardner, Chandler, and assorted other '30s tough-guy writers. Issues were scarce as hen's teeth.

"Believe it or not, I've never seen one." This coming from a mystery buff was as embarrassing as admitting to being a virgin past twenty. "Boy, I'd love to."

"And I'd love to have you."

"And you might, cutie pie," I thought. If the kid played his cards right, I might wind up calling Nick the Dick "Dad" too.

"Guess it's time for the big sleep," I said, turning the key in the lock. Reluctantly.

A highpockets, already well juiced, pulled open the door to the topless. For a few seconds we heard Gloria Gaynor belting out "I Will Survive" on the Wurlitzer.

"Guess so," Nick said. He bent his head and brushed his gills against mine. Sexy without being pushy. Where did the guy get his sex appeal? From the dick?

"I'll give you a call in the next couple of days" was what

Nicklette said before leaving. The lights from the Pussy Cat illuminated him as far as the corner. He jammed his hands deep into the pockets of his bomber jacket. He crossed Church Street and was heading toward Sixth when the fog took him.

The Big Knockover

I was thinking about what Ross Macdonald said about fictional detectives being idealized versions of their authors when I rang his bell. I knew Kid P. was watching my new skirt follow my gams up the stairs to his apartment. My high heels sounded like cannons on the parquet. I was nervous and felt as exposed as the brownstone's brick. Nick was casual—old jeans, Etonics, Health and Racquet Club T-shirt. The arms looked strong. Nautilus machines? Squash? His hair was still damp from a recent shower. He smelled as good as I remembered. Maybe better.

The pad was a theoretical one bedroom. Theoretical because the bed was in the living room, and the living room wound up less lived in than the bedroom, which was now the writing room. The borderline between life and art is always fuzzy. The contents of the workroom were inching their way into the living area the way the Chinese are taking over Little Italy.

Nick had bought some goodies from a swank gourmet mart. White plastic containers gleamed on the chrome and glass coffee table. The only white I was interested in was in powder form. Nose candy. I needed the blow to relax.

I catalogued the bookshelf. Blake-free and housing every detecto work known to man or beast, some in first edition. Also *Detective Tales, Ellery Queen's Mystery Magazine, Dime Detective, Mike Shayne Mystery Magazine, Spicy Mystery*—and those seven-by-ten-inchers were just the tip of the iceberg.

The liquor cabinet was almost as well stocked. Figured. Writers are supposed to drink. Ray and Dash sure as hell did.

After I cased the joint, we sat down on the Castro. We weren't talking much but we were saying plenty. Nick pulled out the *Black Masks*. Issue #1, April 1920, we were thigh to thigh. May 15, 1923, the aftershave moved in. June 1, 1923, the inkslinger's hand stroked my trams, slowly gaining altitude.

Breathing became heavier. Nick whipped out October 15, 1923, but I wasn't paying attention. I can pat my head and rub my stomach at the same time, but I can't read with someone's gash glued to mine. Hammett's literary debut, neglected, slid to the floor. Nick slid off my sweater. He held me in his arms. Definitely Nautilused. Gallagher's arms were more sinewy. My nips stood up like cadets at the Point.

Then Nick zipped off my skirt, canoodling and kissing me all the while. Good coordination. Squash, obviously. I was now in my black lace camisole, matching tap pants, garter belt, and stockings. We seemed to have all the time in the world and intended to take it. A hand slithered into my underpants. Whoever said it was better to give than to receive?

Hours later, or what seemed like it, the lingerie had been stripped off and flung. The garter belt nussled the pâté and a stocking veiled the stuffed mushroom caps. I was ready to get off the receiving end. I wanted to see the athletic equipment under the jeans and the tee. Some exploratory hand action under the belt felt promising. I took my time unwrapping the package. He was blockier and hairier than Hank, more muscular and athletic. A nice present.

We joined the *Black Mask* on the floor. I was being stroked, licked, sucked, rubbed, and bussed everywhere it counted. Right side up, upside down, every which way, and I was giving the same A.P.B. back.

It got to the point I thought I'd jump out of my derma. Any more lubrication and the rug would be a swamp. It was time to put the pistol in the holster.

The phone rang and I came to. I was lying in my bed. I released the shudder button and got on the horn. "Hello," I said. Breathy. The voice on the horn twanged, "Hi, it's Nick." But which one, goddammit?